CINDERELLA, NECROMANCER

F.M. BOUGHAN

Month9Books

Copyright © 2017 by F.M. Boughan

CINDERELLA, NECROMANCER by F.M. Boughan
All rights reserved. Published in the United States of America by Month9Books, LLC.
No part of this book may be used or reproduced in any manner whatsoever without written permission of the publisher, except in the case of brief quotations embodied in critical articles and reviews.

Trade Paperback ISBN: 978-1-946700-33-9
ePub ISBN: 978-1-946700-34-6
Mobipocket ISBN: 978-1-946700-35-3

Published by Month9Books, Raleigh, NC 27609
Cover by Najla Qamber Designs

Month9Books

To my elementary school teacher, Mr. J. White, for letting me stay inside at recess and write my weird stories.
To my middle school English teacher, Mr. T. Colp, who—after reading the very first writing assignment I handed in—asked what I wanted to be when I grew up, and when I told him I wanted to be an author, said "Yes, I believe you can."

CINDERELLA, NECROMANCER

I

The Ending

B^{*lood.*}
The blood of my enemies drips down my forearms, fleeing the confines of the spaces between my fingers, traveling toward freedom on the cold, stone floor.

Red and hot and sticky and sweet—ah, how sweet the air smells—and I can't help but wonder if things might have turned out differently.

For me.

For them.

For us.

It tickles as it pools at my elbow, the many bright rivulets joining as one before that final leap.

I understand their need for freedom. Would that I could simply slip away and escape, but no, not this time.

This *was* to be my escape—and yet, standing here with bloodied hands and flesh beneath my fingernails, I wonder.

Was I wrong?

1

Was this truly the only way?

No one deserves to die, my father would have said. As cruel as a person might be, only a monster wishes death upon their enemies.

Ah, Father.

If only you knew.

If only you'd seen.

If only you'd met my sisters.

2

The Beginning

On the morning of my fifteenth birthday, my mother died.

It was a cruel and terrible death, wrought with pain and suffering and moments of relief between the screams.

When death finally took her, the darkness hovered like a plague over our home, my father and younger brother and I only moving and breathing to survive, though if anyone had asked us why, we couldn't have given an answer.

On the morning of my sixteenth birthday, the darkness descended in a form incarnate, though at first, we couldn't see it.

Why should we have?

Father thought he'd brought me the best birthday gift a father could give his daughter: a new mother.

I saw nothing but a vile attempt to replace someone utterly irreplaceable.

I screamed, threw the pot I was holding at his head, and locked myself in my room for three days.

On the fourth day, six-year-old Edward knocked on my door.

"You can't stay in there forever," he said, his small voice wavering. "Father is threatening to call the locksmith. Mother—"

"Don't call her that or I won't speak to you," I said.

He paused before continuing, an awkward pause that made me wonder—no, suspect—that *she* stood outside my door too.

"*She* is threatening to take a hatchet to your door," he whispered, so soft I could barely hear.

Was she now? I wanted to see her try. Difficult, though, being on the other side of the door.

"And ruin Father's fine craftsmanship? She wouldn't."

But I didn't know if she would or not. After all, I'd only caught one glimpse and hadn't even seen her face. Or looked in her eyes. I'd been a fool.

One's eyes say so much more than most people suspect. While the superstitious bustle about, trying to hide their true names—for they believe there is power in names—they should really be wearing dark glasses and learning to speak while gazing at the ground.

Names? Please. Child's play.

To learn the state of one's soul, find their gaze and hold it.

But I'd thrown a pot and run away.

How differently things might have turned out if I'd only followed my own rule.

A deep, calm, female voice penetrated the safety of my walls and wormed its way into my inner ear. "Ellison, please open the door. You must be starving, and I can't imagine how—"

"I have a window."

Edward sniggered, and I knew he'd been thinking the same thing. Just because there was a chamber pot in the room and I hadn't come out, didn't mean I hadn't at least thought that much through.

She sighed. "I can't even imagine what you're going through, Ella dear."

I flinched. *No one* called me Ella. No one but my mother.

"And I'm certainly not here to replace your mother," she continued. "I hear she was a wonderful, outstanding woman."

Outstanding? When my mother smiled, flowers bloomed. When she cried, the skies wept. When she spoke, seas parted. No phrase on God's green earth could even begin to describe her.

"But I'm afraid I'm here to stay and, at the very least, I hope we can be friends."

Afraid? No, this woman at my door wasn't afraid. Fear makes people tremble and weep and piss themselves, and *she* did none of those things.

No, *she* stood outside my door and fed lie after lie on a silver spoon to my brother, and to me, just as she'd no doubt done to my father.

"I have two daughters who are about your age, Ella." Her voice grew soft and warm. I shivered at the change. "They'll be arriving soon, as soon as school ends for the term. I just know you'll get along splendidly. Won't you come out so I can show you their portrait? I've put it up in the parlour, just above the fireplace."

Above the fireplace? Father's rifle went above the fireplace, not some hideous painting of strange girls in no doubt too-frilly dresses.

Ah, but curiosity and temptation are evil things when they join forces. They crowd one's brain and push and pull until nothing is left but an ache to do exactly that which you know, beyond all doubt, you should not, under any circumstances, do—but at the same time, how could you ever *not* do it?

The inner self can be so cruel.

I allowed myself a quick glance around my room. No one could say I lacked for anything—I had clothes and dresses for every occasion, a wardrobe that would be envied by the Queen herself, books upon books upon books, jewels to rival the brightest stars, and mirrors wherever I turned.

To remind yourself that you're beautiful, no matter what state you're in, morning, noon, or night, my mother had said.

But what worth was beauty, and what wealth were jewels, compared to the comfort of a mother's touch? I would have given all worldly possessions for that alone.

And so, with trembling fingers and a heart screaming of betrayal, I opened the door.

3

The Betrayal

Her smile was full of teeth, her lips red and full and inviting. I still did not meet her eyes. Though I thought myself a fool and coward for not doing it sooner, I admit I was afraid. Afraid of learning a terrible truth, or worse, discovering that no terrible truth existed beyond the reality of a new mother.

I looked to Edward, but his innocent face was flushed and rapturous as he gazed upon the intruder.

"Come along, Ella," she said. "I'll have your girl draw up some tea. She won't be with us much longer, just until Charlotte and Victoria arrive and get settled. No need paying for a housemaid when there are plenty of able-bodied women about, hmm? Frugality is the Lord's delight!"

This should have been my first hint at what was to come.

"I'm not in the mood for tea, if it's all the same to you," I said, still looking at Edward. He might as well have been a glowing firefly, for all the attention he paid to her. What *had* she done during my self-imposed isolation?

Not-Mother waved her hand before placing it on my shoulder—long, pale, slender fingers curling around my flesh like icy tendrils. But they weren't icy at all. Her touch felt warm and strong and as much as I hated myself for admitting it, reassuring. Was this the beginning of Edward's devotion?

"Edward," I said, perhaps a little more forcefully than warranted.

His gaze snapped to mine as though my speech had sliced through a taut line.

"You're out!" he shouted, a smile spreading across his face without reservation. "You'll love what Mother has done to the parlour, come see!"

Off like a shot, Edward disappeared from sight in the manner that little brothers often do.

What had she done to the parlour? I looked to her for the meaning behind Edward's outburst and caught her eyes.

We froze, she and I.

She gave a tiny gasp, so quiet that I might have missed it were I not looking for any clue or hint or indication as to the nature of this woman we were to now call *Mother*.

To this day, I know not what she saw when she looked in my eyes. My heart, however, remained in my throat, for I saw something that both terrified and intrigued me in the same blow.

I saw *nothing*.

"The place simply needed a woman's touch, don't you agree?"

I ignored her veiled insult, choosing to focus my attentions on the abhorrent display of extravagance and wealth that had overtaken our parlour in a matter of days. Our comfortable chaises, Grandfather's tea table, and the practical, heavy window drapery, all gone. In their place? Ornate, delicate seats with barely a hint of cushion for padding, exotic dark-wood furniture, and swaths of fabric so heavily beaded and gilded that I feared robbers might break into our home and live for a year on one drape alone.

I prayed that this woman had spent her own wealth on such a display, for Father would never approve. While we lacked for nothing, he saw no value in decadence, nor the need to flaunt our blessings.

How ungrateful that would seem, my dark beauty, he would say, *when there are so many others who have so little?*

Not-Mother flew to the window and grasped the corners of a flimsy ivory fabric, pulling it tight across a sliver of sunlight that threatened to invade the dim-lit room.

"Isn't it marvelous?" She sighed and drifted to a portrait on the wall of three women. I recognized her, but not the two younger girls beside her. They stared out of the portrait with an unnerving intensity, and I pitied the artist they'd sat for. The smiles on their lips did not extend to their eyes, and it did not take much deduction to conclude that they must be Charlotte and Victoria.

Our new sisters.

The portrait presented a convincing enough façade, no doubt, for the likes of Father. What was he thinking, bringing this woman and her wretched darlings into our lives?

Not-Mother cleared her throat, waiting for a response.

I couldn't help myself. "I admit, I preferred the rifle."

To Edward, I whispered, "And with so many beads about, I'm afraid to sit down lest one lodge up my—"

"Ellison!" Not-Mother gasped, but at that very moment the front door slammed, both saving and damning me in one breath. I knew those footsteps like I knew nothing else save my own hands.

Father appeared in the doorway, a thin smile plastered on his face. It wavered ever so slightly as he took in the renewed parlour, a flinch at the corner of his mouth at seeing the replacement above the fireplace.

His gaze shifted to me and his true happiness returned. "Ellison, you've emerged."

I hoped he would run forward and envelop me in one of his consuming embraces, but he refrained and offered a tilt of his head instead. Was he embarrassed to show affection to his own children around *her?* I hoped not. We'd all been restrained since Mother's death, but I saw no necessity for this level of ambivalence.

"I got hungry," I said, hoping to draw him out. "There are very few things worth eating that fit under the crack of a door."

His smile broke free, and a roar of laughter brightened our tomb. My heart lightened and I clutched my mid-section for emphasis, feigning starvation, which made his laugh that much heartier.

It was a beautiful sound, and too long past since heard in the corners of our home.

Of course, our delight was *her* dismay. She couldn't even allow us this one moment of joy, and she strode toward Father with purpose, grasped his arm and patted his shoulder with what should have been a loving touch.

I wish I hadn't been the only other person in the room. I wish I hadn't been alone in seeing Father's face grow slack, his eyes dull and laughter cease like a bow screeching across taut strings mid-note. Where had Edward run off to?

"Darling," she said, "Ella and I were just getting acquainted. I've told her about my gorgeous girls, due to arrive any day now. Won't it be wonderful to have the whole family under one roof?"

I gaped as Father nodded, vacant stare fixed on her visage. It made me uncomfortable to admit—she did possess an unearthly sort of beauty—but surely my father would never be swayed by a pretty face and too-sweet words?

He mumbled some incoherent agreement, or so I presumed, and the rage in my belly returned.

Without another word, I grabbed a jeweled pillow from the nearest settee and hurled it at his head.

Then I fled the room and locked myself away for three more days.

On the morning of the fourth day, everything changed.

4

The Leaving

"I'm leaving for a little while," said Father, his gentle voice drifting through the space between door and wall. "I have business to attend to. It's an opportunity I can't pass up."

I pressed my forehead against the crack. I didn't want to speak to him, but my heart did.

"How long?"

"A little while."

"You're lying," I said. "Lie to Edward, if you must, but not to me. You've never, so don't try to start."

A soft thump against the door told me I'd been right.

"Oh, Ellison," he whispered, "if all goes well, it won't be for long. I truly have a necessary task that demands my—"

I flung open the door, nearly sending my poor father sprawling. "Take me with you."

It seemed the only logical solution.

"I'll make your meals and tend your clothes." Sudden desperation rushed my words. "And you know I'm very good at selling to ladies in the marketplace—"

His smile was sad but kind. "That you are, my daughter. But not this time."

I tried to protest, but he placed a finger across my lips like a seal. His eyes pleaded with an urgency I'd seen only once before. Right before Mother's death.

"Be good while I'm gone, Ellison. Promise me that much. Take care of Edward. Celia will see to it you're well cared for while I'm gone."

I should have stopped him, then and there, but he pressed something into my hand and curled my fingers around it, holding tight to my fist.

"Be good," he repeated, and my puzzlement grew. How could I not?

"I will," I whispered, "but when—"

He shook his head, gaze downcast. "After my business is complete, I will return. That I can promise you."

I nodded, heart aching to diffuse his sadness, while every ounce of my being screamed to cling to him and refuse to let go.

But I did not.

He released my hand and stood, straightening his coat and running a set of fingers through thinning, chestnut hair.

With a firm nod and a glance toward my closed fist, he turned to walk away. At the top of the stairs, he looked back.

"Ellison?"

He sounded weary, though resolute. What had we become in just one short year?

"Yes?" I tried to match his tone, giving comfort in whatever small way a daughter might.

My father took my gaze and held it, growing suddenly intense and, in a way, frightening. "Prove all things. Hold fast that which is good."

He swept down the stairs, leaving me trembling like a newborn lamb.

I plunged my fist inside the pocket of my robe and released the object he'd given me.

I couldn't bring myself to look. Not now.

Believing he'd return soon was a far easier truth to bear.

He left that same morning, quietly, while the rest of the world still slept. I watched from my window as he galloped down the road that would lead him through town, past the King's palace, and out the other side on the road headed north. For years I'd begged him to take me on one of his distant journeys, and after Mother's death, he'd promised his trips would never again separate the family. We had to stick together now.

Celia's arrival had changed everything.

Father and his horse had barely disappeared from sight when someone rapped on my door—three sharp knocks, and a fourth with ominous finality.

I suppose I shouldn't have answered, but at the time, some small part of me must have hoped that Father's leaving had only been an illusion or some semblance of a nightmare, and that he actually stood on the other side of my door once again, waiting.

But Celia Not-Mother stood there instead, hands clasped at her middle.

"Your father has taken leave for several days to do business in Neustadt. Be a good girl and bring me up a pot of tea. Sweet child."

The last she added as an afterthought.

Be a good girl? For Father, certainly. For her?

"That is not my place," I said, for I had no knowledge of

kitchens and pots, nor the necessary interest to deduce what might be needed. "Miss Mary—"

"Is no longer in our employ."

A breath caught in my throat. Father's trail barely minutes cold, and already she'd loosed the woman who'd nursed us and raised us during Mother's frequent convalesces. Miss Mary had no children or family of her own save us.

"You didn't," I said, fists firm at my sides. "You can't."

Celia lifted her chin as though height meant power and folded her arms across the looseness of the blue silk robe she wore which—I swear it, even now—once belonged *to my mother.*

"I can, and I did. A needless expenditure, she. We must be careful with our coins, child."

Tell that to the curtains and pillows.

She tapped a slippered foot. "Tea, child. In my room. I will be waiting."

Indeed she would.

I exited my room without a word, descended the stairs, and slipped out the front door in nothing but my night shift and the light, ivory robe I'd favored during my isolation.

The cool morning air sent a chill through my bones, and though the earth's pebbles stung my feet, returning inside the house for comfort did not once enter my thoughts.

I crossed the courtyard and slid on my belly underneath the front gates, staining not only my robe and shift, but also my own limbs with scrapes that bloomed tiny streaks of bright red blood.

Speed and quiet were my companions, lest Celia burst from the house and drag me back into the kitchen. I expected I had as long as a kettle should take to boil before she realized I hadn't turned left at the bottom of the staircase.

The sting of scratches drove me onward, each piercing stone in my feet a distraction from the pain of abandonment.

I saw few faces along the road, and those who saw me simply nodded and continued as they were. The town knew our family and our sorrow. Perhaps the strangeness of a barely-clothed girl in town spurred pity instead of shock, or perhaps they secretly admired my boldness.

I suspect the former.

A strange feeling crept over me as I made my way down the dusty roads on the town outskirts, where the more fortunate citizens—such as my successful merchant father—had built their dwellings. Living just outside town limits provided more space than the closer, smaller homes, and offered a little more freedom from some of the stricter regulations that, out of necessity, came from living within a well-functioning inner city.

Upon reaching the cobbled streets that led toward city center, I realized that several weeks had passed since I last set foot upon this stretch of road. There to my left? The butcher's shop, from which I'd ordered the foods to sustain us through our period of grief, and there to my right, the quaint storefront of Mother's favourite dressmaker. A lump formed in my throat at the sight of one place in particular.

The jeweler's.

I owned many of the jeweler's skillfully crafted pieces, some which were conceived of and designed by none other than Liesl, his daughter and my dearest friend.

Ah, Liesl. The sister of my heart, she'd endured my mourning, my silences, and my weakness in the past year with a patience that knew no bounds. Indeed, I knew no other person with as strong a will as my dear friend. Her yellow hair and plump figure had caught the eye of several gentlemen in town in recent memory, but so far as I knew she'd held her ground and refused to be swayed by any—despite the advantageous social status a marriage to one of these men could provide.

I did not blame her for her caution. As a jeweler's daughter, it was doubtless difficult to be certain of the sincerity of a proposal, lest the gentleman be more interested in the holdings of the family business.

I had not seen Liesl in weeks. We'd seen little of each other as of late regardless, an unfortunate effect of growing up and of my involuntarily assumed position as lady of the house—but I hoped she also still held me in her heart, in some way. When this— whatever *this* was—ended, I would seek her out and tell her the tale of my subverted freedom. And pray that her patience with me had not fully waned.

I continued along the still-dry streets—a far more comfortable journey than walking unshod would be once the day began and the roads filled with horses and their puddings—and traversed the market square of town center. Several sleepy merchants had arrived early to claim prize positions along the perimeter of the square, though they remained fully engaged in their tasks and did not spare me a glance. I veered right at the King's Arm, and though it was quiet at this time of morning, it wouldn't be long before travellers and town-dwellers alike broke bread together over a pint of ale or beer and a tall tale.

Ah, but young ladies such as myself were not to know of these things, or so I imagined Celia would say. Tell that to my father, who I suspect favored the Sunday evening minstrel for my eventual betrothal. We teased my mother mercilessly about this, before. She would laugh and shake her head, call me a mere girl barely of age to braid her hair, let alone dream of marriage.

I didn't, really. But anything was worth hearing her laughter during the days of illness, and it was a way for both of us to cling to the familiar.

A gust of lavender-scented wind twisted through my loose hair, and I let it carry me further down the cobbled road until it turned to dirt again, and just beyond that still.

My feet came to rest in front of the Church of the Holy Paraclete. The grand cathedral, lovelier than most due to the King's generous donations—or so I'd heard—stood as it had for centuries, its two outer spires seeking heaven. I'd often wondered if they were the only ones.

I had no need of confession this morning, despite recent defiance. I believed God would accept my actions as necessary under the circumstances, and so my visit to the Holy Paraclete held other purposes.

Onward past the cathedral was a field of mournful stones: short, standing, or flat against the ground. Others were carved with images to comfort and celebrate the lives of those who'd gone before.

An iron fence surrounded the field, and although on days past I'd had to climb over it in a most unladylike fashion, on this day, the gate—usually locked—stood open. Whoever had left it so had clearly never heard of the dangers of roaming spirits.

I slipped through the gate and breathed deeply, allowing the scent of hazel and lavender to envelop my being with the peace I sought. I closed the gate.

Under a hazel tree, in the center of the field, rested the one thing I ached for above all else.

"Mother," uttered my lips, as my feet carried me toward the simple, marble stone she'd requested. On one half, her name and year of passing, with a tiny, shallow cross. On the other half, emptiness. It waited for *her* other half, who'd since betrayed us all.

A piercing pain in my right foot sent me pitching forward, knees scraping the flattened earth before my mother's grave.

I pulled my knees to my chest and brushed off the dirt before inspecting the source of pain. A green, spiky seed jutted from my heel.

Devil's weed. I drew the bulbous spires from my flesh. "Did you do this, Mother?"

But she hadn't, though I couldn't have faulted her spirit if she had. With Celia for a replacement, I'd send spiny thorns into my daughter's feet too.

I crawled on the hard, grassy ground until I leaned against her stone, eyes closed, face tilted to the misty gray sky. In the stillness of the early morning, it was easy enough to imagine her next to me. Though certain it was a trick of the mind and my yearning combined, I could have sworn the air grew warmer, the breeze softer with her memory. I felt awash in her spirit as the scent of lavender and hazel grew stronger and stronger, until I had utterly convinced myself that she must be gazing upon me from her place of glory in heaven.

"He's gone," I whispered to her, though who is to say whether the spirits hear or listen? Perhaps they can only see us from far above. "Oh, Mother, forgive us … "

"I'll forgive you if she won't," said the empty graveyard.

My lids flew open as one small drop of saltwater escaped along the curve of my cheek.

A boy—or perhaps rightly, a man—stood a mere ten paces from where I sat, smartly dressed in a navy riding suit and an obtrusive gold medallion, but without a horse in sight.

And although I'd strode through town without a second thought for my apparel or lack thereof, I drew my robe closer and tighter and pulled the long shift overtop my ankles.

He stared with an intensity that rivaled a priest at mass.

I did not speak.

He did not bother to understand my subtle hint.

"What are you doing in a graveyard in your night clothes?" His voice was rich, deep, and twinged my nerves.

When I didn't respond, he sighed and slipped out of his long coat. He held it out toward me and stepped closer.

I must have cringed, for he stopped and raised his other hand in surrender.

"I'm not going to hurt you. I just thought you might be cold in that, ah … "

"I'm fine." I didn't want his coat. Nor his pity. Nor even a slight measure of his company.

"Please," he said, still advancing, "a girl like you shouldn't be out during these early hours unaccompanied, let alone in your state. People might talk."

A girl like me? In my state?

I would have asked after his meaning, had I cared. Instead, I stated with patience, "Please go."

"I'd be a terrible gentleman if I did."

"And you fancy yourself one for gaping at a girl in nightclothes once she has asked you to leave?"

He laughed and I admit, it was a sweet sound on a dark morning.

But I could not have him here.

"I suppose you're right, miss, but there are terrors about these days, and it'd be a sin to leave you to them."

Terrors? "I haven't heard of anything."

His eyes grew wide like saucers, as though terrors were as common as cows. "What about the royal proclamation?"

"What about it?" I spat the words rather than acknowledge my ignorance. Nearly a week locked in my own room and the world had fallen to terrors, whatever they might be.

His brow furrowed as he watched me like some kind of newly

discovered curio. "I don't mean to frighten you if you don't know. It's best I let your father tell you on his own time."

Mother, give me patience. "Frighten? Please. Do try."

Another laugh, and a toss of the coat in my direction. Rather than allow it to lie in the dirt, I picked it up and draped the heavy fabric across my shoulders.

"I won't," he said, "but it's regarding spirits and death and so forth. Not something a lady ought to be bothered with, in the end."

I would bet one silver coin that *he* left the gate open. And he thought to lecture me about spirits?

I uncurled my legs and braced against Mother's stone to stand up. Without another word, I crossed the space between stone and gate, ignoring the ache from where the thorn had pierced my heel.

At the gate, I slipped off the coat and draped it across the first link of iron fence.

Foolishly, I spared him a glance, for it occurred to me that once again, I had forgotten about the eyes.

"What's your name?" I asked, though I didn't care.

A smile replaced the creases of worry, and he touched his forehead while placing an arm across his middle to bow in the formal manner of noble men.

"William. At your service, my lady."

He drew upright to meet my eyes, and afterward I thanked God that the iron gate had been there to halt my backward stumble.

Like a crack of lightning in the clear night sky, there was nothing sharper in his eyes than pure, unadulterated goodness.

But more than that, something stirred within my belly as our eyes met.

Something I could not afford, nor did I want any part of.

I had learned all too well that the allowance of love brought nothing but sadness.

5

The Coat

Ileft William and his warnings in the graveyard, with a fervent prayer that our paths never cross again.

I couldn't bear it.

As an afterthought, I had taken William's coat off the fence and draped it back across my shoulders, though at the time, I knew not why.

Now, I can see as through crystal: I was trying to keep a piece of him with me, a reminder, perhaps, or a promise that he might need to seek me out to retrieve it.

As I walked home, however, the stirrings were easily ceased by the journey, for the town had finally awoken and come forth to conduct the day's business. The town square was awash with stalls of fresh fruit, vegetables, and foreign cloth in a variety of colors unseen in common garb. Several familiar faces nodded in polite recognition, and one gentleman struggling under a weight of iron pots—why he didn't sell them in a shop, I cannot say—called to bid me good health and happy morning. I replied in kind, though my torn feet and the circumstances which brought me to the town square at such an hour defied both his blessings.

I noted, as I passed by, that the door to the jeweler's shop stood open—and as my friend had no love of rising before dawn had well passed, I continued onward.

I arrived home, feet aching and further bloodied from the devil's weed, leaving trails of precious red liquid in my wake. Would that those were the only trails of blood to my name.

As I crossed the threshold, Edward bounded down the stairs, wild and panting.

"Ellison!" He stopped a mere hand's breadth from where I stood, the worry on his face almost more than a sister could bear. "Stepmother is very upset with you." He took a heavy breath, full of panic and fear. "She's threatened a whipping."

A whipping? For a lack of tea?

She wouldn't get far on her threat, seeing as how we didn't own a whip. Not for horses, nor for people.

"She won't." I spoke with all the confidence of an impudent child. "She wouldn't dare. If Father found out, he'd divorce her presently." A thought occurred. "Though perhaps that's not such a bad idea—"

I stopped the jest at seeing Edward's blanched face and knelt to embrace him instead. If Father wouldn't hold us, I saw no reason not to do it ourselves. I certainly couldn't see *her* ever doing so.

His tiny eyes filled with tears as we pulled apart, leaving me to wonder what she'd dared say in his presence.

Words bubbled from his pouted lips. "Stepmother says Father has gone to market. And Miss Mary—"

"Will return in due course." I'd make sure of it. "And Father is on one of his trips, is all. He'll be back before you know it."

God forgive my lying tongue.

Edward sniffed and blinked as one does when crying, and I sought a handkerchief from the pockets of William's coat. I found one inside the inner breast pocket, but as I drew it out, a small object slipped from between the folds of fabric. It plummeted to the floor, bouncing three times before skidding to rest underneath the grandfather clock.

With a shout, Edward dove to the floor and reached for it. I admired his lack of hesitation. In my hand he deposited a wide-banded gold ring with a circular, engraved face.

The ticking of the clock ceased.

My blood flowed like syrup.

The face of the ring was engraved with a seal. I had seen this before, on bulletins in the town square, on sealed letters, on a flag that flew high above the people on a tower even taller than the heaven-reaching church spires.

This was the royal seal.

I had met the Prince.

I tightened my fist and smiled at my brother, though truly I fought to contain the contents of my stomach.

I might as well have walked into the palace, insulted the Queen, and stolen the King's crown. I might as well have asked to be arrested.

No. I would not allow Edward to be left here alone with that woman.

"What is it?" Edward peered at my fist and tapped a knuckle. "Can I see?"

I shook my head and searched for yet another lie. "Just an old bit of brass, nothing more. Thank you for retrieving it."

It was then he noticed my coat. "Are you wearing a man's clothes?"

I tousled his wild hair, the color of breakfast tea, and slipped the ring into my robe pocket. I remembered only then that this pocket already had an occupant—the item Father pressed into my hand that morning.

I still hadn't dared look, lest it speak a truth I was unwilling to hear.

"Does Celia still want for her tea?" I asked.

As children are wont to do, he'd already forgotten his first question.

"I don't know, but she's very angry."

"She didn't hurt you, did she?"

His confusion was all the response I needed. I grasped his shoulders and turned him in the direction of the library. "Why don't you head in there? Choose a book, and I'll come along shortly. We'll read it together. Would you like that?"

"Would I!" Like a shot, he ran full tilt, leaving me in an empty hallway with nothing but a pilfered coat and the royal insignia. I needed a place to hide them. If the Prince came looking—or worse, a contingent of palace guards—how could I explain myself?

No matter if I told the truth. It wasn't my fault that William— *Prince* William—had been so stupid as not to wear it in public. Why he would choose to do so was beyond my imagining, but far be it for a merchant's daughter to cast judgment on a royal.

Regardless of reason or purpose, they could still have my head for it.

And I rather preferred having a head.

6

The Consequence

Curiosity drove me to what I did next, though one might also cite a lack of common sense or some innate need for punishment. I made my way to the kitchen, though I might as well have been heading into an abyss for all the silence.

No longer echoed the joyful raucousness of cook and maid and scullery boy, replaced instead by the creaks and shudders of an empty home.

I stole to the furthest corner of the room and found a darkened cabinet where I shoved William's coat and ring as far back as my arm could reach. Hidden in shadows, no one would find it here until spring cleaning, a boon if by chance I found no way to dispose of it before then.

Elsewhere in the room, a cupboard door slammed. I bolted upright and hope sprung anew, Miss Mary's name on my tongue. I wove around the pots and pans and hanging meats, searching for the source of the sound.

Gretel, our cook, watched me from aside a basket of onions.

"They ain't here," Gretel said, wiping oily hands on her soiled apron. "I'm all what's left."

Hope vanished like a wisp, replaced by disappointment and a tiny spark of anger. I should have smothered the spark and let it die, but naivety won out and I fanned it instead.

"It won't keep," I said. "She hasn't the place to do this kind of thing. Once Father returns, he'll set it right. Or *she* will, once she minds the stench of her own waste."

Gretel's eyes, thin and full of sorrow, revealed a nature of strength built by hardship, melancholy wrought with acceptance to her own fate.

She lifted a tray off the counter, set primly with a teapot, cup, and saucer. Steam rose from the pot's spout, and I regretted every ill thought I'd ever spoken about eating Cook's cabbage or squash.

With a sigh, she placed the tray in my waiting arms and patted my head as though I were a doll about to be broken by rough children.

"Peace be with you," she said, and with her right hand, touched her forehead, chest, left shoulder then right, as if the Almighty cared about a girl giving tea service to a woman she despised.

I doubted the Lord cared one whit about this tea.

Still, I turned from the kitchen and, with unsteady hands, navigated the curving staircase to the second floor.

At the end of the dim, windowless hallway—for none of the lamps were lit, nor the doors to other rooms open with curtains drawn back, as had been our custom for as long as I could remember—I lifted a hand to tap twice on the door to my father's, and now Celia's, bedroom.

"Come in," said a voice from within.

I regretted my decision to bring the tea up the instant I stepped into the room.

Celia stood at the window, watching something through a slit in heavy, black curtains—curiously, these were nothing like the gauzy film that covered our parlour windows. Her hands were clasped behind her back and she stood ramrod straight, deep gray gown flowing past her ankles to pool on the floor like a train.

The room, lightless and lifeless as a tomb, urged my feet to turn around and leave.

But they did not.

"Your tea," I said, lacking an address. I wouldn't acknowledge her place in this house.

She didn't stir from her place by the window. I thought it just as well and left the tray on a small tea table in the center of the room, though the temptation to cough or drop a cup to provoke a reaction—any reaction—grew stronger with each passing moment.

With one step remaining to freedom, the tide turned.

"Ellison."

I froze, heart thudding within my chest.

"Turn around, please."

I did as told, stupid as I was. *She* hadn't moved.

"You are very late with my tea. I've been waiting."

What could I say? "It's hot, I assure you. I needed help. I've never had to make tea before."

She turned her face halfway, the light from the split between the curtains casting a menacing shadow across her profile, spoiling her beauty.

I took immeasurable delight in the sight of it.

"I see. Would you mind fetching something for me? I've heard there's a lovely edition of *Faust* in the library, and I'd like to read it with my tea."

Faust? How peculiar. "It's not in the library at the moment. I have it on my night table."

"Bring it to me, please."

Perhaps Father had mentioned it to her? I couldn't see how else she'd have learned about it, as the volume had been in my room during the entirety of my isolation.

Once in my room, I plucked the book from its place on the night table. It was a heavy, illustrated edition with gilded pages, a gift from Father in my twelfth year. Although I didn't want her beguiling fingers on its pages, I did want a moment's peace for Edward and myself.

But in that instant, as I turned toward the door and saw that Celia stood there with a pitch-dark scowl, I realized the truth.

She had been in my room.

My cry was silenced by the slamming of my door and the click of a key in a lock that should not have been there. I dropped the book—my precious book—and flew to the door. I turned the knob, and met resistance.

The lock on my side of the door was gone, and in its place, a flat sheet of iron.

She'd trapped me inside and changed the lock, but when?

"*Let me out*," I cried, and pounded both fists on the door.

The shadow of her lips appeared at the crack between door and wall.

"Disobedience is not tolerated in my household, Ella dear. We take our duties very seriously."

How *dare* she? "It's not *my duty* to bring your tea."

She tutted and lowered her tone until it slipped like molasses through the cracks. "Nor is sass becoming for a young lady. You will stay in your room and think about what you've done. When you are ready to do as you're told, I will release you."

Do as told! By her! I hadn't yet reached *that* level of desperation. I'd already spent a week in this room, what would be a few more hours? Surely Gretel would slip food to me as before.

I ran to the window, one final detail in my resolute plan.

As I turned the latch and pushed against the panes, my nerve began to dissolve. The panes did not move.

"I do hope you have a strong constitution, Ella," said Celia, "as you needn't bother with the windows. Can't have vulnerable young ladies wandering about on their own, hmm?"

For a brief instant, it occurred that I might ask why—did she know of the terrors William had mentioned, or was this simply part of my punishment?

Oh, *William.*

I couldn't stay locked up. I had to retrieve his coat and ring and hide it elsewhere, for if Celia had the audacity to intrude upon one's personal space, how long would it be before she found his belongings and began to ask questions?

And truth be told, I wouldn't last long in a room with a full chamber pot and no means to escape the growing odor. To confirm my suspicions, I pulled my pot from under the bed—and shoved it back without hesitation.

No house staff, no emptied pot.

I returned to the window and pushed with all the might I could muster, but still it refused to budge. My feet and forearms ached from the pressure.

Ah, yes. I needed more than to have my pot emptied and to fill my empty belly with food. The scrapes and wounds on my limbs needed tending before they became something far worse.

I sat on my bed, knees pulled to my chest, recalling the comfort of Mother's strong stone against the curve of my back. Poor Edward! He would wait in the library for hours. Celia would turn this to her advantage, wouldn't she? It was the perfect opportunity to poison him against me.

The very thought of her touching him, holding him on her lap, and capturing even one of his smiles made me leap from the bed and pound on the door once more. Pride be damned. I could not remain in this room while that woman roamed our halls.

I beat my fists against the door, over and over in endless rhythm, shrieking like the Devil himself, pounding flesh upon wood like a war drum. It might as well have been, for I saw it as a declaration of my defiance, a warning that while she could hold my body captive, she couldn't have my spirit.

And yet both remained, captive and held indeed, until I collapsed on the floor with burning lungs and bloodied hands.

Spent and broken, I slept.

7

The Passage

I awoke with a pounding in my skull and an ache in my veins. The hard floor hadn't made a very good pillow, and each limb protested in its own way.

If I was to stay captive here, some strategizing was required. Though I had neither water nor sufficient food, I did have a small store of apples at the back of my wardrobe.

Strange, perhaps, but they existed as a late-night collection for evenings spent reading by candlelight on an empty stomach. Inspection of the wardrobe revealed six apples, though one had a large, brown spot, making it more suitable for sauce than lone consumption.

I chose a bright red apple with amber stripes and bit into it with near religious fervor, devouring it with as much devotion. Its soft, gritty sweetness did little to sate my hunger, and I tossed the spent core onto the floor. On retrieval of *Faust*, I returned for the fifth time to the exploits of the poor doctor, as the room contained little else to occupy the hours. And so, a plan formed: When Cook brought food, I would put in a request for a different, unread volume.

But as the shadows lengthened and the growl of my belly grew to a roar, I feared that perhaps I had, on this occasion, misjudged my opponent.

I don't know how long I waited in that room, though the chamber pot, hunger, thirst, and pain of torn feet and hands were nearly enough to consider Celia the victor.

As resignation crept like a poison through each set of limbs—lifting me from the bed toward the door and an undeservedly given apology—my progress was stilled by the sharp, fevered cry of something below.

I looked down.

My heel, in its clumsy gait, had trod upon the string-thin tail of a tiny, gray mouse. Resourceful, this mouse, for it carried the browned core of my apple.

Rather than screech, as most girls tend to do in the presence of vermin, I pitied the poor thing, for it hadn't asked to be born in such a state … roaming the floors of our home for scraps instead of delighting in the joy and freedom of some farmer's field.

And now, in avoiding the fate of becoming some hawk's meal, he'd stumbled into my path during my own effort for survival.

I lifted my foot and released him. "Apologies, Sir Mouse."

As quickly as a mouse can when burdened by an object as big as himself, he scampered across the floor and slipped beneath my wardrobe. The small lip at the base of the unit afforded him and the core just enough room to fit underneath.

"But what will you do there?" He couldn't have been living there, and now in seeking refuge he'd leave a half-rotten apple core behind to be overrun by ants and whatever else.

"Sir Mouse, I believe you could have made a wiser choice."

I have never thought myself strange for speaking aloud to creatures unlike ourselves. After all, are they not afforded the same respect as other living beings? Celia, of course, excepted.

Curiosity beckoned, and so I found myself on my knees and forearms, peering beneath the wardrobe. Where I expected a mouse, a gust of cool air brushed against my cheeks. I saw no small rodent, but instead the faint outline of a hole.

Imagine! A family of mice living in my walls.

I lay down on my side to get a better look, reaching one hand under the lip of the wardrobe to pull myself closer.

My fingers pressed against some manner of lever or latch that sunk into the wardrobe like an unsuspecting thumb into a moldy peach.

The wardrobe shifted.

Thrusting myself backward, I rolled across the floor as the enormous wardrobe—amid a series of scrapes and grinds and metallic shrieks—swung away from the wall. Inside, my apples thumped about, no doubt bruising and becoming entirely inedible for anyone save my vermin companion.

More important, however, was what stood behind the wardrobe. Where there should have been a blank, solid wall, was …

Oh, but I couldn't tell at first. I stared with disbelief at the impossibility of a shifting wardrobe.

Once I regained control of my senses, I saw it. Faint but clear, if one should happen to look. I approached the wall and pushed. A panel in the wall, about Edward's height and as wide as Mother's stone, swung open.

I stared in.

Darkness stared back.

An escape? How *marvellous.*

Naturally, I proceeded, but on further thought ran back to my bedside table to retrieve a short bit of tallow and matches.

With a lit flame and near-blinding disbelief, I stepped through the wall.

The passageway—for indeed I found myself in a narrow passage—extended mere steps forward before presenting a choice. To the right was a shorter section of passage with an opposing door. I supposed that must be the way into Edward's room, but rather than confirm my suspicions, I thought it wisest to uncover all options first.

After all, a secret such as this wouldn't stay hidden for long in careless hands.

I went to the left, took three paces, another twist right, and forward—

My foot dropped through the air and in that instant visions of landing broken inside a wall, undiscovered for centuries, pierced through my calm. I might have screamed had my foot not landed with a thud on solid ground again, jarring my bones and nearly pitching the tallow out of my hand. Instead, I leaned forward and shone the light to find a set of stairs leading downward, presumably to the ground floor of our home.

Had Father known about this? He couldn't have. What would be the purpose for building such a thing? Secret passages and hidden doorways are the stuff of children's tales, and I had long since left the carefree state of childhood, not necessarily by choice. After Mother's death, we quickly learned that there were some tasks even servants could not do on behalf of the lady of the house. I had become she.

And though child no longer, I had never known of these

passages—nor had Edward, I assumed. My brother, owing to age, has never been particularly adept at secret-keeping.

Dust and dank air swirled about my nose, tickling with each breath, teasing the senses as if to dare a sneeze.

After reaching the base of the steps, I navigated passage upon dark passage, circling our home from between the walls, guessing at which room might be on the other side of each small door panel.

The kitchen wasn't difficult to find, but the sound of Gretel singing discouraged the thought of revealing myself for the sake of William's coat. I would try the library instead.

And yet when I reached the passage where I suspected the library might be, a door on the other side confused my sense of direction.

To decide, I closed my eyes, spun around three times, and stopped. The door I faced was the door I would open. A childish manner of choosing, to be sure, but embraced by the darkness between those walls, I felt a giddy rush of pleasure at this act of defiance.

A lever to the right of each door provided a way back into the rooms.

I prepared to pull with all my strength—after all, does metal not rust with disuse?—but it came down with ease as though recently oiled.

Grinding and squeaking and crunching came from inside the wall. I hardly dared to breathe. God willing, Celia wouldn't be on the other side.

When the grinding ceased, I pulled the door panel open and, once again, stepped through.

8

The Book

I was not in the library.

I had arrived in my father's office.

Fear and shame and the thrill of the forbidden rushed forth as a tide, for Edward and I were never allowed to stand alone in this room unaccompanied. Father's business was his own, save by invitation. That we'd always understood.

But Father was here no longer, and some bit of fate had brought me through the passage to find—

What? Another book to read? As I was to be under lock and key, perhaps I could survive on the bourbon and rye that sat atop his desk in the center of the room. And while I didn't think apples and rye would provide the necessary sustenance for survival, truth be told, I didn't think at all.

Instead, I stepped further into the room, swung the open bookcase easily back against the wall, and pushed until a heavy click revealed it had latched.

I began my inspection of the office.

Shelves surrounded every wall, packed with books and papers and curious objects. A sword here, a pile of gems and stones there, bits of string, and more books besides. As I pulled a small box decorated with pearl inlay from the center of a dusty shelf, the door handle turned.

The box slipped from my fingers and crashed onto the floor. I imagine it broke into thousands of shards of wood and pearl and whatever else, but I saw nothing save the turning of the handle and—to my utter dismay—the bookcase where I'd exited, flat against the wall.

Have I mentioned what a fool I can be?

Ah, so I have.

It's no secret, then, that a foolish girl would also waste precious seconds—as long as the turning of a key—searching for the latch under a bookcase, instead of finding a suitable place to hide.

The moment the door swung open, I dove underneath Father's grand desk, pulled up my knees and realized, only then, that I still held a burning flame.

"Curious." Celia—who else?—entered the room, her footsteps light as a cat and menacing as a bear. God help me should she discover what I'd done.

"If there are mice about, I'll have that cook's head." She sniffed the air and I snapped a hand overtop the flame of my tallow, sucking in breath through my teeth as the fire extinguished against bare flesh.

A shrill female voice pierced the space beyond the room. "Mice! Oh, Mother, no!"

Who on earth was that?

"You mustn't jest so," the voice continued. "If this house has mice, why, I won't be able to stay a minute longer. I'll take the first coach back to—"

"You'll do no such thing, Charlotte. I'll have a trap set in the morning."

"Will you?" The waif sounded breathless, and as squeaky as a mouse herself.

Celia's footsteps echoed away from me, though I dared not breathe. Dust from the passageway still sat in my nostrils and I pinched my nose until my eyes watered.

"Yes, my pet," she said to the mouse-girl. "I'll have it taken care of. Off you go. I'm sure you need rest after your journey. Wait in the parlour, and I'll send someone down to fetch your bags."

Fetch her bags?

But Celia had loosed the house staff.

Ah, but not *all* capable hands were now beyond her control. At least one set sat underneath a desk in her father's office, fearing the wrath of a usurping boor.

It appeared my new sisters were here, and I was about to meet them whether I liked it or not.

I scrambled forward from beneath the desk, though my limbs felt like sacks of flour under the weight of panic. How could I reach my room in time?

Though I suspected my desperate prayer would go unheeded, still I offered the promise of confession and penance should Celia be delayed long enough for my return.

Hit the latch, swing the bookcase. Light the candle. Exit the room. Take the wrong turn.

I might have wandered for days, lost between the walls, had I not turned left instead of right and tripped over an object on the ground. Both knees and hands slammed sharply onto the cold floor.

The tallow rolled away, snuffed again, but I kept silent.

Beneath my throbbing knees, I felt a large, *Faust*-heavy book. Though tempted to curse it for adding injury to injury, instead I lifted it in my arms, accepted the candle's fate, and returned the way I'd come.

Seconds were as hours, and minutes as days. Surely, Celia had discovered my absence by now. Surely, she would leave me in my room to starve and find a way to block every passage.

Surely, she would be my end.

I ascended a set of stairs—finally—and turned left. Pulled the lever to my right and prayed I'd chosen correctly, and that it wasn't too late.

In the same breath, I entered the room and shut the wardrobe back against the wall before diving under the covers. The instant my toes met the sheets, Celia strutted through the bedroom door.

"Your sisters have arrived," she announced. "Get up and come down to greet them. You'll fetch their bags and carry them up here to the landing."

Secrets made me bold. "I'll do no such thing." I sat up in bed and pulled the blankets tight to my chest. "I'm too weak from hunger. Can't they wait? Master Bert—"

"Is no longer in our employ." The fury on her brow sparked and burst into flame. "You will also cease your insolence immediately and do as you're told."

"I'm not strong enough." If she wouldn't listen to reason, then perhaps practicality.

She glared, all trace of softness gone. Oh, for Father to see her in this state.

I blamed myself, and still do, for I should have told him my misgivings the moment he declared his journey.

But as I hadn't done so, the intensity of her gaze and the fear of my secret being discovered were enough to send me to my injured, burdened feet.

She looked me over, wrinkled her nose, and sniffed. "Change your clothes, too, girl. You look like rubbish."

I folded my arms across my stomach and matched her stare as she left the room. How I hated her, then. I did, in that moment, believe it couldn't get worse. Though the portrait above the fireplace had shown naught but empty shells of girls, surely they couldn't be worse than *her*.

Still, I did as I was told and changed into a simple robin's egg blue dress, with ivory lace at the bodice, sleeves, and hem. My obedience only extended so far, however, and I chose to slide the passageway book out from under the bed rather than rush off to play servant to girls I was supposed to call sisters.

With a heave, I laid the book on the bed and ran two fingers across the embossed leather binding. Dust had collected in the creases and ridges of the spine and cover, and the faded gilding along the page spine suggested an age to the book far beyond anything I'd seen before.

Yet these stole the least of my attentions, for on the side, holding the book closed as though it contained some terrible secret, was a thick metal clasp.

A tiny keyhole in the center of the clasp piqued more than a simple measure of curiosity—I *needed* to know what was inside.

A tug on the clasp proved unsuccessful, though in truth, my physical strength left much to be desired. A stronger woman might have broken the lock and turned the pages, but I stood staring and yearning and aching for knowledge. One secret this day was not enough.

My inner self nudged and I sprang for my robe. From the pocket, I drew the object Father had tucked into my hand that morning.

A shout from below suggested Celia would wait no longer for my presence.

I opened my hand.

A key about the length of a child's finger rested in my palm, its polished cream length ending in teeth as sharp as knives. This key was not iron or bronze or copper, as keys should be.

No, this key was made of bone.

And it fit inside the book's clasp.

9

The Sisters

As time did not favor me, I slid both book and key beneath my bed before leaving the safety of my room. Soft slippers covered the fresh scabs on my feet, but even long sleeves and a pleasing smile couldn't hide the cuts on my hands and bruised chin.

Without time to wash, I looked quite the opposite of a regal daughter of the nobility.

"Here she is," Celia proclaimed as I descended the stairs. The three ladies entered the front entrance hallway as I hit the bottom step. "She'll take your things to your rooms."

"She looks a fright," said mouse-voiced girl, whom I assumed to be Charlotte. "I'm not sure I want her touching my things." Her cinnamon-brown ringlets bounced as she tilted her head this way and that, studying my approach as one might observe a monkey at the zoological gardens.

"Presuming you haven't brought a bag of bricks, I'll do my best," I said, though I doubted I could even do that much.

"She speaks!" Charlotte whipped her gaze from me to her mother and back again. And then, without an inkling of prescience on my part, she stepped across the floor, pulled off a white satin glove, and snapped the back of her hand against my cheek.

I gasped and clutched my face, the shock of being struck more painful than the actual sting. I'd had far worse many times on this day alone.

"Charlotte," huffed Celia, "meet Ellison, your stepsister."

No rebuke for her daughter? Not even a pretense of apology?

"Oh," said Charlotte, pulling her glove back onto a pale, delicate hand. "How do you do?" In a quieter tone, she added—with a surreptitious glance at her now-gloved fingers—"Your face is filthy."

And that gave one a reason to strike another? Why I remained silent is a mystery to me even now, but I wonder if some small part believed that if I didn't acknowledge *their* existence, they would not, in fact, exist.

"My bag contains no bricks," said a soft, feminine voice from behind Charlotte.

By deduction, Victoria.

Her ebony hair, much like her mother's, cascaded in an elaborate plait down to the small of her back, with sections pinned and twisted in strange ways to hold up a colourful, feathery hat.

I offered no retort, and both Charlotte and Victoria took their leave to the parlour. As they passed, I noted the brilliance of Victoria's hat, but a second look revealed that the feathers were, in fact, entire wings. Some milliner had crafted a hat from a dead bird's wings and, if I saw correctly, several entire birds' heads.

I felt ill at the sight. *This* was high fashion?

"Once you've carried the bags," Celia cleared her throat and fixed upon me like a snake, "as punishment for your delay and your refusal to apologize, I wish you to change the sheets of each bed and refill the wood stack next to the parlour fireplace."

I would never be clean again, at this rate.

"May I have some assistance from one of my sisters?" The last word stuck behind my teeth, and I pushed it out with force and regret. "Following the afternoon tea, of course. So that we might get to know one another better."

And though I didn't want help at all, mild familiarity sounded preferable to being slapped across the cheek at someone's whim.

Celia folded her arms and offered up the pretense of a smile. "We shall see."

From the parlour came a shriek of aggravation. "Mother! I'm tired and I must have tea. I can't stand another moment without it, I swear, I'll die."

I took this as a sign of the conversation's end. I had work to do, for until it was finished, the book waited alone.

<hr />

From that moment until sundown, I carried bags, fetched tea and desserts, scrubbed the entrance hall, and changed the sheets in every room. The stack of wood was forgotten amid the scuff, though it appeared that Charlotte delighted in asking small tasks of me under the guise of wanting assistance.

At first I preferred it to being locked away, though as the day wore on, I thought solitude a more appealing alternative to unceasing labors. Only once did I see Edward, timid and yet bursting with anticipation as we dined at our finest table, eating from Mother's china and drinking from Father's crystal goblets.

No doubt Edward thought the prospect of two more sisters to read him stories and bring him sweets as thrilling as a white Christmas morning.

"How is your schooling, girls?" Celia sipped her beetroot wine and tapped the glass for more. Only when she tossed me a fierce glare did I realize she meant *I* was to refill her glass.

Was she so helpless?

"Dreadful," said Charlotte, guzzling her own. "Did you know we're expected to do our own wash? And iron our own dresses? It's ludicrous. I shan't return."

I might have expected a comment about education and not the hardships of housework, but those were early days and I remained foolishly optimistic concerning our future.

"You poor thing," Celia murmured. "If all goes well, you may not have to." I started, nearly dropping the wine. Whatever did she mean?

Victoria cleared her throat with a polite cough. "How about you, Edward? Do you and your sister attend an academy?"

As Edward's mouth contained peas and potatoes, I thought to answer for him.

"We have a tutor." Though doubtless Celia would release him as well. "We receive lessons during the winter months, and are free to explore our own interests during the rest."

Victoria stared as though she'd thought me a mute. "I didn't speak to you."

"Now, now," said Celia, "no need, child." To me, she added, "We can't have that, now, can we? The Devil finds work for idle hands."

Talk of the Devil and he's sure to appear, I wanted to say.

Little did I know.

"I'm sure we'll find something to occupy your time." Celia dabbed the corners of her mouth with a napkin.

I set the bottle down and returned to my seat, though my tongue could not be contained. "And Miss Charlotte and Miss Victoria, will they find their time occupied as well?"

The girls snickered as though I'd said something amusing.

Celia folded her hands on the table. "Doubtless so."

They stopped their twittering.

"But seeing as how they've just come off a tiring journey and months of tedious schooling, I believe some slight recreation is in order."

My mouth opened of its own accord, but Celia continued to speak.

"Don't trouble yourself about it, child. You'll have plenty to fill your time, and you may begin by clearing our table. Edward may assist, if you like. Come, girls. Evening tea and cakes in the parlour, Ellison."

With smarmy glances and wicked grins, the three rose and took their leave. Edward and I remained at the table.

"Shall I help?" he squeaked, appearing more perplexed than I. The poor child was unaccustomed to being left out.

"No," I said, lifting a plate of uneaten pheasant and potatoes. They'd barely eaten enough to fill a teacup. Father would never tolerate such waste.

"I can," he urged, "then you can read to me. Stepmother said you didn't want to read with me anymore, but that's not true, is it?"

The pheasant teetered in my hands. "Of course it's not true. I'm so sorry, Eddie. Celi … *Stepmother* had, ah, other plans for me. Did you wait long?"

He grinned and bounced on his heels. "No, she read to me instead! Though I didn't much like the story. She didn't read it like you do."

How *dare* she. So she was a liar and a thief, if trust and time could rightly be stolen.

"We will read together. Let Cook know we need another pot of tea and some thin cakes, and change into your nightclothes. I'll finish here and be up before you know it."

I hoped I was right.

IO

The Key

My hands trembled as I drew the book and key from underneath the bed, candle at the ready. With the rest of the household abed—including Edward, who'd lasted all of three pages into a tale of a racing hare and tortoise—I finally had a moment's peace. Though my limbs ached for rest, how could I with such a mystery at my very fingertips?

I grasped the bone key and twisted. It turned easily in the lock and the clasp released with a gentle sigh. I took hold of the cover, held a breath, and opened the book.

The room plunged into darkness.

I relit the tallow and returned to the book.

Again, darkness.

Three times I relit the wick, and three times the flame died.

On the fourth try, I did one thing differently, as strange as it seemed. I begged the candle to stay alight—the words of a desperate girl in need of some happiness, if only for a moment.

The tallow remained lit, and I resolved to place a linen beneath the wardrobe from now on to stop the drafts from extinguishing my small fire.

The opening pages of the book were yellowed and rippled with wear, crackling as I turned each one. Upon seeing the Latin phrases that covered the second and third pages, my eagerness waned. Had I waited all this time to find nothing but the *Vulgate*?

Or perhaps not, for dedications and warnings in Latin and German sprawled across the pages that followed, though in my impatience, I did little more than glance at the words.

At last on the seventh page, a title: *The Book of Conjuring.*

Beneath that was a faded stamp containing a barely legible inscription, though enough of the lettering remained to make its point clear. This book belonged to the *Bibliotheca Regia Monacensis*—the Royal Library of Munich.

What had my father been doing with a book from the palace archives, let alone possessing the key to open it?

Pleased as I was that the book had not been another text of the Holy Scriptures, as I turned still more pages, many of the words and phrases seemed reminiscent of those used by a priest at mass.

But not quite.

On some pages, circles were drawn within circles, words between each line. On others, I found strange symbols such as double crosses, lined boxes, and pentangled shields with names listed in each corner.

There were many circles, and many names.

I didn't understand.

A heaviness settled across the room as I read, and each breath became thick with effort. My hands trembled as I touched the next page, and the next.

The book was not right.

I shivered with fear for what it might be, but I couldn't stop.

Something led me onward, glued my fingers to its surface, refused to release me from this pressing need to *understand*.

I turned page after page after page without ceasing until, like a hawk alighting on its chosen branch, my fingers came to rest on a near-blank leaf, save for one simple line which read: "For the Conjuring of Illusions."

I turned the page.

There, the text's author had depicted another circle inside a circle with writing between, and a name in the center.

"To reveal that which is hidden, or hide that which is revealed," I read, striving to keep my place despite the tallow's flickering flame. "In the third hour of night, and dressed in white, find a secret place on level ground. Trace a circle as such appears here, without deviation, writing all that is shown amidst it."

I couldn't help but glance at my wardrobe. What would I do, should Celia discover the passage?

And while I didn't understand its lure, nor why my simple curiosity had grown to a lusting wonder, in that instant I felt compelled to do as the words instructed.

Was this magic?

I knew little of such things, but what I did know of it didn't inspire confidence. While forbidden by priests and clerics and the Scriptures, it had never seemed quite so different from the sorts of miracles performed by the Christ in his day.

Was this, then, a book of miracles? Or simply a fanciful tome, meant for children and left in the passage by mere chance?

Whatever its purpose, the pain of the day and the toll of hours stolen increased my yearning for this moment of peace. I could not stop reading.

"When this is done, place a measure of ash in the west of the circle, and in it a bone no longer than a man's finger and no smaller than one joint. When you have done this, kneel facing the east, and with an unwavering voice say—"

I ceased to whisper aloud. Should I dare speak these words without a circle, ash, or bone?

But why not? I didn't believe in *real* magic.

And although I didn't understand the book, or the passage, or the rumor of terrors roaming our streets, I wish I had, for I would not have done what I did next. And though I didn't believe it *could* be done, I did not care.

I marked the page with a finger, lifted the book, and pressed the latch beneath the wardrobe.

I planned to hide this passage, if only in my own imagination.

But first? I had to gather cinders.

II

The Circle

I found the parlour without much difficulty, though the heightened need for complete silence—so as to not wake a sleeping household—caused me to step even more carefully than before. I couldn't afford to fall this time.

When I pulled the lever to enter the room, I was seized with panic, for I had forgotten about the scraping and grinding. Once upstairs, once here below. How long until someone came to investigate the noise?

Rather than risk discovery as I did in Father's office, I closed the fireplace—for that is what opened onto the parlour—just far enough to provide semblance of illusion, should someone glance inside, but far enough from the wall that I could dash back into hiding at a moment's notice.

Moonlight glinted through the gauzy curtains of the room, setting the jewelled adornments to sparkle like stars. It was, I admit, a beautiful sight. My fears of discovery eased as I took in the room, the silence, and the calming charm of the night sky.

I set the heavy book on a nearby chaise and reread the instructions. Knowing where to stand would be simple enough, as the rising sun caught these windows early each morning. But what would I use for the circle?

Lacking sense, I used the closest thing at my disposal. I climbed across the backs of the couches and chairs near the window and, using those implements fully intended to stoke fires and not indulge careless young women's fancies, lifted the curtain rod and pulled down the fabrics.

I twisted the curtains until they became thin, rolled lengths that nearly begged to be curved this way and that, forming two small circles—one outer, one inner—about the width of skirt hoops in the middle of the parlour floor.

From the fireplace, I gathered handfuls of cinders and ash, the powder and burnt shards coloring my hands a mournful shade of gray. I placed these in the circle facing east and, in a stroke of genius I still pride myself on, took a stick of half-burnt wood that I might—without regard for discovery, consequence, or damage— copy the words from the book between the lines of my circles. Legible they were not, for charcoal and Persian carpets don't do any favors for one's penmanship. I hoped it would do.

In the center of the circle, as clear as I could make them, my hand formed six letters: Curson. A name, but one which sounded foreign to my ears. I dared whisper it aloud as I checked the writing and a tremor ran up my spine at the sound of it.

Only at that moment did it occur to me that I might be playing at something, well, otherworldly. But the concept of danger wasn't yet a reality, and truthfully, the possibility of real danger might have heightened my determination if it did anything at all.

Tasks complete, it was left to my ivory night shift and the book's key to play the roles of white robe and small bone. On the surface, I knew I was being both silly and reckless. Looking around at the curtains on the floor, my charcoal scratches, and my ash-stained hands, I couldn't help but giggle at the absurdity of it all.

Father gone. A new, cruel stepmother and her obstinate daughters. Rumors of terrors in the town, whatever those might be. And strangest of all, secret passages in our home! I placed the bone key in the center of the ash pile, covering it enough so that only the very edge remained visible.

I stepped to the center of the circle, quiet laughs escaping with every movement as though life itself was naught but one extended jest at my expense. I turned to the west, knelt, and placed the book on the floor inside the circle. Leaning over so that the candle would illuminate the words, I read with as strong a voice as one can, when whispering into the night's dark shadows.

"I, so-and-so, conjure … oh." I stopped, for I'd made a puerile error. I began anew. "I, Ellison, conjure you, O Curson, powerful and illustrious spirit, in whom I place every trust, by the one and only undivided and inseparable Trinity—" I rolled my eyes at this, for I doubted the Father, Son, and Holy Ghost could be bothered to listen to a girl kneeling inside a circle of curtains, "—that you should come forth humbly and with restraint, sworn to carry out whatever I ask and make hidden that which has been revealed, or reveal that which is hidden."

According to the book, I was to wait until my summons received an answer, at which time I should present my request. No, my *command*.

I sat in darkness for some time, enjoying the flit and play of shadows against the far wall. Without curtains across the glass, the moon's rays acted of their own accord on the elaborate adornments of the parlour.

I waited and waited, growing wearier with each passing moment as the novelty of my adventure waned. I was beyond tired, for the exhaustion of the day caused me to teeter as I knelt. Sensing my imagination's indulgence was about to come to an end, I made one final effort. I repeated the summons, this time in a clear and firm voice without whispers, as weariness had made me careless.

The moment I finished the recitation, I closed my eyes, yearning to succumb to sleep if only for a moment. The warm comfort of darkness called to me, that I might take its refuge and replace the curtains in the morning instead …

The air hissed.

There was a softness to the sound, and my eyes flew open at the thought that perhaps a garden snake—or worse—had wandered into our home.

The hissing grew louder, sharper, until I realized that it wasn't a snake at all but something that *spoke my name.*

"Ellisssssson."

I leapt to my feet and spun to face the uncovered windows, looking toward the circle's east. The bone key and the pile of ash pulsed with a dark light, if indeed there is such a thing. It was as though all joy, all happiness, and all hope had been sucked from the room into the little pile of ash and cinders, which burned with an unflamed fire.

A tendril of black smoke rose from the center, curling through the air, rising and rising, until it rested directly in front of my trembling face. The smoke hissed my name once more.

"Ellisssssson."

I nearly lost control of my functions, as crude as that is. But it is important to understand this: beyond all else, however the book and key and passage might have excited my curiosity, I was more afraid in that moment than at any other.

I wanted to believe I stood in a dream. That I'd fallen asleep, that I dreamt all that occurred.

But I did not.

The smoke grew thicker as I stood, rooted, shaking inside the circle. I tried to lift one foot, to move away, but the hissing grew louder and louder until I was certain the entire town would come running to my aid.

Tendrils of smoke curled around my ankles and wrists and a scream caught in my throat, for when I looked back at that which hovered before me, I thought I saw two eyes, glinting within the blackness, looking into my own.

Something within the swirling mass of smoke could *see*.

And it waited.

"Command me, mistress," it said.

I did not hold back my scream, then.

I dove for the bone key and ripped it from the ash, fingers burning at the touch as though they'd reached into tongues of real fire. A hand of smoke clasped over mine, cold and rough and firm as flesh. It pushed against my own, and in surprise I allowed the bone to re-enter the ash for only a moment.

"Command me, mistress, for I am yours."

I cried out a second time, tears springing to my eyes as I pulled back the bone with all my might, kicked at the ash once, bent to grab the book, and ran back toward the passage as if the Devil himself had appeared in our parlour.

For all I knew, he had.

My feet tripped over the circle of curtains, tangling around my ankles. I shook them off, dove through the passageway door, and fell aground gasping for air.

From the parlour, silence.

My labored breath was the only sound I heard, though I dared not peek out, should that ... creature ... be there.

And in that silence, the truth of the matter became clear.

I had conjured a spirit.

Oh, Mother, what have I done?

12

The First Spirit

How long I remained in the passage, I cannot say. I slept with my back to the wall, clutching bone and book to my chest for some time. On waking, I had a choice: Peek out to see if the spirit remained, or return to my room and risk Celia's wrath when she found the mess in the parlour.

And as I'm not known for my ability to resist the temptations of curiosity, of course I chose the former. The morning sun's earliest rays peeked over the tops of the trees, and another panic seized my breast. I had slept for longer than I thought. Celia would awaken at any moment.

As there was no spirit in sight—and truly, daylight tends to wash away even the deepest frights of darkness—I burst from the passageway and began futile efforts to right the room. How could a young woman whose talents did not extend to growing upward replace the high curtains? Or clean the stain of ash and charcoal from the carpets?

My tears returned, sending droplets of water spinning down

to pool at my chin, where they slid into the ash. Every drop left a small, circular dent in the pile, and I might have laughed at the spotted ash had I not been facing certain death—or at least, some manner of painful punishment.

"Need help?"

I sprang to my feet at the sound of Cook's gravelly voice, a sharp release of fear in my gut. I faced her and I must have looked a fright, for she smiled at me as one does upon seeing a stumbling calf in a farmer's field. She glanced around the room, taking in the curtains, the carpets, and—to my horror—the displaced fireplace.

"I was ... I didn't ... " What could I say?

"It's all right, Miss Ellison," said Gretel. "Let's get them curtains righted afore the lady comes down."

And to think I'd often dismissed Cook as a pleasant but simple woman. She had more perception and sense than I in those days. I accepted her help, and she assisted with hanging the curtains, sweeping the carpet as best we could—which she then took for washing, despite the laundering not being her job—and at last she inclined her chin at the fireplace.

"Best you get back to bed, girl. The lady'll have my hide and yours if she finds you out of your chamber."

I shook my head, heart swollen with gratitude, but also a mite fearful that Cook knew my secret.

"Why are you helping me?" I couldn't leave without knowing.

She smiled, a genuine smile as I'd never before seen on her round, flushed face. "Your father be a good man, miss, and you and the little one not far behind." She nodded toward the book, which I'd dropped at the edge of the passage. "And though I be sworn to secrets of his own, I'll keep yours as well, seeing them as they are."

"But why? What can I give you in return?" I needed some assurance, at least.

Gretel brushed her hands across her apron, smudged despite the day's early hours. "Naught but that my place in the house continues."

"But I can't—"

"I know, girl." She placed a finger against her lips. "But I know you'll do your best until the master returns. Likewise, I'll help you in your, ah … " She glanced at the floor where I'd laid my circle. "Otherworldly doings."

She crossed herself, shooed me into the passage, and shut the fireplace behind until it latched. Though bewildered that Gretel seemed to have some knowledge of what I'd attempted, I was ever the more grateful for her help—and this gratefulness only increased tenfold when I reached my room and slid inside, for footsteps down the hallway revealed that Celia had indeed arisen and was headed my way.

A key turned in the door. *Ah, so she locked me in overnight.*

I might have been enraged, had I not been preoccupied with presenting a picture of innocence.

She opened the door to find me sitting abed, perusing *Faust*, hair askew.

"Get up, child. Laziness isn't becoming. Go down and make ready the dining table, and fetch breakfast and tea."

I could hardly be accused of laziness if locked in the room!

"For three?" I asked through clenched teeth.

Celia stiffened. "Don't be foolish. I will dine alone. My daughters will dine when they rise."

She said "my daughters" to emphasize, surely, that I was not to be included, despite the pleasant words we'd exchanged only the week prior.

I couldn't suppress my sigh, and once loosed, why not dig myself a further grave? "Is it really so difficult to retrieve it yourself?"

Celia entered the room, walked across my floor, and plucked

Faust from my hands. I couldn't read her expression, her face a blank canvas. "You ungrateful child. After all your father has done for you, you can't be bothered to help his poor, new wife adjust to life in a strange place?"

Whatever was she on about?

"You should be ashamed of yourself, lying about, selfishly loafing whilst—"

"It's hard to do much else when locked in one's room. Please return my book."

Eyes flashing like a cat's in the night, she lowered her face to within a finger's width from mine. "Lest you wish to see yourself and your brother on the next carriage to Saint Antony's, I suggest you still that insolent tongue and do as you're told."

With that, she swept out of the room still holding my book, a precious lifeline to memories of better days. I clenched my fists as anger rose from deep within.

Saint Antony's? *Oh yes, because Father would certainly approve of his children entering the priesthood and the nunnery before they're old enough to guide a carriage through the streets.*

Her threats were sorely lacking.

Still, in an effort to spare Edward from her misdeeds, I rose and did as asked. It hadn't escaped my notice that today, she'd included my brother in her threat. I had hoped it would take longer, but as cruel as she seemed, Celia was not stupid. If she couldn't control my will through threats to my person, she could do it through threats to the one I loved most.

I dressed in yellow lace and wore a necklace of one tiny pearl that rested in the center of my breastbone. Just because *they* wore hideous fashions didn't mean I had to follow suit. I had a wardrobe full of perfectly wonderful gowns and more than enough adornments to match. Better a simple pearl than a lavish hat made from expired creatures.

The early morning passed, and I hadn't yet seen my brother. I had a moment of fright around late morning tea that perhaps Celia had made good on her threat after all, but I stole away from the tasks demanded to poke my head into Edward's room.

I loosed a sigh of deep relief at seeing him there, still lying abed, but the relief didn't last long as a moan escaped from beneath the sheets. I flew across the room and knelt by his side, placing a hand on his forehead. It felt warm to the touch, though not so warm that I could affirm a fever.

"Eddie," I whispered, and pulled back the covering that shielded his sleeping face. He stirred, blinked sleepy eyes, and yawned a great yawn.

"Ellison?" He turned to his side but made no effort to sit.

"Are you well?" For I saw then that his face was pale, eyes unfocused, and his tiny lips too dry.

I stood and opened the curtains, allowing warmth and light to spill into the room.

"My stomach hurts," he said, his little hands disappearing beneath the blanket folds to clutch his belly. "I don't feel good."

This was most inconvenient, and more than a little worrisome. "I'll send for Doctor Hofstadter, yes? Where does it hurt? Can you show me?"

He pushed himself up onto his elbows and I drew the blankets back all the way, my heart tightening as he shivered. Edward held his stomach as one does after a full meal. "It feels like I ate too many sweets, but I didn't! I promise I didn't. Not even one."

I gave him a smile, though more for his sake than mine. My

insides shook like fresh jelly, for how could I care for an ill child while keeping house? Surely, Celia would understand and allow me to spend my day here. But first, the doctor.

"The doctor will have you righted before you know it," I said, smoothing a hand along his forehead, "and you'll be up and about in an instant. I'm sure it's a bit of bad beef or a spring cold."

Edward wrinkled his nose and slapped a hand over his mouth. "He won't make me take any of his medicines, will he?" How he knew of the doctor's ill-tasting medicines was beyond me, though I suspect he recalled Mother's reaction at the foul-scented concoctions the doctor had suggested during her early months of illness.

I prayed silently that Edward had simply caught a short bout of stomach ache. Overreaction, perhaps, but not for me. Not for our family.

I offered him reassurances, retrieved a book for him full of pictures and familiar words, and promised to return as soon as I could. I had Cook send for the doctor and took my pleas to Celia. I found her standing in the parlour doorway, staring into the room.

My blood froze.

I stepped backward, hoping to remove myself from notice, and collided with someone behind.

"Watch where you're going, you clumsy oaf," squeaked Charlotte, fanning her face in false shock. I mumbled an apology and pushed past as she sniffed in disdain.

"Ellison."

How that woman's voice could stop me mid-stride, I may never know. Or worse, how she always seemed to sense my presence. It might have been impressive under different circumstances.

"Come here, please."

I did. Charlotte's eyes glinted with pleasure at my summons.

"Yes?" I stopped just short of the doorway. I didn't want to see the remnants of my nighttime excursion in full daylight. Particularly not if Cook and I had failed to adequately disguise my doings.

"Cook tells me raccoons entered our home last night and made a terrible mess of my beautiful parlour." She turned to me then, not angry but resolved. "She has done you the favour of seeing to it the rug is restored. You, on the other hand, will clean out the fireplace."

I'd do what?

"If the disgusting vermin return, at least they won't track ash all over my Persian rug and draperies."

Ah. Cook. How I underestimated the woman even still.

"Edward feels ill," I protested. "I've had Gretel call for Doctor Hofstadter and I plan to spend the remainder of the day with him."

Surprise flickered in her eyes, but she recovered quickly. "You called without my permission?"

Certainly Father would *not* overlook this when he returned. "I didn't think it necessary to get permission to treat one's illness."

"It costs money, child."

"Family is priceless."

I matched her, stare for stare, until she relented. "Very well. I'll tend the boy while you sweep the cinders. Doubtless he needs a mother's touch."

I couldn't contain myself. "You are *not* his mother."

She laughed. Yes, she *laughed.* Deep and strong and full of cruelty, but she laughed. "We'll see about that."

She swept from the room, leaving me with Charlotte and a task that required me to swallow all memories of the night before. Charlotte, however, eyed my yellow lace dress and pearl necklace. I didn't like the way she looked at me, so I moved away with intent to begin my task.

There was a firm tug at my throat and I felt something give. I gasped, whirled, and found Charlotte carefully folding my necklace into the palm of her gloved hand. I reached to snatch it back, but she pulled away and shook one finger in my face as though scolding a disobedient puppy.

"That's mine. Please return it immediately." I attempted tact at first, though I doubted it would be effective.

Charlotte raised her eyebrows, tucked my necklace into her bosom, and lifted empty palms heavenward. "Whatever do you mean, sister?"

The woman was nothing short of a thieving cow, if cows could be thieves. "Return my necklace now."

She shook her head. "You must be mistaken. Might it have been lost in a basket of laundry? Or perhaps somewhere in the kitchen? I imagine you must miss it terribly."

Yes, I did.

So I plunged my hand down the front of her dress, touched the object in question, and pulled it out as Charlotte screamed with the lungs of a banshee.

"You brute," she shrieked, naturally just as Celia thundered down the stairs and into the room. "Mother! Mother, this ... this ... *beast* attacked me! I was only trying to make conversation, oh Mother ... "

I couldn't speak. How had this turned on me in an instant?

Charlotte spilled tears as she launched herself into the arms of her mother, who glowered at me.

"Ella, I thought better of you after our talk this morning."

And I had thought young women were beyond such displays. "She stole my—"

Charlotte wailed again, louder this time, though she flashed a wicked grin between cries. Celia's teeth clenched, her red lips shining all the brighter as she condemned me. "Once you finish here, gather your things."

"But—"

"Silence."

"She stole—"

"Quiet." If she had been any closer, I believe she might have slapped me as her daughter had on first meet. "It's time you learned what gratitude means. Pack your bags. Victoria will have your room. From today forward, you will sleep in the attic."

13

The Attic

S he would not let me see Edward.

She would not tell me of his illness.

Instead, I snuck out through the back door on pretense of emptying the bucket of cinders and ran after the doctor, my skirts flying every which way and billowing up clouds of dust and ash with every step.

I caught the doctor as he climbed into the carriage, and I breathed a sigh of relief that Celia had not loosed our regular driver as well.

I suspect cooking and driving were the two things she was not willing to risk at my hands.

"Miss Ellison, how do you do?" The doctor appeared somewhat taken aback by my emergence, though even now I suspect it had more to do with my outward appearance than anything.

I curtsied, though not necessary under the circumstances. Rather, I did so to convey my own efforts at courtesy in comparison to that received from the new ladies of the house. "Fine, thank you, Doctor, though I'm uncertain whether I can say the same for Edward. Please, how is he?"

The doctor removed his floppy black hat, twisted the brim, and replaced it on his head. "A bit of influenza, I believe. It seems quite mild and he's a spirited boy, so I'm sure he'll recover rather quickly."

Thank the Almighty! "You're quite sure?"

The creases of weariness around his eyes softened. He had kind, gentle eyes. I had always liked Doctor Hofstadter, even if his visits often meant something terrible had already befallen—or was about to befall—one of us. "He'll be all right, Ellison. Please give your father my regards, will you?"

I nodded, but thought to inquire further. "Doctor, my deepest thanks for coming with speed. Please, have you heard these rumors of terrors in the town? No one will explain—"

His expression darkened, brow furrowing and closing him off like a veil. "Don't you listen to rumors, Ellison. Your father is a good man and I don't believe a word. As for the terrors in the night, well, we seem to have had some respite these few days. Perhaps it's over." He lowered his face to mine, voice quiet and scratchy like sand. "Be careful, Ellison. If that woman should prove to be more than you can bear, remember I'm but a carriage ride away. I've seen too much suffering in your family to stand idly by."

And with that, he doffed his hat, stepped up into the carriage, and awayed.

I stood in our carriage drive, no further to understanding William's rumors and yet relieved at the news of Edward. While I appreciated the sentiment of the doctor, he left me staring after him with more questions than before.

What had Father to do with any of this?

I did not dump the ashes.

While some part of me urged to do as I'd been told—more to prevent myself from repeating the events of the previous night—something deeper grabbed hold of my sense.

I admit, I was curious. The terror of the spirit, or being, or ghost's appearance had eased until the memory felt like a hazy dream, and the temptation sprung forth that I might try—as I was assuredly better prepared now—to repeat my success to the fullest. After all, I'd gone to all that trouble and hadn't even asked for anything. Clearly, I needed the passages hidden before it was too late.

A nastier request crossed my mind at the memory of Charlotte's claws at my necklace, but I chided myself with a stern reminder: I could not *become* them, lest I lose myself. Cruelty would be no punishment in return, so I would turn the other cheek and seek a better way to co-exist with them.

A way that would keep Edward and I safe and healthy. A way that would preserve our integrity and humiliate theirs.

Don't laugh.

I am well aware that I failed.

I hid the bucket of ash and cinder in the attic behind a cracked mirror that had been propped against a dust-coated chest of drawers. The attic smelled of damp wood and dry leaves, accented by dust and grime that coated every surface and floated through the air when disturbed. A mattress rested in a far corner, doubled over and full of mites, or so I suspected. A plate-sized window that looked toward town provided the only light, and I feared that open candle flame might set the whole room ablaze.

I moved several boxes of old books and Lord knows what else—carefully, as I didn't yet have the physical strength to lift them—to create a makeshift bedframe for the mattress, distasteful as it seemed, as well as a small end table and a desk. The latter I constructed from two of the wardrobe's drawers and a cracked wooden door.

While I didn't intend to give up my room and passageway access—for I very much doubted I'd find a passage entrance in the attic—I thought it best to utilize the time given to move rooms constructively, just in case.

In the midst of my attempts to make the space liveable—or at least, not inherently dangerous—my stomach began to complain, a reminder that I hadn't found opportunity to fill my belly since the day before. With Celia's attentions elsewhere while I moved from bedroom to attic, I wondered if perhaps I could sneak a morsel or two of the sweet cakes the rest of the house's ladies indulged in several times each day.

All ladies but myself and Gretel, that is.

I traversed the creaking staircases with care, and came to find Gretel struggling under the weight of firewood for the ovens. Her face was flushed and brow damp with sweat. I rushed to her without hesitation, for she had not hesitated to help me.

"Let me assist," I said, lifting several logs from her arms and placing them atop the kitchen's near-empty pile. "Surely you can afford fewer logs per trip? It might add a mite of extra time, but—"

The pile dropped from her arms in a heap and she bent over at the waist with hands on knees, breathing heavily.

"Time for nothing, girl. You know as well as I." She nodded at the firewood. "But you may be right. Dropped a piece or two along the way in, anyhow. They send you to fetch something?"

"Ah, no, I was merely hungry … " I realized the selfishness of my request. Celia worked the both of us to the bone, and Cook had helped me on borrowed time. How could I ask anything more of her?

But she must have sensed my hesitation, for she gestured to the back door with a nod. "I'll find something for you if you check my steps and bring back the pieces what fell on the way."

I agreed with a greater enthusiasm than the moment warranted, but empty stomachs and guilty consciences have a way of motivating even the most stoic of individuals.

For the second time that day, I left my now-stifling home and stepped outside. About five paces away from the door was the final piece of wood that had tumbled from the load, and several more beyond. I decided to make the short trek into the stables and start from the pile, collecting pieces as I moved back toward the house.

But when I drew close to the stable door, several snorts from within stilled my steps. The horses certainly would not greet me, nor their keeper, in such a way. Horses do not complain for nothing, and with the rumors of terrors about, perhaps I should have taken greater care. But who gives heed to dark rumors in broad daylight?

Still, the horses' warning gave me cause to search the ground nearby for an object I might wield in protection, but all of Gretel's dropped logs were behind me. I could turn about and race back to one of the pieces of wood on the ground, or continue only a few steps forward to an entire stack of splintery weapons—though these were just inside the door of the stable. Either choice might place me at risk.

It is strange even now to recall that not once did I consider running back to the house for help. Perhaps some part of me knew the danger I walked toward couldn't be worse than what I already endured—or perhaps I simply couldn't bear the thought of losing something else, even if that something happened to be a four-legged creature.

The decision came easily and I filled my lungs with intention to count to three, lunge forward into the stable, grab a log, and use it however necessary to defend our horses—while calling for help, of course, though with all our staff dismissed, who else would come beside Gretel?

"One … two … three … " I leaped forward and reached for a piece of wood, but snatched my hand back with a start. "Oh!"

A hooded figure crouched in the darkness next to the wood pile, a log in each hand. The figure appeared to be searching for something amid the wood, but as I burst through the doorway, he dropped both pieces and rolled backward in the same instant that I recovered and closed fingers around a thin-chopped spike—and swung it toward the figure with a scream rising in my throat.

He leapt to his feet and at that moment, the hood fell from his brow to reveal—

"William?"

I stared after him, incredulous. His expression mirrored my own, and he glanced from me to the spike in my hand and back again. I thought to drop it but only lowered it instead. I am not sure why.

What was the Prince doing in our stable? I hoped Gretel had not heard the beginnings of my cry for help.

"Uh … hello." His mouth gaped open as mine surely had, and I almost laughed.

"William *is* your name, yes?" I noted the long cloak he wore, dark and billowing and ending at the knees, as if the garment intended to obscure the identity of the wearer. His gold medallion, hung around his neck, sparked a memory. Fear flared in my empty gut. Had he remembered and come searching for his cloak and ring?

I chose my words with care, for if he'd come to personally claim his belongings, he might still wish to keep up whatever strange ruse he played at. "What are you doing in our stable?"

"I'm ... I ... "

"If you've come searching for treasure, I'm afraid we don't keep our valuables hidden among the horse puddings, nor the firewood. Be honest, or I might complete the swing." I drew back the piece of wood in my hand and fought the smile that struggled to betray me.

"No, wait." He held up his hand and stepped closer. Did he truly believe me? Curiouser by the moment. "I'm looking for something. I, uh ... my coin purse was stolen on my way into town and I thought I saw the culprit dash in here."

That had to be one of the poorest—and stupidest—stories he could have possibly given.

"It was stolen on your way into town?"

He nodded. "That's right."

"We're not on the way into town, if you hadn't noticed. There's no major road that leads from the south, as the central roadways draw travelers in from the east or west as a matter of defensibility."

He really should have known that.

"I ... hadn't noticed." His throat bobbed as he swallowed, glancing from the wood I held to me.

"And you say the culprit ran in here?"

"Yes!" William's nod became furious. "Small boy, I think. Youngish. Ten, perhaps."

"Did he come by way of the road? You know, the one into town?"

"Yes?"

By all things, whatever was he doing here? I gripped the wood tighter. "Despite living on a gated and locked property."

"Well—"

"And I suppose you saw this thief drop your coin purse into our *wood pile*? Because that's what thieves do, of course."

He swallowed again, harder this time. "Look, I didn't know you lived here, but … " He paused for a moment, his expression becoming thoughtful. Without warning, he sprang forward and tore the piece of wood out of my hand before throwing it back on the pile.

"Oh!" A sharp pain in my hand revealed half a finger-length of splinter lodged in the skin of my palm. I bit the inside of my lip and silently cursed myself for not seeking Gretel's assistance immediately. As a mule tied unwillingly to a cart, I am as stubborn, but I would not take the blame for this injury. "First, you bother me at my mother's grave, then you break into my family's stable for heaven knows what reason, then stab me with my own—"

"I didn't stab you!" The look he offered was one of incredulity, so I held up my hand. Color drained from his porcelain cheeks and he grabbed my palm. I flinched at his touch—a warm, soft hand. Nothing like mine, which was now slightly roughened and worn raw in places from several days of hard labor under Celia's rule. "I'm very sorry, I can't seem to do anything right around you, can I … "

His voice trailed off as he pinched the skin at the splinter's base, holding my hand with his own. Indeed, the action was entirely improper, but I didn't believe it any worse than having been seen in my nightclothes. We seemed to define the very notion of impropriety.

Gently, so as to not leave any smaller remnants, William drew out the splinter and tossed it to the floor.

I pulled my hand away from his in an instant. "You haven't finished answering my questions."

His shoulders lifted and sagged. "That's because I don't have a good answer for you."

His surprise at seeing me was long gone, replaced with the same effortless self-assurance of our first meeting. My stomach tightened and stirred as a slow smile spread across his face. He glanced at my clothes and shook his head, and I wished that for once, he might catch me wearing something clean and appropriately befitting for meeting a prince.

"You had me going for a moment," he said, a true laugh escaping this time. "Honestly, I'm not here to cause trouble, but I *am* looking for something."

"Did you ever think to use the front door?"

"It's not that kind of something."

So he hadn't come for the coat and ring after all. "Would you be so kind as to enlighten me? Or shall I call for the constable?" Never mind the constables rarely made their way to our district.

"Girl? You all right out there?" Gretel's shouts from the house told me I'd been too long already. I peeked around the corner of the stable door to return her call.

"All is well. Thought I'd say hello to the horses while I'm here." She'd understand—I hoped.

"Hurry back," was all she said, and so I assumed she had found something to sate my hunger.

"Please excuse me, but I have to go," I said, turning back to William with a witty reply on my tongue.

But when I looked back to where he'd stood, he was gone.

14

The Claim

Dismissing thoughts of William—for I had many questions that could not be answered—I filled my belly with Gretel's generosity and headed back to my true room to, at the very least, move *The Book of Conjuring* from passage to attic in case I lost this small battle. If I did lose, I felt it wouldn't be for long, and truth be told, I simply wanted to return to the book and look a little more deeply at the contents.

In my eagerness last night, I'd neglected to consider what else the volume might contain, or even check if there were instructions on how to handle one's first-time spirit-conjuring experience.

I couldn't believe I was considering such a thing, either. The day prior I'd questioned the existence of God, and today I sought to conjure a spirit from the Otherworld by His name.

That should provide some indication as to the level of desperation I felt at Celia's inclusion of my brother in her morning threats, and the anxiety only increased the moment I returned to my room.

Victoria stood at the wardrobe pulling dresses from inside, holding each one up to her silk-wrapped body and admiring herself in one of my many mirrors.

"What are you doing?" I blurted, losing all sense of composure.

Victoria started, stared at me, and then continued to ignore my existence. Was I so beneath her? I stepped further into the room, a sense of boldness creeping up my spine and wiggling into the spaces between my teeth.

I blamed Charlotte's bosom.

"I said, what are you doing?" I reached for my green velvet walking suit and yanked it from Victoria's hands before she could realize my intent. Her mouth dropped open in a silent gasp before snapping shut as a crocodile does its jaws.

She reached to pull it away, but I saw her bony fingers coming and drew it behind my back. She lunged again and again, and still I held it from her reach. After too many tries, she glared and pulled a pale, rose-colored satin dressing gown from the wardrobe.

I reached for it as well. She was ready this time.

"These are my things," I said. Not that material goods meant to me what I presumed they did to Victoria or Charlotte, but it was the very principal of the issue at stake.

They'd taken my home, my father, and my freedom. They could not have the very clothing off my back, too.

Finally, Victoria spoke. "You don't deserve them."

If one could spit daggers from their tongue, she would have buried twenty in my neck. But I caught her words with reckless daring and hurled them back.

"You don't belong here."

Victoria's grip on my gown tightened. "Your skin is far too sallow to wear this shade and your hair looks like an overturned mop. If anyone deserves beautiful things, it's me."

Shallow and vain. What delightful young ladies my sisters were. As though linked by thought, she and I lunged at the wardrobe, flinging our arms around as many garments as we could, elbows pushing and jarring into ribs and sides. I didn't spare her my shoulder either and slammed it against her breastbone as she reached for a hatbox on the top shelf.

She screamed and fell backward. Her bottom landed with a thud on the floor, and the layers upon layers of her garish silk gown cushioned her backward tumble. She didn't smack her head on the bedpost, though she came very close.

Part of me regretted wishing that she'd been only a few inches to the left.

But only part.

"You witch," Victoria hissed, stumbling to her feet. "This is our home now."

"You live here," I corrected. "There's a difference. It's our house—mine, Edward's, and Father's. You happen to be a long-term guest. And this is *my* room."

I should not have mentioned my brother. I knew this the moment his name left my lips.

"Edward?" Victoria whispered, her eyes drawing to narrow slits. "Still abed, is he?"

Her tone was menacing in a way that even Celia had not achieved.

My throat grew dry.

Yes, it is true. I felt afraid of her, though I didn't know exactly why. Only that whatever she said next would be unbearable.

She took a feather pillow from my bed and turned it over in her hands.

"I do hope he recovers." She flicked her gaze to mine. Loathing oozed from every corner. What had I done to deserve this? "It would be a shame if he took a turn for the worse."

She stopped spinning the pillow.

And then I understood.

Lord, have mercy. "You wouldn't." The words barely passed from my lips before being swallowed by the air. She smiled, set the pillow down, and picked up the rose-colored dress.

We stood there in silence as the day's moments passed.

What could I say? What could I do?

I couldn't watch Edward all day and all night. And while I didn't want to believe that Victoria was capable of carrying out her threat, in truth, I did not know these women at all.

How could I know what they were or were not capable of doing?

15

The Encounter

That is how I found myself in the attic with but a scant few tattered dresses Victoria deigned to toss my way—pieces I'd kept for sentimental reasons or which I had planned to fix someday or turn into curtains and pillows. They weren't lovely garments, and neither did I have my jewelry, brushes, or even a blanket to warm myself on the moldy mattress.

Perhaps worse, I had lost easy access to the passageways. What if Victoria discovered them by accident as I had? Sir Mouse couldn't be depended on to make the distinction between she and I. Or worse yet, what if Celia attempted to move the wardrobe in a fit of redecorating?

I spent several days scouring the attic for some way—any way—back into the passages, but found nothing. I did as Celia asked, performed the most demeaning tasks—yes, I emptied the chamber pots—and slept in the attic with the whole court of mice, scampering cockroaches, and acrobatic spiders. I didn't mind the brown ones so much, for they appeared to be ridding the attic of other less desirable crawling things.

I said nothing and did everything with obedience and a modicum of patience. I prayed Father would return, and quickly.

I also prayed Edward would recover. He improved, certainly, but spent most of his time in his room or on Celia's lap. And while I would never admit it to anyone else, I did all this out of fear for his life. Victoria often flounced about the house in my gowns, sending false-shy smiles in my direction, or purposely calling me into my room—her room—to lace her up.

I refused to be provoked. My brother's life depended on it. How long I could exist in this state, I didn't know, and I hoped I wouldn't have to find out.

Indeed, I spent more than one morning sitting at the fireplace, sweeping cinders and aching to press the hidden latch and flee into the passages. Did *The Book of Conjuring* have an invocation that might still my sisters' tongues? Even Celia no longer bothered to give me tasks, busy as she was coming and going at all hours of the day and night, dressed in her finest. I had tried to ask where she was going two nights after sleeping in the attic.

She denied leaving.

The following morning, my attic window had been papered over. From the outside.

Finally, one evening in utter frustration at my lack of freedom, I loosed a quiet and highly unladylike screech in my lonesome attic chamber. Foolish to the last, I lashed out against an innocent wooden trunk that sat in the middle of the floor, striking it with the toe of my soft slipper—and even softer toes. It shifted by only a pace, but the urge had been satisfied.

In regret, I bent and clutched at my foot to soothe the ache and a breath caught in my throat. On the floor, so faint as to only be noticed by someone who looked for it, was a straight-edged crack. No, not a crack—a cut. Intentional. Foot forgotten, I pressed my fingers against this cut and followed it, a spark of hope worming its way into my being … for it wasn't long before the cut ended and took a sharp right. With my shoulder, I moved the trunk further across the floor and bent low over the cut once more, tracing it with two fingers as it took another right, and right again, until …

I wasted no time. There had to be a way to open or move this square of floor, sized just right for someone who regularly traversed the spaces between house walls. I pressed on each strip of wood inside the square, pins of dying hope striking me at each unmovable inch, until finally—finally!—one thin board released with a click.

I dug my fingernails underneath the lip and pulled the board away. An iron ring underneath begged for my touch.

With a sharp tug, the section of floor gave way, opening to reveal a dark chasm in the midst of the attic. A reach inside presented hand-width wooden blocks nailed to the wall—a ladder, of sorts—which I'd no doubt missed on my travels through the passageways for one simple reason: I hadn't been looking for it.

I guessed that this section of passage would bring me to the space between Celia's room and the smaller guest chamber where Victoria had slept before usurping mine. The discovery granted a thrill of victory. Without a moment's hesitation, I swung my legs over the edge, turned about, and climbed down.

Within minutes, I'd managed to traverse through the walls, down to the ground floor, and into the kitchen. Gretel would be long gone for the night, and everyone else abed for at least long enough to drift in and out of several dreams—provided I had not woken them with the process of my discovery.

Tiredness could not have gripped me, however, if it used iron shackles. My freedom had returned—in one way or another.

But where to go? Though I wore my dusty day clothes still, and light slippers on my feet, there were few options. My mother's stone? I'd find little comfort anywhere else these days, but if I kept my wits about me, I'd be there and back again before accidentally stumbling across Celia during one of her nighttime excursions. I could not fault her for that—she waited until she thought us asleep before venturing forth. In her position, I would do the same—in fact, did I not do that very same thing right now?

Carefully and quietly, I crawled under the locked gate, this time taking care to knock away the sharper rocks as they pressed into my palms and knees. Little worse for wear, I made for the church via the town square as before. I am not certain why I chose this path at this hour, for unlike an early morning journey wherein none save a few merchants traverse city streets, walking the cobbled roads in new moonlight would surely result in an encounter with other folk.

I blame my natural inclination toward imprudence.

Though, perhaps I simply needed a reminder that the world continued to exist apart from the confinement of life at our estate. Perhaps I needed reassurance that the world still moved on without me.

Whatever the reason, it kept my feet moving forward in the dark, down the empty streets, toward the center of town. I gave brief thought once again to the terrors William had mentioned, but little care. Why should anything bother with me? Of more concern was the Prince's daylight venture into the family stable. That posed a far greater question than the truth of a vaporous rumor.

I kept to the shadows, moving along the sides of the buildings and staying out of the gleam of moonlight. Traveling alone at this hour might have been reckless, but I am not a fool in *all* things. Each soft step brought me closer to my mother, yet as I passed a row of two-storied buildings that during daylight hours housed merchants and crafters of all kinds, the sound of laughter, music, and voices filled my ears.

The King's Arm. Of course it would be occupied at this time of night, terrors or not. In a better time, I might have been there too, sitting on Father's knee or in a tall seat beside him while he whispered that we were not to breathe a word of it to Mother in the morning. I'd first heard many a now-legendary singer or storyteller that way.

Drawn to the light like a moth whose wings beat closer and closer to flame, only at the last moment before stumbling directly upon him did I notice a large, swaying man who lay in my path. He'd gone to ground out of the light, and a moan escaped his lips as I hopped back to keep from treading on his outstretched arm. In one hand, he grasped a flask, which he raised to his lips with concerted effort—once, then twice, attempting to absorb the drink through his nose before finding his mouth.

From within the tavern, a song began anew—lyre, I thought, at the tone of the strings—and a round of fresh laughter burst forth at a comment I could not hear.

If only I could look through the window for a moment …

But the closest window sat directly above my drunken, shadowed companion.

I am not sure why such a curiosity overwhelmed me in that moment, but the longing for something familiar and the immediacy of opportunity turned my mind into thoughtless sludge. I stepped up to the man, placed one hand on the window ledge, and said, "Excuse me, sir."

His attention snapped to me, and he flinched in alarm before settling back into his drink-driven stupor.

"Where'd you come from?" His words slurred and he waved his flask about with a distinct lack of control. "D'they send you out t'keep my mouth shut?"

The scent of his breath wafted toward me as he spoke, and I suppressed a gag. He stunk of liquor and rancid meat.

"I assure you, sir, that I want nothing to do with your mouth."

"Eh? What's that?" He poked my leg with the flask. "Konrad send you?" Filmy eyes gazed upward, and the stupidity of my actions became immediately apparent.

"Never mind, sir. My apologies for disturbing you—" I turned to move away—to head down the street and continue on my journey to the Church of the Holy Paraclete—when a hand closed around my ankle.

I gasped and froze, but not because of the boldness of a stranger. Rather, I thought I saw something move in the darkness beyond.

I blinked into the shadows, but saw nothing. Had I imagined it? The man who held my ankle mumbled words that might have conveyed some meaning had his flask not been as empty, but I preferred not to remain at his mercy longer than necessary. With the heel of my other foot, I stamped down on his wrist.

He released me with a shout and a curse, and a burly gentleman with wheat-colored hair poked his head out of the door and glanced around, even as a commotion from behind sent another man sprawling forward down the short set of tavern steps.

"Help's off limits tonight, Konrad," wheat-hair said. "You're done, too. Go join your brother and you can lurch home together."

Brother? *Ahh.* The man clutching his wrist at my feet, no doubt.

"Devil take you, bastard," slurred Konrad. "She was askin' for it."

"Shut your mouth or I'll shut it for you." Wheat-hair disappeared back inside, leaving the three of us wishing the same thing—that we might be inside, too.

Konrad climbed to his feet and staggered several paces away from the tavern door, grumbling. "Georg? Where'd you go?"

What on earth had possessed me to stop here?

I should have continued onward—but once more, my curiosity overtook my sense and I did not move. If either man advanced toward me, I would run. Home, if need be. I could return on another night, perhaps one where self-preservation had a foothold in my skull.

"Konrad!" The drunk next to me—Georg—moaned and shook his flask, the few drops inside plinking quietly. "You too? They don' understand … "

Konrad turned and peered into the dark around the tavern entrance, the light from inside certainly blurring the space where brightness gave way to shadows. "Brother?"

Cold wind rushed past my ears, blowing my loose hair forward about my shoulders, and a sense of dread washed over me like a too-heavy blanket. The air grew thick with foreboding.

I needed to go home *now.*

"Georg, where are you?" Konrad held a hand above his eyes to block out the tavern light and stepped to his left, though this took him deeper into the surrounding darkness of the square. "Ah, there you—"

His words cut off with a choke as a deep shadow, darker than the rest, *moved* across his body.

His head fell from his shoulders.

It rolled toward the place where Georg and I hid.

My scream escaped before I could think better of it, and I turned to run with no thought but escaping whatever it was that had silently taken Konrad from this world. I managed to flee but a few steps before I collided with someone else moving through the shadows, and my scream began anew. I stumbled backward even as a hand wrapped around my shoulder and another covered my mouth, stifling the noise into silence.

I could not move, for whoever held me did so with a force that defied escape. I drew back a heel to slam it into my assailant's knee—

"Quiet." A voice hissed in my ear, a voice so familiar that I might have lashed out in surprise regardless of the command, had he not tightened his grip and spoken again. "Be quiet as if your life depends on it, for it very well may."

I tried to nod, difficult though it was with a hand clamped around my mouth. Sensing my relaxation, he released me and turned my shoulder to face him. Though dark, I could not mistake that form and voice together. "William?"

He wore the same dark, hooded robe as in the stables, with his medallion glinting overtop. Three other men, larger and taller, stood behind him. Two wore robes similar to William's, and the other, a riding coat like the one I'd stashed away after our first encounter.

But it was not the time to think of coats and robes.

"You?" William's pitch rose to give away his incredulity. "What are you doing here at—it's not important. Peter, Lorenz, take her inside the tavern. Don't let anyone see her. Take her to the back and choose a table."

"What?" It was my turn to reveal surprise. "I can't just—"

But he wasn't listening.

"Cromer and I will see what we can do out here." He spoke to the men, not me, and while I wanted nothing more than to yell at him and demand an explanation, the vision of a man's bloodied head rolling in the dirt stayed my tongue. And also turned my stomach.

Had he seen? "The terrors, William. I think ... I think they're real. Something just killed a man, he's dead, we have to leave—"

He glanced from me to the men. "I know."

And with that, he vanished into the square's shadows with Cromer. I moved to shout after him, but one of the others touched a finger to my lips and growled.

"Don't say a word, if you want him to live."

Who *were* these men?

While I had the thought to break free and run home on my own, I would abide William's request for the sake of his own safety—despite how desperately I wanted to beat my fists against these men and demand the truth. Why would a prince be here in town, *now?*

It made as much sense as a prince in a field of gravestones, I thought.

Peter and Lorenz—both tall enough to take root in a forest—stood shoulder-deep to each other, with me between. Should anyone have viewed us from the front or back, I suppose they wouldn't have seen me, though at the time I thought any attempt at shrouding a woman from sight within a tavern seemed a futile task.

I said nothing as we walked up the steps to the King's Arm, and though I ached to stare into the shadows to find William, the weaker parts of me wished not to see Konrad's headless body—or his head, for that matter—and so I resisted curiosity this once.

They led me inside, where it seemed only a few had noticed the strange goings-on outside. The minstrel kept singing, tankards clinked, and laughter continued to pierce the air.

I thought I might vomit if I didn't sit down.

Several words were exchanged with the occupant of a secluded table in the rear of the room, and I sat with shaking limbs in a corner-positioned chair. I folded my hands on the table. Perhaps seeing them there would stop their trembling. Peter and Lorenz chose to stand, facing the room.

It was all very strange, and I couldn't imagine how William would talk himself out of this one without some revelation or another. For that matter, I failed to see how he might enter the room without revealing himself—or appearing very suspicious under a hood—nor why he would choose to do so in the first place.

Yet of greater importance was the question of what he was doing skulking around in city shadows.

Though seated, it took some time before I caught my breath, and though I could not shake the image of a man's severed head rolling across the ground toward me, I managed to cease trembling long enough to still the churning contents of my stomach.

It felt like an age before William pushed between the men he'd left to guard me and sat down on the other side of the table, hood raised. In the dim light of the tavern, even I could make out the flush of his cheeks and hear his quickened breath.

"Are you all right?" His words came in a rush and he dropped his hood, shielded as he was from view by the men standing in front of the table. "Were you hurt?"

Only if nightmares are counted among injuries. "No, thank you. Though I imagine it will take some time to remove the sight from memory." I looked into his eyes and saw it, then. He *knew* something. "What *was* that? Whatever could do such a thing?"

He shook his head, and my fright once again became a slow descent into anger.

"It's nothing. It's … shouldn't you be at home, asleep? Or," he said with a tight smile, "sitting in a graveyard?"

I scowled at him. How could he joke at a moment such as this? "Shouldn't *you* be out looking for your coin purse in strangers' stables?"

It was not my most brilliant retort, I admit.

"We're not strangers, you and I. Didn't we cover this already?

I'm William, which you already know." I remained silent as he gestured toward me. "This is the part where you tell me your name. You are ... ?"

"Wondering why I'm sitting at the back of a tavern instead of running home."

He planted his palms on the table and leaned forward, speaking so softly I could barely hear him, save for seeing the words formed on his lips. "Remember when we met? I told you there'd been rumors of terrors in the town."

I didn't respond.

"These are they. One came here, tonight, and killed that man outside."

The shaking returned and I tried to quell it, swallowing so hard upon my own throat that it seemed to close in on itself. The ache must have shown on my face, for William reached across the table and placed a hand on mine.

I flinched and pulled away, the intensity of his gaze and earnestness of his touch more than I could bear. I would be lying if I said I couldn't still feel the press of his hand against my mouth in that moment.

"And I suppose you're here to save us all?" I tried to put a light-hearted laugh behind it, though it escaped as a cough instead.

William's gaze flicked over his shoulder and back. "You wouldn't believe me if I told you."

Presumptuous, he! "You know me so well to assume what I will and will not believe? I hadn't realized you were also an intuitive."

He sighed and rubbed both hands across his face and back through his hair, sending strands poking through his fingers like bits of straw.

Not that I looked close enough to notice.

"I'm no intuitive. But I am someone who cares about this

town's citizens, and I go where I am needed."

A flutter in my stomach made me curse my weaknesses. "And you believe you're better needed here than outside, where the terror stalks innocents and takes their lives without warning?"

A frown marred his features for an instant. "It's gone, for now. It has already killed and taken the body. There'll be no more disturbances tonight."

Realization dawned. "You've seen this before."

"Perhaps."

"You said they were *rumors*."

"I shouldn't have said anything at all. It's not my place."

"I might have died, and it would have been your fault."

"But you didn't, *did you?*"

"No thanks to you!" I folded my arms across my bosom and refused to meet his eyes. He sighed heavily and I might have felt a pang of guilt, had I not just seen a man's head separated from his shoulders by nothing but shadows. I tried, how I tried, to shake the memory, but the small portion of courage I'd stored upon seeing William this night vanished with the weight of a man's death.

The corners of my vision blurred, and I blinked away the liquid that welled up, unbidden.

"I'm sorry," he said. "I should have realized you're not the kind of lady to sit at home and barricade the doors at something so fleeting as a rumor."

One of my mother's favourite phrases came to mind, and as it fit the moment, I deigned to speak to him again. "A life spent idle is no life at all."

"Agreed."

He grew silent again, and I felt a warmth spreading through my fingertips. What I truly wanted to know, I could not yet ask— why would the Prince be risking his life in the dark amidst known danger? Still, I didn't feel the time had grown right to give myself away. He would tell me in his own time.

If ever.

"Are you certain it's gone?"

"Yes." He looked down at his hands and back at me. "It's late, and you've seen enough tonight to lay low a person of weaker constitution. May I—may we escort you home?"

The request jarred me from my wondering. An escort home with the Crown Prince? If my father had seen me returning home late at night with any man, no doubt there would have been trouble enough, but if Celia were to see *this*? I wouldn't be long for this world.

And perhaps worse, William might wonder why I had to crawl on my belly to slip under our gate and return to the house.

I set the bait, instead. "I have a better idea. You tell me why you were really poking around in our stable, and I'll let you take me home."

He sighed yet again, and shifted seats until he sat next to me rather than across. It was strange, having him so close—and the warmth in my hands spread to my chest. Despite how infuriating I found him, I admit that I was growing not to *dis*like his presence.

He intrigued me, after all. William didn't exactly act like a crown prince, so far as I could tell.

"I really wish you'd tell me your name," he said, a hint of a smile returning to his face.

The intrigue wore thin, for that I kept to myself. I needed one secret, at the very least, to hold from him—at least until he revealed himself.

"I really wish you'd cease pressing the issue," I replied.

William shook his head and propped an elbow on the table, resting cheek against fist. "You're quite the mystery, you know that?"

I did. "Neither of us seems particularly inclined to reveal more than necessary to talk to each other. Perhaps we should each take that as a hint, and turn the topic to other matters?"

He did laugh then, loud and full, earning a look of alarm from Peter and Lorenz. He waved off their attentions and gazed past me for a moment, thoughtful.

"All right, then," he conceded. "We'll talk of something else. Do you have any brothers or sisters?"

"A brother. Somewhat ill, but recovering."

"Older?"

"Younger."

"Ah." He grinned. "I should have guessed. An older brother would have figured you out by now and either kept you safe at home or come along with you. And your parents?"

"Oh, no." I shook my head. He would not come to learn of me that easily. "Your turn. One thing at a time, if you please. A lady shouldn't babble on, revealing her whole self at once. What about you? Brothers? Sisters?"

But of course I already knew the answer.

"None, and I consider it both a curse and a blessing, depending on the day. I had a brother, I'm told, but he passed on before I was born ... my mother told me once, when I found her crying in the garden under a lilac tree. She remembers him every spring, even now."

That, I hadn't known. "I'm sorry to hear it."

I couldn't envision life without Edward, but knowing what could have been? I imagined his mother must have her heart torn out again and again with each passing spring. "What happened?"

He shrugged and sat straighter in his seat, placing both palms flat against the table. "That, I don't know, but I suspect it was something less than peaceful. No one speaks of it." He grew quiet, flexing his fingers on the table's surface. "And to be honest, I'm not quite sure why I'm telling you of it right now. But, enough sadness. It's your turn."

Of course it was. I wanted to hear more about his brother, but he would have none of it and indulged his own curiosities instead.

"What do you do when you're not wandering around at all hours of the night and morning, or catching trespassers in the yard?"

A calmness descended as I told him of the books Edward and I read together, and of the copy of *Faust* I'd loved so deeply before Celia stole it from between my hands—a detail I conveniently left out. He appeared surprised that I could read, and it occurred to me that William—likely due to my haggard appearance and soiled clothes each time we met—believed me to be in the employ of those who lived at my home.

I did not correct him, nor did I steer him to believe otherwise. If he would not be forthright concerning himself, neither would I.

Still, he told me of his lengthy schooling and the books he enjoyed—mostly adventure stories, of which I was not surprised—and beyond that, he spoke of his journeys to other cities and provinces. I recounted several tales of days spent in our own town with Liesl and my mother, and we both pretended that the other did not know his true identity despite the entourage and I forgot, fully, that I had seen a man murdered that night by an unknown foe—and that Celia and her daughters waited for me at home with tasks that no doubt required a full night's rest to complete.

It was only when I felt my eyelids droop with heaviness and Peter or Lorenz or Cromer turned to William to suggest we take our leave of the establishment that I remembered what had happened, where I was, and who I sat in the tavern with.

And it was only when I caught myself nodding off in the midst of William's tale of menacing wolves and the Black Forest that he remembered these things, too.

"Come on," he said, standing and pulling his hood up to conceal his face. "Let's get you home before you're noticed missing."

Sleepily, I took his extended hand and allowed him to help me to my feet.

But once I stood, he did not let go.

"Why is it we've never met before? I suppose the opportunity simply wasn't there." He spoke more to himself than I. "How circumstances change … "

At the time, I didn't understand his meaning, but I didn't have mind to ask—I only knew that he held my hand, brushing the back of it with a gentle thumb, and that I did not pull away but found myself secretly wishing he might hold it for the duration of the journey home.

And when he finally sighed with the slightest of smiles and let go, some part of me felt hollow in a way I also did not understand.

"Let's go," he said, and so we did.

I fell into comfortable step alongside William, and though I could not bring myself to tell him so just then, I had forgiven his interruptions and trespassing of our prior meetings. I wished he would speak to the truth of those occasions, that I might understand, but for tonight? This was enough.

We spent the walk home in silence, for it felt too strange to fill the empty space with words while others were close enough to listen. And what is more, I did not feel quite the same as I had when the sun first slipped from the horizon that night. Though one man's death had seared an image of gruesome endings upon my memory, some other strange foe had taken root and settled within … for when William looked my way, I wondered what he saw and hoped he was not disappointed. I admit, I may have wished for him to continue looking, and considered with sharp anticipation that our hands might brush as we walked alongside.

I had thought, for quite some time now, that I didn't want this. This connection, this touch, this closeness with another as my father had with my mother. And yet, here I was, betrayed by both heart and body. Cruel conspirators, they.

We reached the house gate and I remembered that particular method of entry required of a locked gate. But, just as I resigned myself to crawling upon the ground in William's presence, one of his attendants—Lorenz?—came forward and busied about the lock for no longer than a woodlark's call. The gate swung open. Lorenz stepped aside and gestured to the now-open space.

"Thank you," I said, to Lorenz and William in turn. Despite the dryness of my throat and the strange weakness that had come upon my limbs, it would have been rude not to acknowledge William's contribution to my safety. "Contrary to what you might think, I'm grateful for your intervention tonight. The events prior to your arrival were … most disturbing."

He stepped closer and took both my hands in his, ignoring the unsubtle throat-clearing of Peter or Cromer.

"I'm glad you're all right. It's not safe for you to be wandering around after dark these days."

I couldn't resist one final nudge. "Are you saying I can't take care of myself?"

"No! Of course not. You're clearly quite capable of that, it's just—"

I smiled to let him in on the jest. He returned it and squeezed my hands, both warming and cooling them at the same time.

"It's obvious I won't be able to keep you inside the house, but would you promise me one thing?"

I knew I should not be making promises to anyone save my brother, but my head, heart, and mouth refused to cooperate as the moment deepened. "That depends."

He shifted his weight from one foot to another. "Don't go out at night. Between the sun's disappearance to its reawakening above the horizon in the early morning sky, remain indoors."

"You know very well I can't promise that."

"When the sky begins to grow light again, it's safe. At least, safe from what you saw tonight, if not anything else. I'd prefer you indoors until the sun's full face—"

"You'd *prefer* it?" My tone grew shrill, admiration giving way to annoyance. Who did he think himself, to demand such a thing? It was a prudent request, and not without merit—I had promised myself inasmuch the moment that man's head fell from his shoulders—but if William thought he had any claim on me in an official sense, he was sorely mistaken. Particularly if he continued to refuse to disclose himself.

"I don't mean to force claim," he sputtered, confusion wrinkling his brow, "but I fear for your safety and I don't wish to see you come to any harm."

And I didn't wish to involve myself further with someone who could not be honest about their true self. "Good night, William."

He bent slightly at the waist, as if to excuse himself with a formal bow, but realized what he did before completing the gesture and pretended to brush dirt off his coat instead. Upon straightening, I received a decidedly informal nod.

"Good night … " His voice trailed off, expectant.

I knew what he waited for, and I supposed I owed him that much.

But first, I turned to leave and walked several paces toward the house before allowing a final glace over my shoulder.

"Ellison," I said, "but you may call me Ella."

16

The Invitation

The morning that followed crawled by in a slow haze, for my continued lack of sleep meant I had little strength to protest Celia's requests—nor did I wish to risk the punishment of additional work for a moment of defiance.

But the hours wore on as they tend to do, and as I sat cleaning ash and cinder in the warmth of late afternoon, there could be no mistaking the sound of hooves and wheels, venturing closer and closer down the drive. My heart leapt at the sound, for we didn't have visitors anymore. Celia invited no one for tea, and after the doctor's visit, no one called.

I resisted the urge to bolt from my seat on the floor and peer through the curtains, for both Victoria and Charlotte sat in the parlour as well and seemed to have forgotten about me for the moment. I preferred not to remind them.

The clopping of hooves stopped abruptly. A carriage door opened and shut, and three sharp raps on our door were followed by a fourth with great finality.

Neither sister stirred.

"Who do you suppose that is?" Victoria folded her hands in her lap, setting aside needle and embroidery.

"Who cares?" Charlotte flung her piece of fabric at the ground. "I hate needles. And napkins. And visitors. Ugh, it's not like I'll ever need to be able to do this after I'm married anyway."

I wanted to tell her that in that case, she'd better keep at it but another set of knocks—more urgent this time—stilled the words on my tongue.

Charlotte stared at me. "Well?"

Did the girl lack even the tiniest bit of sense? "You want me to represent the family?"

She continued staring, and though I looked to Victoria, she maintained her habit of pretending I didn't exist. Unless she had want of me for something, of course.

With a sigh and a shrug, I rose and headed to the door, where the knocks came a third time. But this round was accompanied by a loud and ocean-deep voice.

"Open, by order of the King."

I froze, and my fingers turned to outstretched icicles against the handle.

William's coat. The ring. Had he finally remembered? I had been a fool to choose the words I did at our parting.

"Who is it?" Charlotte shrieked from the parlour.

Perhaps I could pretend as though I hadn't seen either item. Or that I had a twin who'd taken them away, or that it was Victoria, not me, who'd met him—

My fingers closed around the handle, for not to answer the door at all would doubtless do nothing but serve to reinforce whatever notion the visitors might have about us and what we—no, I—had done.

I opened the door. My life was full of doors opening and closing, but up until that particular door, none had been more important. None. Believe me. None.

A rotund, blue-coated man stood on our front step, dark beard trimmed nicely to cling to the corners of a thin moustache. On his head, a teacup. At least, it looked like one, turned upside-down and plunked on his head, if teacups were blue and starched cotton, and lacked handles.

What I mean to say is, his hat looked so ridiculous that I might have laughed, had the fear of seeing a royal messenger on our doorstep not caused me to clench my thighs in fright.

Remember, fear makes one tremble and weep and piss. The second I held back out of hope, the third out of necessity.

I curtsied to the messenger. "Good day, sir. Won't you come in?"

The stern eyes softened as he regarded me, and for the second time since Celia's arrival, I wondered at my appearance. My cheeks grew warm as he appraised my outfit. It wasn't *my* fault I wore a stained, dirty dress. Necessity warranted certain sacrifices.

I didn't want his pity.

He inclined his head, a gesture I surely didn't deserve or expect. "The same to you, kind miss. Is the man or lady of the house about?"

I began to answer, but my words were drowned by the screeching voice of my favourite sister.

"Who the hell is it, you lazy, cinder-sweeping wench? I swear, you're—" Charlotte rounded the doorway from the parlour and stopped, mouth agape.

"And good day to you as well," said the messenger, catching my eye with a sly wink as he addressed the gaping git.

"Why, hello." Charlotte recovered with a deep curtsy. "Greetings and good health to you, sir."

I tried to catch her eye myself, but she appeared mesmerized by the insignia patch on the gentleman's coat. I cleared my throat instead.

Charlotte glared at me. "What?"

"Perhaps Cel—uh, Stepmother should be here to greet our visitor."

"Perhaps." She continued to stand in the hallway like a stunned deer.

"Could you retrieve her?" Had she never received any training in something so simple as manners?

She sniffed. "That's not *my* job. You find her. I'll entertain our guest." To him, "Do come in, please. Don't mind her, she has no place speaking to a man of your obvious standing, I—"

He held up a hand to silence her nattering. "Actually, if you don't mind, I'll stay right here. I'm delivering a message across town, not here for a social call. I promise not to take more than a few minutes of your time. If one of you could retrieve the lady and return here with her, I would be most appreciative. And if there are other eligible ladies at home?"

At the word *eligible*, Celia appeared at the top of the staircase like a ghost revealed. I held my breath at her appearance, for it was she who would either hold our family's reputation or destroy it with the words that followed.

I wished I'd been wearing something more appropriate. And brought Edward to the door with me. And possibly neglected to admit the others' existence.

"Greetings," Celia announced, sweeping down the stairs. As she drew closer, I noticed she wore a gown of deep violet lace, with a high-buttoned collar and two strings of pearls around her neck. Her hair was perfectly curled and pinned high atop her head, and rouge lightly colored each cheek, accenting her natural stunning beauty.

She'd seen him coming. Of course she had.

I burned with jealousy.

She glanced at me with casual dismissal. "Thank you, girl. You may go."

Girl?

"Actually, lady, I would prefer that she stay." The messenger's smile held kindness and sincerity. "This concerns all the young ladies of the household."

Celia's eyebrow raised as she reached the bottom step. "Oh? Well. If she must."

If eyes lit fires, Charlotte's glare would have burned me where I stood. Celia called for Victoria, who glided into the hallway with her nose high in the air and enveloped in silent haughtiness. With the four of us in the same place, I became acutely aware of my own situation.

How I ached for Father.

How my face burned with shame for what I'd allowed them to make of me.

"Well?" Celia's words dripped like boiled honey, making my teeth hurt and my stomach turn. "Here we are. Are you sure you won't have any tea?"

He shook his head, drew an envelope from a leather satchel at his belt and a scroll from the inner pocket of his coat. The scroll he unrolled with dramatic flair and another wink in my direction.

"To the King's Loyal Subjects," he read, "by royal decree, on the twelfth of May, the royal family has declared the commencement of a festival which is to last three days. The King encourages much merrymaking by all, and would be delighted to host any manner of entertainers, musicians, and tale-tellers at court for the entertainment of all the kingdom's citizens. Prince William will attend to the guests on the evening of each festival day at the Royal Balls, and the festival will culminate with an extraordinary announcement that shall be made in celebration of Prince William's seventeenth birthday, on the third eve."

At this, the messenger paused and looked at Victoria, Charlotte, and myself in turn. "All young ladies of eligibility are encouraged and invited to attend these three balls with their chaperon."

Three gasps in the entranceway.

My heart dropped into my shoes, and though I willed it to return to its place in my chest, it didn't listen.

The messenger rolled the scroll, replaced it in his coat, and handed the envelope to Celia in one smooth, practiced motion.

"We're honoured," Celia gushed, "and of course we'll attend." Her minions nodded with such forceful eagerness, I feared their heads might pop off. "Do convey our appreciation and acceptance to the Royal Family."

"Of course," he said, bowing his head. "And with that, good day, and I expect we shall see the four of you in your finest on the twelfth of May."

"Four?" Charlotte cried.

I saw Celia's elbow drive into Charlotte's side, though I'll never know if our guest did.

"Indeed," Celia oozed. "All four of us will be delighted and honoured to celebrate the Prince's birthday. And, I assume, to compete for his hand, yes?"

The messenger merely smiled. "I've only been instructed to read the announcement, and can't say I'm privy to any other information at this time. However, one may draw certain inferences from the wording ... "

"Naturally." Celia brushed past to open the door and usher

him out. "Thank you so much for your attention. We won't miss it for anything."

He touched his hat to bid farewell, but as he turned to leave, we shared a private moment of understanding—he, determined that I should know that I, too, counted among those invited to the affair, and I, grateful beyond my own apprehending that someone should acknowledge my worth apart from what had become the daily trials around the household.

And with that, he left.

Celia clapped her hands together as the clop of horse hooves grew ever further away. "Isn't this an interesting development, hmm?"

"My God, Mother. Imagine that." Victoria's fervent murmur cut through her mother's enthusiasm. "An invitation to the palace, and balls besides. You realize what this means, don't you?"

Celia's placid smile morphed into a deep, curling grin that, oddly enough, enhanced her exquisite features. It was a good thing *she* wasn't eligible. Pity the prince who married one of her offspring, however.

"Girls. Darlings. This is it." Celia placed a hand on each of her daughters' shoulders, sending me back into oblivion. "This is what we've been waiting for. Our moment. Do you understand?"

They nodded as one, heads bobbing like fish toward bait.

"But, Mother, what will we wear? And what of our shoes and hair and ... there's so much to do!" Charlotte's expression grew frantic, eyes squinting until I felt sure she'd never see again.

Celia patted them both. "There's little time, and much to accomplish. I'll see to it you have new gowns made, and I'll bring in one of the etiquette tutors to review your dance steps and the finer points of speech. One thing is for certain, however. One dance with either of you and he *will* be ours."

"Ours?" mumbled Victoria.

"Our family, dear girl. With a royal marriage comes power and influence, and a prince's riches will make this place look like a pauper's hovel."

Their eyes grew round and greedy, and I imagined they'd dream of coins clinking in coffers tonight.

"You *will* meet the Prince. He *will* choose one of you. Do you both understand?"

I stifled my own cry of surprise as both Charlotte's and Victoria's eyes lost their light, faces growing slack and dull at the sound of Celia's voice and her hands on their shoulders.

The same way Father's had, that day in the parlour.

I hadn't imagined it. I had not been wrong.

Something about my stepmother was very, very wrong, and in only a few days she would stand in the same room as the King himself.

And with William.

I had to warn him.

17

The Second Circle

"I should like to go, too," I said, though a wiser part of me knew the folly of the request.

The girls' vision cleared as Celia lifted her hands and turned to face me. I stepped back, away from her reach.

Just in case.

Charlotte began to laugh. "Surely you jest. You're far too pathetic to even set foot outside our gate, let alone the palace."

"Now, now," Celia said, folding her arms. "The invitation was extended to all eligible girls."

"But, Mother—"

Celia's glance stilled Charlotte's tongue. "Ellison, so long as you complete your daily chores and have something suitable to wear, I don't see why you shouldn't attend. Right, girls?"

A wicked, wicked grin inched its way across Victoria's fair visage. "Of course, Mother."

Charlotte refused to comment, for which I felt relieved. If only two of three plotted against me, all the better.

"Thank you," I said, and curtsied for good measure. "I'll be sure to do just that." I left the room to resume my work among the ashes.

And so, I felt no surprise at Celia's announcement a short time later that she and the girls were headed to town to have gowns, hats, and the Almighty knows what else made for the upcoming festival. The moment they were out of sight, I ran to the kitchen, retrieved William's coat and ring, and bolted back to the parlour. With a swift hand, I pressed the latch and released the fireplace from the wall, crept inside, and closed the door.

Through the passages I went, back to the book. I retrieved it and the bone key and, with as much haste as possible, hid them both on the passage floor outside Father's office. I prayed they would be safe there.

But as I emerged from the passageway and into my former chamber, soft thumping on the stairs lifted my spirits to a place I'd thought had disappeared forever.

"Edward?" I burst from the room and ran to the stairs. "Are you up?"

His beautiful face, so innocent of the madness around him, peered up at me from the center of the staircase. He sat with a model tin carriage in one hand and a carved wooden horse in the other, running them up and down the steps with fervor. Scattered about were several toy soldiers and at least one of my childhood dolls. A part of me yearned for the days when my greatest concern was what I might dress each doll in for the day ahead, but only a part. One cannot live in innocence forever, insomuch as I wished it for my own brother.

"Ellison!" He smiled at me and my heart turned to jelly. "Come play with me."

I joined him on the steps and chose a well-loved soldier whose paint had seen better days. "How are you feeling, Eddie? Better?"

He nodded, and ran the horse down my leg. "Much better. Stepmother has been looking after me, though I still don't like the way she reads our stories. She lets me have extra biscuits, though."

Did she, now? So she still wasn't above buying his favour. "Are you all right, for certain? I mean, with Father gone. You must miss him terribly. I do."

It was cruel of me to bring it up, I know. But what could I do? A sister has to reclaim her family somehow, and sometimes brief pain is the only way to draw one memory forth over another.

"I wish Father would come home," he sighed, and I delighted in his sadness, if only because it meant he hadn't forgotten us.

"And what of Charlotte and Victoria, do they read to you? Or play games? Toss the ball, or sing you to sleep?" In truth, I knew they didn't, but I craved reassurance.

He laughed and threw his arms around my neck, and I pulled him onto my lap, though I'm sure we both knew he'd grown a mite big for it.

"No," he said, "but I don't think I'd want them to. They'd step in a puddle and scream, or run at the sight of a housefly."

My turn to laugh. "That, I think, is exactly the truth." I plucked a small, red ball from the pile of toys on the step below. "But *they* aren't here right now, which means *I* am privileged to a moment of my own. Shall we?"

He tore the ball from my fingers, rolled it down the stairs, and leapt down after it.

"Meet you outside," I called after him. Though I might lose my dignity and my freedom at their hands, I would not lose my brother, too.

They returned as the sky grew dark, and because I had spent my day with Edward instead of cleaning or mending or—Celia's newest favourite task for me—shovelling dung in our stable, I received one verbal thrashing, one slap across the cheek, and a revoking of the night's dinner. Little did Celia know, Edward and I had already feasted, thanks to Cook's generosity and good company. Of course, the three of us swore it to secrecy.

And little did they all know, I minded not the tasks so much with each day, for they grew a mite easier as my strength increased. But I would not tell them that—surely doing so would invite even more burdens, and I barely had enough time and patience for those already given.

But after yet another threat to my brother's safety—this time from Charlotte—I spent my evening in a mad scramble to finish the day's chores. Even as the rest of the household packed away the remains of the day and retired to lay down their heads, I remained at my final task, once again at the hearth, sweeping charred ash and cinder from a fireplace that I'm sure they used purely out of spite.

Who lights a fire in the flush of May?

My limbs ached and eyelids drooped, so I gave in to the peace of closing one's eyes only once or twice, though my mind knew I shouldn't. My body had other ideas. And, as no one seemed to notice that I hadn't yet climbed the stairs to my attic prison, I awoke mid-night to a darkened parlour with moonlight streaming through the gauzy curtains and soot all over my face.

I'd fallen asleep among the ashes.

A notion crept up my spine, resting just below my common sense before overwhelming any inkling of self-preservation I might have had.

For as frightful as the events were of several nights past, I had spent the days since wondering what might have happened, had I not lost my head and fled. After all, Father gave me the key, and though the book had been hidden, I wondered if he hadn't a reason for wanting to keep both safe.

And he wouldn't have given me a gift so dangerous, certainly. Perhaps he even intended for me to find the passageway, like a puzzle to solve. Perhaps he'd be proud when he returned and I revealed my success.

Success that was, as of yet, incomplete.

I burst from the ashes and opened the passageway, tearing through the darkness until reaching the book and key. Back in the parlour, I followed form: curtains, writing, pile of ash. My undergarments were as white as I might have for the moment, and so I found myself in the center of the circle once more, this time nearly naked, but not so naïve as before.

I prayed for courage, begged for forgiveness from the Almighty—for inasmuch as the conjuring invoked his name, I still felt unsure—and plunged the bone into the ash.

Recited the prayer.

And waited.

18

The Mist

He came in hisses and whispers, flitting in and out of each ear, squeezing my senses until I believed I would faint if it continued one moment longer.

"Command me, mistress."

Although I trembled, I remained in the circle. My feet stayed planted, despite the urge to run, run quickly, away from … from … this.

With a shallow breath, I faced the rising smoke, its black tendrils curling around each of my wrists, snaking to envelop my neck like a lover's embrace.

Not that *I* know of such things.

Yet.

Eyes, red and gleaming, took shape in the smoke.

I pulled one wrist away, though I didn't mean to show fear.

The eyes vanished. I remained still.

They reappeared, but the less I pulled, the greater shape the spirit took.

Nose, mouth. Thin, gray lips. Black hair, deep as shadows and flitting like dark fire. Skin like gray ash, unclothed across his torso, arms, and—

I shied away as panic rose in my chest. I couldn't deny the stirring, so different from what I'd felt before.

This ... spirit? God Almighty, could he be an angel? He was *beautiful.*

And he demanded *my* attentions.

"Command me, mistress. You have called. I have answered."

His voice echoed between my ears, radiant and terrifying. "What—what are you?"

Ah, the brilliance of my own tongue.

He—it—no, *he,* for reasons I will neglect to detail for the time being—smiled, and if I had thought Celia's smile a fright to behold, it was but a clown's act compared to this.

My knees weakened. Sharp teeth like tiny daggers glinted in the surrounding mist.

"I am yours."

I didn't know whether to praise heaven or cry out for mercy. "Why have you come? Who are you?" Again, the genius of my speech cannot be denied.

"I am Curson, who reveals things hidden and conceals that which may be revealed. You called my name, and I have come."

"Are you a spirit? An angel? A ... " I couldn't bring myself to entertain the third option. Father would *not* be party to that.

"What do you say I am?"

Oh mercy, mercy.

The misty tendrils around my wrists shifted into fingers, delicate and yet cold as ice against my flesh. He—oh yes, he— leaned toward me, drawing his lips toward my own. My breath quickened, and warmth rushed into all my cold places.

His mouth brushed my ear, and I shivered at the chill and at—
But that is not important.

"What would you have me do, mistress?"

May the Lord forbid the world ever learn what I thought then, for I banished those notions as I was certain, so certain, that the great Abyss would open up and swallow me whole in an instant.

Not that I would have minded, were *he* with me.

Body frozen, my eyes swept across the room, desperate to recall what, if anything, I had truly called him for. A jewelled pillow, glinting in the faded starlight, brought to mind the first day I'd set eyes on this changed room. How Edward had laughed at my jest concerning the beads.

How Father had betrayed our trust.

"No," I said, stepping back from what would surely be my damnation. Indeed, I knew nothing. "I need you to hide the passageways in this house. Hide them from my stepmother and stepsisters, that they may never discover them of their own accord."

Curson's smile vanished, and as he pulled away, it was as though someone had grabbed hold of my very spirit and wrenched it through my chest. A deep, aching hollowness filled my secret places. My cheeks burned with shame.

"Very well. As you wish."

I wanted him to touch me again, but for the sake of all things good and holy, I knew I would be lost if he did.

"How does this work?" I cleared my throat, wishing I had chosen to obtain at least some kind of over-garment before engaging in this foolish venture.

"You call and ask. Then it is done."

How very helpful of him. "When?"

"The moment of your request."

"So, it's done?" He inclined his head, and I shivered once more.

"Can I call you again?"

I was an idiot.

This time, he glanced down—and while I was not about to follow his gaze, I hoped he looked at the circle or something within it.

"Not with that. You have used the last of its ability to conjure forth. You'll need another talisman if you wish to call one of us again."

One of us? "What do you—"

"My time is at an end, mistress." He tilted his head. *"Unless you have another source of power?"*

I didn't.

"Until next time, mistress."

And with my next breath, his body burst back into mist, tendrils swirling around my stunned form until, like water drawn into a drain, the ash sucked the mist down, down, down into its core.

I stood, staring, for a long moment.

Whereupon I collapsed in the very place I'd stood, legs void of the ability to stand, breath shaking and finally, finally, beset by the fear held at bay.

Had he done it? Had I done it? I could only trust that I had.

And my only regret? That I hadn't asked for more.

Once I'd recovered my strength as much as possible, I reset the curtains—with some difficulty—and rolled up the carpet before hauling it to the laundry. I would speak with Cook on her arrival in the morning.

The grandfather clock in the hallway showed half past three. A spark of shock jolted me back into wakefulness as I realized my stupidity—I had performed the rite without knowing whether or not Celia had left on one of her nightly jaunts. What if she had returned while Curson stood in the parlour? In future, I would be more careful.

Yes, I had already decided: I would ask for something else, but more tangible. There would be a next time. I needed assurance it could be done.

But as I found myself in a rare moment of freedom and silence, and more awake than I could recall feeling in days, I desperately desired to take advantage of the moment ... despite Celia, my underclothes, the terrors that were rumors no longer, and my knowledge that ladies should never, *ever* venture throughout town in the middle of the night, regardless of circumstance.

Still, I replaced my soiled dress over my undergarments—for I suspected I might catch a chill otherwise—and left the house. Despite better judgment, I admit, but I left and strolled with confidence through the silent town toward my mother's grave. I prayed I wouldn't come across Celia along the way, but the surge of assuredness I felt at what I had already accomplished that night was enough that, in truth, I didn't concern myself with anything beyond the end goal.

And when I reached the graveyard where my mother's stone stood strong and firm, both relief and sadness were enough to build strength upon strength for a time.

The gate was once again open, but I didn't care. I strode in— no, I ran—and threw myself down against her stone. I closed my eyes and basked in her memories, drinking in the scent of the earth and trees and blooms. The lavender soothed my aching bones from the long days of labor with little rest.

I imagined my mother there with me, seated at my side, and thought of all that I wished to tell her. Of Celia, Father, and

Edward, of William and my discoveries.

"I wish you were here, Mother … " I whispered into the darkness, though again, I gave no heed to whether she might actually hear me from her place in glorious heaven.

In a breath, the air cooled, and for a moment I feared that the terror had found me—but no, this felt different. Like a gentle touch, like the wind blown from pursed lips upon a scalded finger.

The moonlight upon the earth began to shimmer as the smell of hazel strengthened like a storm, and I swear it—oh, I swear it— my mother's face began to form in the swirl of light and wind and scent and I heard her call back to me from some distant place and then—

The crunch of footsteps sent me bolting upright.

Had I fallen asleep?

The air felt still and quiet, with the gentlest of breezes rippling through the hazel tree.

The footsteps fell again, and I held my breath. They came from behind.

"Mother?" I breathed her name as if a prayer. "Are you there?"

But it could not be her, for the steps trod too heavily for a woman.

"Ella?"

Oh, no no no. Not him. Not now, not here.

"We've got to stop meeting like this." He laughed—chuckled, really—and I squeezed my eyes shut. Perhaps if I ignored him, he'd go away. Or think me asleep.

"I know you're awake. I saw you come in."

Curses. I did look at him then, with the cruellest glare I could muster.

"Don't look so glad to see me," he said, and sat down next to me. A tremor seized my stomach and my shoulders tensed. "Barely keeping promises, I see. Twilight's not far off, but you still shouldn't be here. I suppose I should be grateful it's not midnight."

I couldn't stand it any longer. "Please go away, William." Please, please, lest my heart break completely. "I'm here to pay respect to a memory, and you're not helping."

"Your mother?"

I nodded, despite my wish to scream and run away instead.

"I'm sorry."

I did look at him, then. "Why?"

His eyes grew wide. "What do you mean, why?"

It seemed a perfectly reasonable question to me. "Why should you be sorry? You didn't know her. You barely know me, apart from a few chance encounters. What if she'd been a horrible, puppy-kicking monster who beat me each night?"

He grinned and leaned back against the stone, gold medallion once again glinting in the rays of moonlight. "Then I highly doubt you'd be here in the middle of the night. I bet she was a wonderful woman whom you loved very much, but present circumstances prevent you from visiting during, shall we say, normal hours."

Hrmph. "I suppose you think you're clever."

"Of course I am. And what we have is hardly a few chance encounters. Friendships are based on less, other things on ... not much more."

Yes. I *know.* "Tell me, William, what are *you* doing out in the middle of the night again? At least I have a reason to be here, but you've continually neglected to enlighten me on your own exploits."

How I wanted to tell him I knew. But perhaps I could catch him in a lie instead, and take some of the blame off myself if he recalled our first meeting in this place and what he'd lost.

"I'm ... exploring."

"Liar."

"*What?* Do you have any idea—" He stopped himself. "I mean, what kind of accusation is that?"

An easy one, in fact. "If you were an explorer, why come here? You've already visited this place, so you should be elsewhere."

"Oh." He laughed softly and picked at rocks in the dirt. "Then would you believe I'm here to spite my father?"

That, I had not expected at all. "Whatever do you mean?"

He sighed and tossed several pebbles back and forth between his hands. "My father is ... he's a good man, but severe. We have, well, a family legacy of sorts, and lately he's been on me about ensuring I live up to it."

"I couldn't imagine."

"He's set a rather difficult task for me that's coming up quickly, and I don't ... "

He grew silent. That he spoke of the festival and three balls, I had no doubt. But to hear that they weren't something he wished? That was a surprise.

"So tell him," I offered, preferring to gaze at the shining moon instead of his warm, kind face. It calmed my nerves.

"I can't." He dropped the pebbles and pulled his knees up to his chin. "It's not really optional. What's worse is that the future of the kingd—uh, our family's legacy in the kingdom, I mean ... we're one of the old families ... depends on it."

A sad recovery. Why wouldn't he just admit his identity? "I'm sure it's not that important. What will happen if you refuse?"

I felt his gaze on me then, intense and hot and firm. "The world may fall to pieces."

Well, knock me down, but he thought highly of himself! As though the world would end if he didn't take a wife by the changing of the season.

"I doubt that," I said, returning his stare. "Even these terrors, they haven't caused the world to fall to pieces, so how could one small task laid on you by an overbearing father?"

He swallowed, his Adam's apple bobbing up and down. I tread on dangerous ground, knowingly insulting the King, regardless of William's ignorance to my awareness of his identity.

His hand crept across the ground to cover mine, and I shivered. "Believe me, it will."

I didn't believe him. But I did not say that.

I shrugged instead, stretched my legs, and sat upright, away from the stone. "I should go home. I'm sorry life is so difficult for you with your fancy clothes and whole family, but some of us have greater things to concern ourselves with."

He stared after me as I pulled my hand out from under his, stood, and moved away.

"Ella, wait. I'm sorry, you were here to mourn, and I dumped my own problems on you. I was … it was … I'm glad to see you."

Tiny moths took flight in my belly, for in truth? I was glad to see him, too. Despite myself, I allowed a smile to turn my lips, though he couldn't see. I would have replied in kind, had he not continued on.

"And believe me, I've no doubt your life is difficult, if your appearance—"

"What about it?" I whirled on him, teeth clenched and brow furrowed, enjoying every second of it. I looked an awful mess from the fireplace, what would he have of it?

"I mean to say, I've no doubt you work very hard, and—"

"Are you saying I'm ugly?"

"No! I'm sorry, Ella, it's just that the dirt—"

"I'm dirty?"

"No? Well, yes, but what does it matter? I'm sure you're quite lovely under all that … "

I allowed his voice to trail off as embarrassment took hold. Even in the darkness, there could be no mistaking the shame of his blunder. I turned to walk away again, when he called out once more.

"How would you like a job at the palace?"

That I had not expected.

"It's good pay. You'll be well taken care of, and you can visit here whenever you like. During daylight. I'd … we'd be able to see each other more often. On purpose."

It felt as though the air had been sucked out of the yard. Here I'd been, thrilled and terrified by the touch of his hand, and he offered me a *job?* I didn't know whether to be flattered or insulted, nor did my heart, which pounded its confusion.

"How can you offer that?" I whispered, for though I'd meant to expose him, this hadn't been my wish.

He scrambled to his feet and drew close to me, kind smile melting my heart and turning my cruel game into dust. "I'm … I'm the Prince. The King's son. Prince William. I know I should have told you a long time ago, but things were going so well without the stigma of royalty … I'm sorry, but you have to understand. This—" He gestured between us. "—wouldn't have happened. You and I, we … you would have thought different of me. Ella, please don't tell anyone, and I promise we have a place for you if you—"

We? There was no we. There was just a pompous boy who thought himself above the commoners, as if they couldn't make their own decisions about people and friends and the decency of other human beings.

So I pushed once more, and not because I wanted to tease him. Not this time. This time, I would beat him at his own deception.

"Prove it."

He frowned. "What?"

"Prove you're the Prince."

His mouth hung open, and I fought tears from my own eyes. I shouldn't have paid back kindness with cruelty, but my heart hurt so much at his being here and knowing he would soon be sucked into marriage with—

Should I warn him?

He dug in his pockets, spread his fingers, and checked the medallion chain around his neck.

"That's odd."

I said nothing.

"My ring, it's gone. I usually have it in my coat, and the laundress removes it during wash each day and replaces it." Did he not recall the coat he'd been wearing that day we first met? And had that not been many, many days ago now? *Men.*

"Pity," I said. "Is that it?"

He scowled, though I suspect more out of frustration than anger toward me. "I swear it's the truth. Why would I lie to you, of all people?"

"To a young woman, innocent … gullible … "

"I wouldn't." His eyes grew wide and wild. "I won't hurt you, I'd never hurt you. I swear I didn't mean to deceive, I only thought … Ella, I had to see you again."

Why? Why would he say such things? He knew as well as I of the purpose for the upcoming balls.

"Look, please come to the palace tomorrow. Follow the path around the stables, to a large oak door. I promise you will have work, and you'll be paid an honest wage."

"How will they know who I am?"

He bowed his head, glanced to and fro, and caught my heart in a wink. "I'll meet you there."

"With the servants?" I couldn't hide my surprise.

He shrugged. "What is a leader if not in touch with the needs of the people he leads?"

"So you suggest you're better than me." Why did my lips keep talking?

He blinked, straightened, and coughed. "I didn't—"

"Good day, Sire." I curtsied deeply and stressed the address with something near touching a mock. Whatever possessed me, I know not, though I suspect my heart knew that William's and my time together had run its course. I had already nurtured too deep an affection at our prior meeting, and it would not do.

My heart would be broken soon enough, for in only a few days' time, William would choose for himself a wife.

And for a position such as that, he wouldn't look twice at my dirt-smudged face.

19

The Gown

I spent that afternoon standing atop a stool, serving as a pincushion for Charlotte and Victoria, whose dressmaker had arrived to take fittings and measurements based on the latest fashions the ladies had seen in town. The sketches alone were enough to make me feel queasy, with crepe ruffles, satin bows, lace trim, and enough layers to wrap a horse.

Naturally, once either of the girls got tired of standing—I blamed one too many crème puffs—the garments were draped on me while the dressmaker tacked and pinned and poked me in delicate places. Charlotte giggled every time I flinched.

"Just look at the proud princess," Victoria purred, on one occasion where the dressmaker wound a bolt of satin around the skirt hoop. "How fine you look, sister. A pity you don't have a thing of your own to wear."

I wouldn't have wanted to wear one of those monstrosities, even if offered ten pieces of gold and a forty-acre field.

"I have plenty of my own gowns," I replied, for ignoring her would simply lead to greater taunting and provocation. "I'll wear one of those."

Victoria raised a single eyebrow, and I shuddered at the likeness of her mother. Charlotte, however, nearly sprung from her chair.

"What on earth do you mean? You're not attending, surely."

"The invitation was for all eligible ladies," Victoria said.

I nearly stumbled off my perch.

"If she has a suitable gown, I don't see why she shouldn't go." Victoria leaned forward in her seat, elbows to knees, propping her chin in one hand. "I don't suppose you have a particular gown in mind?"

As a matter of fact, I did. "I have a lovely, canary yellow gown with gold and forest green trim. And matching slippers. My mother had it made for me before … "

I caught myself. Victoria and Charlotte were rapt. Or so it seemed.

Doubt seized my chest. "Or, of course, I have a blue—"

"Oh no," said Victoria, "the yellow sounds perfect. I don't suppose you'll model it for us later, hmm?"

"Well, I don't—"

"Oh, please," squeaked Charlotte, matching her sister's glances with equal enthusiasm. "We can help advise on it. Perhaps I can loan you some jewelry, or a hat."

I couldn't believe my ears. "Perhaps."

Victoria clapped her hands. "It's settled, then. When this is finished, we'll see your gown. You'd make a fine catch for the Prince, wouldn't she, sister?"

Charlotte's expression grew dark before she saw the mirth behind Victoria's eyes.

I saw it, too.

She was not being kind. Something else stood behind her intent, and I'd waltzed directly into its path.

Edward did not rise that day. He stayed in bed, and though he remained in good spirits, it seemed the illness had returned. Once released from the fittings, I raced to his room with sweets and a story, and spent the evening at his side. Celia didn't try to remove me, nor did the sisters make good on their insistence to see my gown.

Indeed, Celia's absence continued throughout the remainder of the day, and when daylight turned to night, I still had not seen her. Not that I minded. Still, to preserve myself in case she continued with her nightly forays, I stayed out of the passages after dark, and for the few nights that followed. Days became a whirl of dress fittings and hair dressings, with Celia appearing infrequently to pile tasks upon my head and praise her daughters for how lovely they looked.

An etiquette tutor came to the house in the mornings to school Charlotte and Victoria in the finer points of interactions with royalty, and my mornings were spent with Edward, who steadily grew stronger once again. I feared, however, that he had fallen prey to Mother's penchant for illness, and though I begged God to remove his sickness and take me instead, my requests went unanswered.

I thought of calling Curson again—indeed, I longed for the feel of *The Book of Conjuring* in my hands—but for what purpose? I feared what he did to me, how he made me feel, but craved it all the same. It was nothing like being around William.

Ugh. I had to stop thinking about him.

Of course, I could not.

Instead, my thoughts were stronger as the festival grew closer, and I wondered whether he'd forgotten about me. I didn't go to the palace, so I did not know if he'd made good on his promise to meet me in the kitchens. But how could I, with Edward so ill? Perhaps I would once he recovered a little more. Or sooner.

I recalled Edward's delight the day prior, when I'd told him of our stepsisters' new, garish dresses.

"They sound truly awful," he'd said, "which means *you* will be the most beautiful of all."

I'd offered him a smile born of sadness. "Alas, no. I won't be going. Not this time."

His eyes had grown round with surprise. "Why not? You could marry the Prince! We could live in a castle, Ellison. A castle."

I'd had to laugh, then, for small boys truly understand little of marriage, royalty, and the ways of the world. "I'd rather live here with you and Father, all told," I'd said, "and I'm sure the castle isn't as wonderful as it seems. All those rooms? Just imagine, I bet you'd get lost just finding the kitchen. Or you'd want to go to the library and end up in the cellar! And don't forget, there's no playing with toys on the stairs. What if the King tripped and fell?"

He'd wrinkled his nose and shaken his head. "I still think it would be fantastic. You should go. You don't ever get to have fun anymore."

Oh, to be as perceptive as a child!

I'd stroked his hair and released a sigh, and for the first time, allowed myself to actually imagine what it might be like to put on my canary gown and stand in the palace's grand ballroom.

And to see William, finely dressed. Would he recognize me? Would he feel embarrassed for his previous offer? Would *I*?

The thought was both delicious and painful, and I banished the notion with a wave of my hand.

"Of course I do," I'd said. "I'm spending time with you."

And then the day came.

The sun rose. The clouds parted in the sky, and from the town came the sound of trumpets to announce the beginning of the festival.

In the house, clouds descended instead. Celia made her appearance first thing in the morning, armed with more tasks than I could ever be expected to complete, and rather than endure as I had since the day of Father's leaving, for the first time, a bitterness crept across my tongue and infected my thoughts.

We—all of us, across the kingdom—were due three days of celebration and rest. And in a moment of fury, I told her so.

"Oh?" Celia cocked her head as if an inquisitive pup. "My dear child, if everyone is expected to rest for three days, who will provide the food we eat? Where do you suppose our water will come from? Would you have the horses starve?"

"I wouldn't," I told her, "but everyone in this house can go without every item of clothing laundered for at least three days. And there is no need to polish silverware when doubtless you'll dine on rich tarts and trifles at the palace. As for the fireplace—"

"Wait." Celia held up a hand. "You're right, of course. The palace awaits." Her eyes glimmered with some unspoken delight, and I wondered how much it hurt for her to say that, even if in jest. "But whatever do you mean, *we* will dine there? Are you not attending?"

Surprise shot through me like a spiny arrow. "I hadn't thought ... "

"Victoria mentioned that you have a lovely yellow and green gown with matching slippers that may be perfect for the occasion."

She had?

"And haven't my daughters generously offered to lend you their jewels?"

They had. Not that I needed any, as I had plenty of my own—despite their location in my former bedroom with Victoria. "Yes, but—"

"So," Celia said, clasping her hands together, "if you finish the most important tasks and ready yourself in time for tonight's first ball, you may come."

But I hadn't planned on going. Truly, I hadn't believed Celia would allow it.

If I went, perhaps I could warn William to stay away from the sisters. I could warn him to avoid Celia, to fear her touch, and perchance he would listen and believe the words came from a true place and not from the jealous or vengeful motives of a dirty, ragged cinder-wench he'd met in the graveyard.

Yes, I would go.

"Thank you," I said, purpose blossoming in my chest. And with that, I ran to give Edward the good news.

20

The Rending

I raced through my chores.

My heart pounded with every hour that passed, and though the bitterness of not being able to enjoy the festival remained, I could not recall a day when I had felt so much anticipation and joy.

Yes, joy. A foreign concept at that time, to be sure, but the thought of seeing William again while I wore a clean dress with a washed and primped face was enough to keep a smile on my lips and my heart light, even through the most menial of tasks. Chamber pots included.

And as the shadows grew longer and the sun began its journey toward the horizon, both sisters and Celia began their preparations for the first evening of celebration. As did I.

Tasks complete, I scrubbed away weeks of dirt, stains, and blemishes on my person and my spirit. As each fingernail came clean, so did hope rise. Even if I didn't see William this night, I would have two more chances. What would he say? Surely he hadn't expected to see me there, or he would have mentioned it.

How strange that he hadn't asked if I planned to attend. What would he think?

Would he apologize for our last meeting?

Would *I*?

Still, it would be three nights of merrymaking. Three nights where I could forget about Celia, my missing father, the drudgery of servitude, and the threat on my brother's life—both from *them* and from his illness.

In a gesture of generosity I could never begin to repay, Gretel offered to stay the night these three evenings to watch over Edward, instead of enjoying the town's celebrations herself. I suspect she simply hoped I might outdo the sisters in their garish attire.

When I opened the wardrobe in my former room—*my* room—I loosed a breath of relief that the gown still hung there, untouched, even after the day when Victoria had tried to claim my garments for her own. Its shorter sleeves and higher waist were remnants of an older fashion, but it still shone as brightly as ever and I felt an eagerness to wear it again.

I slipped it on and Cook, in kindness, laced up the back. The corseting hugged my hips and bosom, and I felt faint with surprise at my appearance in the mirrors around the room. I had forgotten what I looked like under the layers of dirt and the grimy house-dress.

We found my slippers, beaded and delicate to match the beading and trim on the gown. From my jewelry box—one of Father's treasures from a trip some years ago—I drew a necklace of enamel-cut pearls and emeralds, with a tiny dragonfly in the center to rest delicately beneath my throat. This had long been my most beautiful necklace, with pearl and emerald earrings to match. Tears sprang to the corners of my unlined eyes as Gretel clasped the necklace into place. It had been a gift from my mother, who had received it from her mother, and her mother before that. Or so the story went.

How I wished she could see me now.

"My, you look a sight," Gretel mumbled, taking me into her arms. She held me at a distance then, and checked me up and down. "If your father were home today, surely he'd lock you away." She grinned and pinched my cheek. "Your ma would be proud of your lady-ness. Any man'd be lucky to have you."

"Thank you, Gretel," I said, returning the embrace. "I do think this is just what I need to lift my spirits."

At the mention of spirits, I thought of Curson—felt heat rush to my cheeks—and fanned my face with a lace-gloved hand.

"Shall we?" Gretel offered her arm, and I took it so that she might escort me down the stairs to the waiting carriage and an evening of blissful freedom.

Celia, Charlotte, and Victoria waited in the front hall, adjusting hats and gloves and jewels, twittering like sparrows that strove to put their nests just so.

Gretel and I descended the first three steps when the twittering ceased. Both Celia and sisters ceased their fidgeting and stared. At me.

For that brief moment—oh, but it was brief—I felt nothing but enraptured delight. I was Ellison, daughter of my noble father, educated and intelligent and beautiful, no matter what anyone else might say. No matter what task might come my way, no matter the storms of life.

Ah, but reality could not keep its grip loosed for long.

At the bottom step, Charlotte's stare became a grimace. Victoria's gasp twisted into a cruel scowl. Celia's lips drew into a thin line, her beauty shadowed by an anger I couldn't explain.

"Are those *my* pearls?" Victoria pointed at the cord around my neck. "And *my* earrings?"

Confusion must have flooded my features. "No, this was my mother's, and grandmother's before that."

Victoria shook her head, voice lowering to a hiss. "You disgusting little liar. You took those from my room, did you not?"

I felt as though I'd been caught in a crosswind. "Yes, but only because it was *my* room, and—"

"Thief!" Charlotte shrieked, pointing a ruffled, purple-gloved finger at my face. "You used my rouge, too!"

I had not used any rouge.

"She did no such thing," snapped Gretel.

"And those slippers," Victoria said, bending at the waist to lift the hem of my dress. "Did you find those in my wardrobe?"

Her wardrobe. *Hers?* She stayed in my room and truly believed all things were *hers?* "It's *my* wardrobe, in *my* room, where *you* are sleeping."

With that, Charlotte lunged forward and grabbed a handful of my hair, where Cook had helped weave tiny white flowers into plaits which we'd then piled atop my head. In one yank, Charlotte pulled out a handful of flowers and released chunks of hair from their places, sending sharp nails of pain down the sides of my head.

"And these are *my* flowers, from *my* garden, you thieving whore."

As if she had ever stepped foot in a garden!

Victoria did the same, pulling out flowers and braids as I cried out in distress, and moments later, I felt the clasp of my necklace release from around my neck. I screamed for them to stop, as did Gretel, but between protests and cries, Celia did naught but stand there as her daughters tore apart my most treasured gown and heirlooms, piece by piece, until every inch lay in tatters on the floor at my feet.

I could not stop the flood of tears this time.

"That's better," quipped Victoria brightly, as I stood before them in my shift. With a laugh, Charlotte ran down the hallway and returned moments later with a sheet from the wash and pair of ancient wooden shoes which Father kept in the library for a lark.

She draped the sheet around my shoulders, moving limp arms as needed, lifting my feet to replace my torn slippers with wooden shoes.

I didn't resist.

I couldn't. What would be gained from it? I'd already lost.

"We told you we'd help," said Victoria, looking to her mother for approval.

Celia said nothing, her face a blank canvas that revealed even less—which I considered a condoning for what they'd done.

"Now you can dance," sang Charlotte, turning in a circle so that her own bluebird gown spun outward and sparkled in the lamplight. "Give us a twirl, sweet sister."

I remained silent.

"Oh, come now," Victoria pouted. "We offered to help. There was no need to steal from us. Is that any way to show gratitude? All you had to do was ask."

I couldn't have responded if I'd wanted to. The tears choked my breath and blurred my vision, but worse than that, I'd been betrayed. What woman needed to ask permission of her own clothes?

And though neither their loyalty nor mine had been mutual or firm, they'd promised me this one night. The kingdom had promised me this.

"Clean yourself up," said Celia, without a hint of emotion. "If you manage to get hold of yourself, you may still make some measure of appearance, but we won't wait for you."

She gripped my chin and pulled until our eyes met, the black nothingness in her own all the more apparent now. "But if I were you, I wouldn't bother. No man will have you. You're not worth it."

With that, she released me, placed one hand upon the vase of flowers on the nearby table, and pushed.

The vase fell to the floor with a crash, sending sharp, porcelain shards cascading across the floor I'd polished only hours before.

"What a mess," Celia droned. "You'd better clean that up too, while you're at it."

And with a flourish, she, Charlotte, and Victoria took their leave, as Cook and I stood staring after.

"Oh, child." Gretel placed a hand on my shoulder. "How she ensnared your father—after all he's been through—I'll never understand."

As the creak and crunch of carriage wheels disappeared down the drive, I took one final, shuddering breath.

And another.

And another.

One breath at a time, I thought, *is the only way I shall manage to live a moment longer.*

But as I stood there, breathing, weeping, memories of the short time since Celia's arrival played as a silent drama through my head. The idle threats and whispered warnings. Her entrancing touch and the bile-filled offspring she called daughters.

My concessions. The thievery and servitude I'd allowed for the sake of Edward's safety.

How debased I'd allowed myself to become.

How far we had fallen. I, the daughter of a noble merchant, reduced to this. Barred from one evening of joy, despite the King's own invitation for all to attend.

No more.

I would allow it no more.

21

The Three Spirits

I turned to Gretel with peace in my heart, a calm that descended like a cool wind to reassure and encourage what I might do next.

"Gretel," I said, no longer trembling, "would you be so kind as to fetch one of Victoria's ghastly bird hats for me? I have need of its … parts."

She hesitated only for a moment before leaving to do as asked, a knowing within her eyes. And I, awaying into the parlour, pulled the curtains and formed my circle, retrieved *The Book of Conjuring* and its now-powerless key, and opened the tome to a page within the book's section marked for illusions.

On the pages following the spell for hidden things, I found these words: *To obtain a wondrous means of transportation.* This, I decided, I would need, but beyond that, what of my appearance?

And what of my sisters?

Ah, all things in good measure. Patience.

As I couldn't find a spell or recitation that might restore my dress, I chose perhaps a more encompassing set of instructions with this end: *To gain dignity and honor.* I believed I could do with a restoration of both. With the circle set, I inscribed the words as the book instructed, though different this time.

The items needed for this conjuring were also different from before, though not difficult to obtain for one who has discovered a renewed determination for justice. Ash was no challenge to find, as I'd hidden a bucket of it in the attic, and from the now-empty stable, I retrieved a bridle according to the instructions. The words also mentioned that fasting was required in order to perform the conjuring, and while I hadn't fasted with intent, I hoped that the lack of time I'd had to consume any food that day would be enough.

I mention this because it is important. I did not awake that morning with intent to call forth one thing or another. All of the pieces simply fell into place. Can I truly be blamed?

Gretel waited for me in the parlour when I returned with bridle and ash. I took the hat from her hands and, with a prayer for forgiveness and pity for the poor creature who'd given its life for such a garment, tugged at a wing until it released from amid the milliner's handiwork. Gretel winced but said nothing as I pulled away the feathers and dried sinew to reveal a thin, delicate wingbone the length of my second finger.

"Thank you, Cook," I said, indicating she should take her leave.

She did not. "Must you really, girl? There're terrible consequences for even the smallest of these acts."

I shot her a sharp look. "How do you know this?"

She said nothing at first, but bowed her head with a deep and mournful sigh. "Do as you must, child, and I'll watch over the young one. But … be careful. I'd hate to think what your father would say, though for all my cautions, he might be the one to guide you through it. Seems, in a way, he already has."

She left, muttering words beneath her breath and leaving me

frozen in memory and questions.

What *did* she mean? Should I go after her and demand that she explain? Surely not now. Later, perhaps, with less at stake and more time to contemplate her words regarding my father and consequence. Otherwise, I might consume my night with further questions and further still.

I would demand the truth upon my return, but for now, there was much to be done.

To begin, I took a long breath, and plunged the bone into ash.

Symbols and letters written as required, I placed the bridle under my knees, faced the east, and read out loud as instructed: "Oh Lautrayth and Feremin and Oliroomim, spirits who attend the sinful folk, I, Ellison, trust in your power and conjure you by Him who spoke and by which all things were made, He who knows all things yesterday, today, and tomorrow. And by heaven and earth, fire and water, the sunlight and the moon's gleam, send these three spirits to me, and let them come gently and without cause to fear, that they will fulfill in its entirety whatever I command and bring it fully to pass."

A shiver ran up my spine as the air grew cold, even while the circle in which I knelt grew hot. Under my knees, the bridle began to tug, pulling itself away from my grasp as a lodestone moves toward blood. I dug my knees in further and returned attention to the book, for there were still more words to recite. Mist, gray and purple and black, rose from the ash and crawled across the circle to my book, wafting fingers of smoke that reached and grabbed and obscured the words on the page.

These fingers touched the bridle, curled around its length and—with a violent tug—tried to pull it from my hold.

I almost broke the circle, for this was nothing like Curson's arrival. He arrived with steady, slow caress, but this—these ...

"Come now," I read, confidence wavering, "without delay, that you must humbly fulfill my commands."

A breeze swept through my hair even though I sat indoors, and the sound of a thousand galloping hooves rose through the ash, louder and louder until the whole house shook and every speck of light from all corners vanished like the descending of night. I bent overtop my knees to keep from falling backward and releasing control of the bridle to the spirits, who still tugged and pulled as if they could not rise without it. I clenched my eyes shut as the world pitched and roiled, mists growing fuller and stronger, hooves and the whinny of horses drawing nearer, and I clasped both hands across my ears for the pain like beating drumbeats and—

The shaking stopped. The noise ceased, and I no longer felt a pull at my knees. As I couldn't afford to waste even a moment, I forced the lids from my eyes, took up the bridle, and stood.

Three spirits surrounded my circle.

I took in the first one. To the east was a spirit clothed in royal garb, a crown of knives atop his head. Blood spilled down the sides of his face in rivers, streaming from the wounds where the blades carved into his skull. I swayed where I stood at the sight of so much blood.

It was to him I spoke the required words. The others would wait. "May the Lord in His mercy restore you to your most deserving status."

With a voice like a hot blade through butter, he spoke the book's reply: *"Mistress, we have come to you, all of us prepared to obey your commands. Command us to do that for which you have called us, and it will be done."*

Red rivers spilled from between his teeth as he formed each word.

These spirits were, truly, nothing like Curson.

I held the bridle aloft, willing my shaking arms to still. "Lautrayth, I wish for you to consecrate this bridle, so that whenever I shake it, a horse will come before me, in whose mouth I shall place it, that I may mount it and ride in safety wherever I desire."

He nodded, took the bridle, and stepped back into darkness.

I approached the second spirit, to the west. He, unlike the others, was without form, his purple mist shifting and swirling to reveal eyes and a mouth, then hands and an ear, and then nothing at all.

I did not fear what I could not see, and so with ease I spoke the following words: "Feremin, I wish to be clothed in a manner that might restore my dignity and honor, that all who see me should be amazed at my presence above all else, unseeing who I am, and seeing only that honor which is due."

My cheeks grew warm as I did what the book instructed, and pulled away my undergarments to hold them before the misty spirit. "By your virtue and power, may you have no leave to harm me by this garment, but may the Holy Christ protect and defend me."

My shift was consumed in an instant as the spirit withdrew into darkness, and so with a hopeful heart I turned to the third spirit.

I started, stumbling back one step and then two.

I saw nothing but a boy, a young boy no older than Edward, with a face so sweet and gentle that one couldn't help but wish to draw him into one's arms—

He reached for me and I screamed. His hand, so small and pale, had not the nails of a human, but the sharp, curled claws of a cat. And as I drew my gaze from hand to boy, my legs became weak and weary.

"You are Oliroomim?"

Fangs like a beast's descended over his lip as he nodded once, and his eyes turned black as pitch without a speck of white. Dark liquid dripped from his fingers, and he cocked his head to regard me as a wild creature to its prey.

"You have no recitation for me?" he asked, his small voice making me yearn to run to Edward, hold on and never let go. Oliroomim sounded nothing like the others. Where their voices had hissed and flitted through the air as if part of the wind itself, leaving no doubt as to their otherworldliness, this spirit spoke with the voice of a child, clear and direct. I fought a rush of pity for the poor being. No child should look this way, spirit or none.

When I didn't answer, he continued. "Dearest mistress, surely you have some need of me."

I did. Oh, I did, but I could not bring myself to speak it.

"I revoke my right of conjuring," I whispered, "and release you from—"

"I'm afraid it doesn't work that way, mistress. What would you have me do?"

Around one finger, I had wound a piece of hair from Victoria's hat. I hadn't required it for the bone alone. "I wish for a mild affliction on the one to whom this belongs."

I dropped the hair into his outstretched palm.

"Mild?" The spirit curled its fingers into a fist and opened them again, an iron nail appearing in the place of where I'd laid the hair. "Inscribe the name."

What? "I don't—"

"Write the name on my hand. You wouldn't want me to choose the wrong person."

"But the hair—"

The child shook his head. "We must be certain."

And as much as I ached to break the circle, I couldn't forget why it had come to this in the first place. I picked up the nail and pressed it into the child spirit's palm. Bright spots of red blossomed against skin and bone that *should not have been.*

"Why do you bleed?" I held my breath. "How can a spirit truly be a spirit if he still bleeds?"

He laughed, the sound so much like a joyous child that my eyes filled with tears as I drew the nail across tender flesh. "Because I like it."

Lord, forgive me.

And so, into the palm of the spirit child's hand, I carved the name of my stepsister Victoria.

22

The First Ball

I arrived at the palace on the back of a black steed, my pockets full of ash and bone. Other guests, arriving in their carriages with driver and steward and matched Arabians, didn't hide their surprise at the appearance of a young woman in a silver and gold ball gown sitting astride an equine of such power that my legs quaked with each step.

I slid off its back and removed the bridle, tucking it into the folds of my gown until I had need of it again. The horse, loosed until that time, took his leave as lords and ladies stared with mouths agape. None moved to stop him, however. I suppose that was for the best, as I shiver to think what might have happened, had anyone else tried to control a steed born of mist and spirit.

The steps to the palace entrance were excessive, requiring much concentration and gripping of skirts to traverse. I feared I would lose my balance going up, and didn't look forward to coming back down. With no rails to assist the journey, the arrogance of such construction drew my hand to the pocket of ash concealed in my dress, where it itched to draw out a pinch and—

No.

I had a purpose here, and it didn't involve the indulgence of petty slights.

"May I be of assistance, miss?"

I started at a touch on my arm and nearly stumbled. Bright, warm eyes caught my own, and strong hands upon my back and arm kept me upright. His request appeared so genuine that I couldn't comprehend he could possibly be asking *me*—until he repeated the question with a kind smile.

"Yes, thank you." I offered him a silk, silver-gloved hand, and we traversed the steps easily. On reaching the landing, I thanked him for his help and he bowed low, touching finger to forehead in the manner of a gentleman to a lady.

"My delight," he said, and disappeared into the surging crowd of latecomers. I remained frozen for several moments, the utter absurdity of kindness washing through limbs that burned like fire for one thing and one thing alone this night.

Revenge, said those feelings I had buried deep.

"No," I said, shaking my head to escape the urging.

"Are you all right?"

My heart leapt and sank at the same time, if indeed that is possible. I knew that voice, though I hadn't heard it for quite some time.

Liesl.

She stood before me wearing peacock blue, setting off her rosy complexion—but not quite so flattering for her yellow hair. Her bosom peeked overtop the dress's neckline like two fluffy pillows, which had to have been her mother's doing.

"Liesl!" I could not stop the exclaim that tore from my lips. "It's quite the relief to see you—"

My words broke at the sight of her politely confused expression. "I'm sorry, have we met? I do apologize, you'll have to forgive me, I get so distracted sometimes. Have you visited my father's shop?"

It's me, I wanted to say, *Ellison. Your best friend of uncountable years.*

But I did not, for it became clear in that moment that Liesl, sister of my heart, didn't recognize me. She saw not who I was, but only … only the "honor which is due."

Oh, it *worked.*

It truly had worked. The spirits had succeeded in this, too. A part of me wished they had not—for I certainly couldn't surprise William with my presence now—but the gladness at spending an evening unknown by Celia and her daughters lifted my spirits enough to recompense for losing the familiarity of my friend's company for a night.

I shook my head and gestured to the enormous, open doors of the palace that rose up before us. "I'm afraid not. Visiting, for the festival. I—I'm sorry, I mistook you for someone else. You say your name is Liesl, too?"

She nodded, still wary, but cheerful nonetheless. "Not uncommon, that one. I know at least three others. I think we're to go through those doors ahead and to the left." Her voice grew softer as she leaned in close. "I'm scared too, but I'm sure we'll be all right. I plan to set myself near an empty corner and snack on pastries all night."

She giggled, and it brought a curve to my lips despite myself. "You don't care for the Prince?"

"Oh no." She shook her head, buttery curls bouncing. "Could you imagine? Responsibility, meetings, sitting on a chair all day listening to people drone on … it all sounds terribly dull."

The revelation was not as surprising as it might have been from another girl. "But you'd never want for anything."

She patted my arm. "Money isn't everything, in the end, but I don't mind the excuse for a new dress, either. I've come with my brother as chaperon, though I suppose he's off chatting up some fair tart already. And yourself?"

The mere fact that she didn't recognize me seemed proof enough that the second spirit had done its work. How would I answer her question without giving myself away?

"I'm ... " My fingers brushed a shard of cinder among the pile of ash concealed in my gown, and it struck me that I could not give my true name if I wanted to maintain the spell's ruse. With a fleeting prayer for forgiveness, I spoke the name that had pressed upon my back so many times—and which I had heard but one man speak in both joy and sorrow, but had never heard him say since the day the illness claimed her from our lives.

"Aleidis." I choked on the sound of it, and fought the rising heat of tears. "My name is Aleidis. Plain and simple. And I've come alone."

"There's nothing plain and simple about you. What a lovely name—an old one, at that." She gripped my free hand with such excitement that I wondered if she might pull it right off. "Shall we enter together? We can be announced together, too. Forget my brother."

I nodded in reply, for it seemed she left me no choice—and after all, some part of me ached to throw both arms around my friend and tell her everything.

But of course, I did not.

My breath escaped me the moment we entered the ballroom.

The room was much larger and far grander than anything I could have imagined. Our home could have fit inside several times over, and with room to spare. Glass chandeliers the size of grinding stones draped from the ceiling, and silk and mirrored tile flowed from one chandelier to the next. A balcony circled the room, with doors leading to rooms on the upper floor.

Grandest of all? The contents of the ballroom itself.

After announcing each arrival, we were to descend even more stairs—a love affair for royalty, I suspect—into the massive hall filled with elegantly dressed guests, carved statues of ice that sparkled like diamonds, a raised orchestra, tables upon tables of food and wine, and all things draped with more silk and gems to rival even Celia's decorative fancies ... yet here, these things didn't seem garish or out of place.

That, I supposed, was what happened when one lived according to one's status and means.

"Isn't it marvellous?" Liesl whispered, gripping my arm as we descended. Our names resonated throughout the hall as the steward announced our arrival, and I shied at the stares and glances thrown our way.

"I believe you may have won some attentions after all," I said, more to hide my own quaking insides than anything.

We reached the bottom step as Liesl turned to me with wide, startled eyes. "Me? Oh no, Aleidis. 'Tis not me they stare at."

At that moment I realized that, despite the innumerable bodies in the room and the strains of violins that had wafted through the air when we arrived, the room had suddenly lapsed into silence.

Complete and utter silence.

I heard only a cough from the back of the room.

Gasps.

Stares.

At me.

The sea of people in front of us parted, one by one. Genteel guests, ladies with dresses and jewels and beauty beyond measure, stood aside. They looked to me and then to where they'd stepped apart, for coming toward me as though he desired nothing else in the world was the one person I feared I was not yet ready to see.

Dressed in gold and silver, just as I, strode Prince William.

Beside me, Liesl couldn't hide her own surprise, and I felt rather than saw her shrink away into the crowd. My heart ached for the sudden loneliness, and a swarm of butterflies took flight in my belly.

Prince William stopped the proper distance away, according to custom. He bowed deeply, and I returned it with a curtsy as required by a person of my standing.

I feared to release even one breath.

"Welcome, Lady Aleidis." His smile was full of warmth and awe, though at that moment I could think of nothing but whether he'd recognize my face without smudges of dirt and grime.

I took the hand he offered and met his gaze. No, he did not recognize me, nor the name upon which I'd rested at our first and last meetings.

I sighed in silent relief, though I admit, some part of me wished he could see the change from the girl he thought he knew in the graveyard. And yet, what would it matter? He hid his true self from me, and I from him.

Had he waited for me in the kitchens that day?

I hadn't much time to wonder, for he drew me close—closer than comfort, for a stranger—until I smelled his breath upon my face, sweet as wine. How presumptuous he acted, I thought. And yet, my body betrayed me and I yearned to be closer.

"May I have the pleasure of your first dance?" He whispered his request into my ear, beyond the hearing of the surrounding crowd. They leaned forward, straining to catch a word.

I stiffened. Celia, Victoria, and Charlotte's faces appeared above the crowd, endeavouring to see over the sea of bodies that encircled us. Poor William—he mistook my reaction for something he'd said.

He pulled back, my hand still in his. "Have I said something wrong?"

"No," I said quickly, for I maintained my sense of self-preservation and the manners taught by my mother. When addressing royalty, one must be very, very careful, and now especially, no matter how much I thought I knew this man—boy?—in front of me.

"I've frightened you." His smile wavered, and he drew my hand up to meet his lips. The crowd gasped. "I don't bite, promise. Just one dance?"

He looked so hopeful that I couldn't refuse. Not that I would have, for without a doubt the King and Queen looked on nearby, watching their son's actions, and I thought they might not take kindly to a refusal. I agreed with a nod and a tight smile, for I could hear Charlotte's uncircumspect whispers of "who is she?" and "what is she saying?" And that, for the moment, was the sweetest revenge of all.

With a breath, William drew me into his arms and the strains of violins and strings swelled above us. The crowd, cued to the wishes of royalty, dispersed to the edges of the floor, though some chose to join us with their chaperons and—I suspected—some with *other* ladies' chaperons.

I fell into the rhythm of the music and William's lead, grateful for having received proper training as a young girl, unlike many who appeared to fumble with their steps. Although, I considered briefly, my memory could have been a result of the second spirit's work. Regardless, it didn't matter.

As we turned, separated, bowed, and joined hands in the dance, William's eyes never left my own. Heat rose in my cheeks, and for a moment, I longed to be back in my room—the attic, even—with a book and flickering candle.

"Who are you?" William touched the small of my back to lead into a turn. "I've not seen you before at the palace, or in town. Have you traveled far?"

"In a manner of speaking," I replied, "but not too far that I can't follow the dances of your court."

He laughed at that, and even the violin's dulcet tones couldn't compare to the sweetness of its sound. "You're a princess, then. Only royalty receives training in court dances outside their own kingdom. Is your father here?"

I didn't rush to correct him, though my throat closed at the thought of Father. "He's not."

We came close then, faces near enough to touch. I thought of the coat, hidden away, to keep from fainting.

"No chaperon? Even more intriguing. How are you enjoying yourself?"

How could he ask such a thing? "I don't know. You caught me before I'd managed to complete my entrance."

He shrugged. "You're hard to miss, even from a distance. Your dress is very ... sparkling."

As we twirled, I caught a glimpse of the King standing on the balcony above, gazing down at his son. "*Your* father certainly keeps a close eye on you." Of course I bit my lip after that, for I spoke with a familiarity far beyond what a lady should who'd just met a prince for the first time.

He didn't seem to notice. "Yes, he does. I suspect he thinks this sort of thing is critical for my training."

"Training?"

"Oh," he coughed, "I mean, etiquette, socialization, that sort of thing."

I almost laughed. "Socialization? Are you man, woman, or horse?"

"Sometimes a bit of all three, I wonder." He frowned. "I'm joking, you realize?"

And at that moment, it struck me—he felt just as nervous and uncomfortable as I. "Of course. But what has a celebratory ball to do with etiquette for a prince? I thought only ladies had to worry about that sort of thing, and besides, a large, public festival doesn't seem to be the best sort of training ground for someone like you ... "

He glanced up toward his father and back at me. "There are certain, ah, customs my family has that are unique to us. Responsibilities, traditions, that sort of thing."

The formality of his speech, regarding this in particular, felt jarring. I pulled my hands away from his.

"You mean finding a wife?" I slapped a freed palm against my mouth. "What I mean to say is ... I ... "

I am continually grateful for small mercies, because he found my blunder amusing. "That's one part of it, but not all. My other duties are considerably less ... attractive."

The comment would have been thrilling, had I not been under a spell that hid me from recognition.

"If I may be so bold, Your Highness, why the urgency? Your father didn't marry until he'd reached his second decade, and even *that* was young compared to his father. Or any other king or prince I know of."

He remained silent and thoughtful, for a time. "The King wills it so. Who am I to question the King?"

William could not have been less believable had he told me a small blue fairy had whispered these orders in his ear. "He's your *father*. Surely that gives even a prince—his own son!—a say in the future?"

With a glance to his father and back again, William shook his head. "I'm afraid it's not that simple, Lady Aleidis. There's more at stake here than you realize."

If he thought me a stranger to family difficulties, he was sorely mistaken. "Is that so? Well, I'm listening."

His eyes grew wide. "I shouldn't have said that, I ... please don't repeat it. Forget it, it's nothing."

Ah, yes. The William I knew had finally arrived. A thrill wriggled up my spine, and I left behind the stiff formality in favor of a genuine conversation with a friend. It was, I realize, a poor decision—but in the moment, with William's fingers gentle on my back and wrist, how could I have been expected to consider the prudence of following impulse?

My thoughts grew cloudy and my tongue took its liberties. "Perhaps we can bargain? I'll forget if you, let's see ... request that the musicians play 'The Golden Sun' for their next number."

Confusion, followed by uncertainty, followed by amusement, flitted across his face. "I do hope you aren't serious, Lady Aleidis. A folk hymn? What would the other guests think?"

I snorted, quite by accident. "I don't particularly care, if we're being truthful. I think it might actually liven things up a bit—help you see who among these women remembers how to laugh when the moment calls for it. And even better, when it does not."

"You're positively incorrigible, Lady Aleidis."

"And you're only pretending to stand on formality because it's expected of you."

He stopped our dance then. I should have stilled my words, but of course, that sort of wisdom continues to elude my better sense.

"Pretending? I'm the Prince. I don't pretend. Look around you—you're at a royal ball. What did you expect?"

"I expected," I went on, "that you might act like yourself,

rather than some stiff-necked marionette without a thought in his own head."

I shouldn't have said it. The ball was his father's doing, not his—he'd said as much. How could I hold him to blame?

I did not, truly. My heart, however, had other opinions entirely. The bloody thing had a will of its own, and it wanted William to cease this fallacious exercise so that we might find some quiet place to be alone and share in each other's worlds once more.

But this was neither the time nor the place, nor did it hold to the purpose for which I'd come.

That purpose, in fact, approached from the far side of the ballroom floor, mother in tow. Escorting them was a rotund gentleman with a thin moustache and a tall, white wig upon his head. He looked our way, and I gasped.

His eyes were empty pools, vapid and unseeing—and his jaw, slack. Lifeless.

He led Celia toward us, she upon his arm.

"Without a thought in my head?"

Oh, *William!* His cheeks had reddened and his brow, deeply creased. Would that I had held my tongue.

He went on. "Who are you to say I can't think for myself?"

Oh, but I had to reply to *that.* "You're scouting for a wife at a ball that you don't care to attend, to find a woman you don't particularly care to marry, all for the sake of some obtuse 'greater purpose' that it appears *you* aren't even entirely aware of. So, Prince William, it looks to *me* as if you care nothing for your own happiness, nor are you the man I'd been led to believe would—"

"Wait." His face was fully flushed now, but it appeared that his anger had given way to an amused disbelief that a young lady— whom he'd only just met—would stand in the middle of the dance floor at a royal ball and berate his execution of free will. "I hear what you're saying, but I promise, it isn't like that."

He touched his gold medallion and rubbed thumb and forefinger against it as I stole a glance toward Celia and Victoria. They were close—close enough to reach us at any moment.

"Mmm," I said, distracted.

"Though I can't say I understand what gives you the right to—"

He stopped abruptly, and my gaze snapped back to meet his. He stared with an intensity that spoke far louder than any words.

"It's almost as if we'd ... "

A pit opened in my stomach. *No. Look away. Please.*

"Do I ... ?" He blinked twice, and stared again. "Have we ... ?"

"Excuse me, Your Highness." A hand grazed my shoulder and I jumped in surprise, so focused I'd been on what I thought—what I feared—William would say.

The pit opened further and swallowed me whole, for Celia and Victoria had reached us, with smiles plastered on their painted faces. My heart began to pound for another reason entirely, but the spell had not failed thus far. It would hold under Celia's scrutiny. I had to believe it would hold.

I hoped William, in his moment of suspicion toward me, would regain clarity to see the lack of sincerity behind these women's eyes.

Of course, he did not.

Their gentleman escort offered his hand to William, who took it in a firm handshake.

"Baron von Veltheim," William said, "thank you for coming. I'm sure my father is very pleased to see you here. How long has it been? I trust the Baroness is well."

"Yes, yes, dear boy," the Baron droned, eyes unfocused. "Very well, very well." His head tilted forward too far, somewhat unnaturally, but William appeared unaffected. I supposed he saw his fair share of oddities both inside and outside the palace, on his travels.

"May I introduce these lovely ladies to your company?" Baron von Veltheim's voice scratched and cracked. What *had* Celia done to him?

William bowed very slightly at the waist, and I saw Celia's elbow strike Victoria in the ribs—an unsubtle suggestion that she might return the gesture.

"Lady Celia and Lady Victoria," the Baron said, as they curtsied. "New arrivals from the south."

If William felt any surprise at being introduced to women unrelated to the Baron—and not his own wife and daughter—he failed to show it. Stoic, he.

Gracious beyond all reason, William turned to thank me for our time together. "Save me one more, Lady Aleidis."

I couldn't help but smile. "As you like." Though, I doubted a repeat dance would be looked on kindly by all the other eligible ladies in the room.

Victoria took William's outstretched hand and feigned a blush. It took much willpower not to roll my eyes. Just as I turned to move away from the couple, my gaze fell accidentally across Celia's, who matched mine with alarming ferocity.

"Good health to you, Lady Aleidis," she said, without a hint of sincerity. And though my own voice trembled for fear of discovery, I replied in kind.

She moved closer to me as the strains of music began once more. "Tell me, where is it you're from?"

Seized by a moment of panic, heaven gave me another small mercy as I didn't have a chance to respond—for at the same time, I caught a glimpse of William and Victoria, who were *not* dancing.

Instead William, attempting to maintain composure, stood helpless as a pink-cheeked Victoria dabbed a once-white handkerchief at her nose. The handkerchief was stained with blood.

Why she didn't excuse herself, I couldn't fathom. The handkerchief grew brighter and brighter, and several other ladies around them finally noticed the presence of blood. And promptly fainted.

I backed into the crowd to escape notice, difficult as that was, but all eyes were on Victoria and the Prince. I hated myself for not running to her aide, but something stopped me. Whether otherworldly or my own cowardice, I can't say, but instead I stood silent, listening.

"Let me call some help," William was saying as he looked around to signal someone, anyone, who might be able to assist.

"I'm fine," Victoria said. The redness poured from her nose still, saturating the handkerchief, traveling across her lips. And then I saw it—a thin trickle of crimson that ran from the inside of her pale, white ear, down the side of her cheek.

And to match, an even smaller drop at the outer corner of her left eye.

"Let's dance," she said, and vomited all over the front of her crisp, newly-made peony gown.

Her eyes rolled back into her skull. She collapsed on the floor in a heap at William's feet.

I was not the only one who screamed.

23

The Illness

I raced out of the palace, heart pounding and guilt pouring from every crevice. I had asked for a mild affliction. *Mild.*

Surely she wouldn't survive such a plight.

Surely she lay dead at William's feet.

Perhaps I can be blamed for running without offering to help, but the moment she collapsed, at least ten armed guards stormed onto the ballroom floor to usher the Prince away, while more still were sent to search the palace grounds for—for what? Treachery? I heard the word "poison" more than once as I fled, but of course, I knew the truth.

And as I was not the only one fleeing the grounds—I fell into step alongside many chaperons either assisting or carrying their charges—none noticed when I stepped through a large hedge, removed the bridle from my skirts, sprinkled it with a pinch of ash, and shook it.

Within moments, my black horse appeared. I placed the bridle around his neck and we flew home, straight as an arrow, invisible to the eyes of those we passed by.

Was I afraid? Of course. I am not stupid. But more so, I feared that I had done something so terrible, so unforgivable, that no amount of penance or pleading on my behalf would quench the eternal fires that surely burned for me.

I shook with a violence born of terror and loathing as I sent my steed back to the spirit realm, after which I righted the parlour as best I could. Once finished, I raced to the attic, exchanged my spirit-woven gown for ash-stained garments, and thundered down the attic steps with every intention of clearing the broken shards of vase that remained in the front entrance.

What else could I do? My guilt wouldn't allow me to rest for even a breath.

Gretel stood at the top of the next stair flight, lips drawn tight against her teeth.

It stilled me in an instant.

"Edward?" I whispered.

She nodded. I raced into his room and thudded to my knees at his bedside, panic rising and thoughts of Victoria forgotten. Edward's eyes were clenched shut, but he thrashed about, tossing and turning beneath his covers. Beads of sweat coated his forehead, though his lips looked pale and cold. Damp cloths lay in a heap on the floor.

"How long has he been like this?"

Gretel entered the room and sat at the edge of the bed. "Only moments after you left, miss. He fell asleep just afore you arrived home."

"How could this happen?" I whispered the question to no one, for no one could give me an answer. "He'd been getting better ... "

Gretel's hand rested on my shoulder. "I'll send for the doc in the morn. He'll know better what to do."

But so did I. And it terrified me, because I had watched a loved one in this state once before, only a short time past.

"I know what you're thinking, girl, and it ain't—"

"You don't know that," I cut in, for I couldn't bear to hear her say anything further. "Whether it is or not, you and I both know there's only one way out from this. It's through or nothing."

For Mother, it had been nothing.

I stood and smoothed the front of my dress. "I'll fetch another compress."

"You stay," Gretel murmured, rising. "He needs his sis."

And I needed my brother.

Later that night, my guilt was assuaged. The spirit had not killed Victoria, and in effect, I suppose, neither had I. She arrived home in a black carriage with two palace guards to help carry her inside. They lay her in my room, and although I inquired after her health, Celia slammed the door in my face and refused to speak to me.

And so I slept by Edward's side, shifting between sleep and wakefulness as easily as a dream.

24

The Festival

The morning brought little relief for either of us. Celia dragged me from Edward's side to ensure I assisted with preparations for the second day of revelry, promising through gritted teeth that she would see the doctor attended him as quickly as possible.

I didn't even pretend at wishing to join them at the ball this time, and did as told.

Hours later, Celia came to me as I scrubbed the floors of our front hall, paying no mind to the freshly washed areas and stepping directly upon them with her shod feet.

I thought to call out a warning to take care until the floor dried, but a struggle within caused my delay and I said nothing.

To my conscience's relief, she didn't slip.

The rest of me envied her superior balance and poise.

"Ella. When you finish here, I have a very important task for you."

Glorious. She began every list of chores with such a statement, as if to temper each order by making it sound imperative for the world's continued existence. I stopped scrubbing and rested the brush against my knees.

"What is it this time?"

I had not meant to spew my venom aloud.

Celia's nostrils flared, though where I would have looked piggish, it made her appear all the more refined. "Ever the ingrate, child? And I thought you might thank me."

I would never have cause to thank her.

"I am fully occupied by preparations for this evening," she continued, "and one of my fair daughters has seen fit to inform me that she absolutely cannot abide the hat I have chosen for her."

Doubtless Victoria had disapproved of the lack of small animals atop her head last night—but surely, after the episode of the previous evening, attending another ball would be the furthest thing from her mind.

"And as we are all otherwise engaged, I need you to call on the milliner for one of the pieces we commissioned."

I nearly dropped the scrubbing brush. *Me?* Leave the house, by Celia's orders?

A smile threatened to turn the corner of my mouth and give away my growing delight. "You wish for me to go into town? Today?"

Celia scowled. "Do you refuse?"

"Refuse? Oh, no." I glanced at my clothes, stained and dirtied. "Shall I go now? I can't wear this, certainly. That might reflect poorly on your household."

Flattery, I hoped, would press her to release me immediately.

"Yes, now. Change out of that disgusting rag and go. Don't delay, this is no time for play. We still have need of you to ready ourselves fully for the evening ahead."

Wordless, I picked up brush and bucket, and set them aside. Only when I had reached refuge in the attic did I allow a squeal to escape. I would see the festival after all, hear the sounds of merrymaking for my own, and smell the sweet and salty air of candied apples and roast meats.

In haste, I chose a beige walking gown and ran a brush through my tangled hair. And because I am a curious creature, I couldn't help but peek into the drawer where I'd hidden the previous night's ball gown, to admire it once more.

But I found nothing inside, save my ivory shift.

My heart seized with surprise. Had someone stolen it? No, for I had given this same shift to Feremin to complete his illusory task. It appeared the illusion did not last beyond its allotted purpose ... and as disappointed as I felt at the disappearance of my beautiful gown, I admitted a relief that I no longer needed to concern myself with its accidental discovery.

My heart grew light as I descended the steps to the front door, but I paused on the landing. *Edward should be with me.* He should enjoy the colors and glee of the festival, not spend his days abed with Celia for sorry comfort.

I thought I might bring him all the same, but relented at the notion that others might fall ill at his exposure. Perhaps returning with a special treat for him would be enough.

It wouldn't be enough for *me*, but might lift his spirits. And if I remained calm and happy in his presence, perhaps it would give him a bit of added strength.

With that, I left my home, the first time in almost two fortnights I'd done so with a modicum of permission. I had a chore to carry out, certainly, but that wouldn't stop my eyes and ears from taking in the revelry in my own small way. Thankfully, I didn't have to crawl under our front gate this time, but I did walk rather than ride in the carriage, following the road into town.

The closer I drew, the louder grew the sounds of festive

celebration, and I couldn't help but be taken by a true and genuine happiness.

And as I couldn't wait a moment longer, I picked up my heels and ran the remaining distance into town, eyes on the mountain-high wooden pole in the center of the town square. Scores of colored ribbons twirled around the pole, and as I came closer to the center of town, I saw that a large handful of young men and women held onto the ribbons and turned them around the pole in time to music.

Yes, music! The town square held many musicians, and though they played from all corners of the square, their music rose as one and joined together like some courtly symphony. In truth, I preferred their lively jigs to the dull and haunting strains of the violin played by the palace musicians.

This music brought a spring to my step, and I danced rather than walked across the square to the milliner's shop. Her door stood wide, with many festival-inspired hats on display: this one decorated with fresh flowers, and that one with lace and ribbon and presumably freely-given feathers. I stepped inside and took a moment to look about as the milliner tended to another customer.

"Ella? Ellison? Is that you? Mercy, it *is* you!"

My attentions tore away from a hat covered in buttons and bows to find Liesl and the milliner staring at me as though I were a ghost. I nearly asked Liesl how she enjoyed the ball last night, but caught myself in an instant.

That had been a different Ella.

"Good afternoon," I replied, my voice softer and far more timid than I'd thought I felt.

"Ellison, it's been ages since … " Liesl's eyes grew sad and pitying.

I returned the look with a smile, for I had long since moved beyond feeling sorry for myself for a lack of friends.

"It has, and I must say, you look particularly charming, dear friend." I hoped she would not chide me for calling her friend after weeks of inexplicable absence.

But I needn't have worried, for she exclaimed with delight and rushed forward to draw me into her arms.

"Oh, it's so good to see you! I tried to pay a visit last week but was turned away. A rather rude woman told me you didn't live there anymore, can you imagine that? How is your father? And Edward? And I've heard you've a new mother, what is she like? Oh!" She pressed a silk-gloved hand to her lips. "Was *she* your stepmother?"

It felt as though we hadn't lost even a moment of time together, but still I didn't want to answer her questions. I didn't know how.

So, I asked after her instead. "Things are different now, to be sure, but look at you! How lovely you look for the festival! Surely the line-up of suitors hasn't slowed one inkling."

She blushed, and I felt relief that she'd accepted the shift in conversation.

"Not quite, dear friend. Not quite. My parents have taken the bait and are currently being rather particular about finding a match that isn't after the family business, but I can't say I mind." She pulled a plump fig from a silk purse around her wrist, and held it to her lips. "I rather enjoy spinsterhood."

She took a bite of the fig and held it to me, but I declined. "You're far from being a spinster, Liesl. But tell me, did you attend last night's ball at the palace? I heard it was … eventful."

Her eyes grew wide and she chewed furiously that she might swallow and answer. "Oh, it was splendid! Would that you were there, but won't you come tonight? There's the most gorgeous princess I met who has gained the Prince's attentions, and another woman had an attack of the vapors right in His Highness's arms! Can you believe it? And the food, Ellison, oh, the food—"

Behind us, the milliner had placed a box on the counter and

gestured to it. When Liesl had finished her exposition on the palace's comestibles, the milliner cleared her throat and we gave her our attentions.

"Order for Victoria?" She lifted the lid off the box and I peered inside. To describe the hat as a monstrosity would do monsters an injustice, for upon the hat sat a severed rabbit's head, with its paws resting amidst the surrounding decoration of pale blue bows and feathers.

"It's hideous," I said, unable to hide my disgust.

"I know," said the milliner. "And what's worse, she asked for fresh rabbit, but I couldn't do it. This one's a stuffed piece from a local shop." She winked at me and replaced the lid. "I can trust you not to say a word, I assume."

What a refreshing change of pace to resume our friendly rapport from earlier days, when I'd come with Mother to place our own orders.

"Certainly," I said, "though truth be told, I can't promise you can trust me to deliver it in one piece."

I shuddered dramatically, and Liesl clapped her hands in delight, fig long finished.

"I know," she said, "you'll come to dinner tonight. Before the ball. Bring your father and we can catch up—wherever have you been? I was worried about you, but none could say they'd seen you about in ages."

How I wished I could. But not tonight. Celia would never allow it, and I could not leave Edward so long.

"I'm so sorry, but I can't."

Liesl's face fell, and I swear she looked sorrier than a fawn that's lost its footing. "Oh. All right, then."

"Oh, Liesl. It's not like that." I pulled her into another embrace to prove my sincerity. "Edward is unwell, and my stepmother is hesitant to care for a child not her own."

A partial truth, at least. "Once he's well, I'll visit. I promise."

And I meant it.

Her smile returned and she kissed my cheeks, radiating happiness. "All right. But I *will* hold you to it. Give my love to Edward."

She stepped from the shop, but turned back once. "I'm glad to know you're all right, Ellison. Mere weeks are not enough to mar a friendship beyond repair, so you needn't worry. I'll be glad to see you when you're able."

I hoped so.

The strains of music wafted into the shop, calling me outside. I thanked the milliner, took the hatbox, and returned to the town square. Although I didn't doubt Celia expected my quick return, this small nudge of freedom sent a surge of willful disobedience through my soul, and I circuited the town square instead.

Stalls selling candies and cakes were crowded by young and old alike, and tall men stood in corners feasting on enormous legs of turkey and barrel-sized mugs of ale.

As I had a few coins to my name still, I found a toy-seller's stall and chose a carved wooden bird for Edward. It looked so true to life that I might not have been surprised had it begun singing.

On a whim, I also purchased a small pumpkin, for I recalled Edward's love of roast pumpkin during festive occasions.

Satisfied with these things and eager to present them, I made my way back through the crush of the crowd, toward the road home. Without warning, a horse appeared from nowhere and reared up in front of me, hooves only a hair's breadth from my face.

I tumbled backward, dropping my purchases and hatbox in the dust. The pumpkin cracked as it hit the ground, and I cried out in dismay for its loss, more than for the pain of falling.

The horse missed descending on my leg by a bare finger width, and the rider leapt from its back, rushing to my side.

"Are you all right?" He took my hand and touched my shoulder to help me sit up. "I'm so sorry, I don't know what ... "

His voice trailed off as I looked up and into his eyes.

"William?"

"You!" His concern turned to a mischievous grin. "Hello again, Ella." He stressed my name as though to gloat at obtaining my revelation.

I pulled my hand from his and pursed my lips. "I'm fine, but my stepsister's hatbox isn't." I pointed at it on the ground several paces away, dented from where it had struck. He retrieved it and returned it to me, mercifully refraining from peering inside. He also found the toy bird, which had rolled away across the square.

"Sorry about the pumpkin," he said, handing the bird to me. "Please, let me buy you another one."

That was the *least* he could do.

I noticed the growing crowd around us, as it wasn't every day the citizens saw their Prince in the midst of town, let alone helping some poor girl to her feet.

"Your Highness," said one of his attendants, also horsed, "we should move to the center of town." Peter, or Lorenz, I thought—I recognized his face from our previous encounter.

William only grinned. "Do you believe me now?"

Whatever was he on about?

"I'm the Prince," he continued, "I told you the truth."

He helped me to my feet and I sniffed, for my nose had filled with dust. I'm certain that was an especially becoming image.

"If you say so," I teased. "Unless, of course, you're only a page from the palace pretending at being the Prince. Or maybe you met him on the road and stole his coat."

William gaped at me. "And my attendants?"

I peered around him as if considering. "Horse thieves. *Now* I understand why you were skulking about in the dark the other night!"

"Horse thieves!" He threw his hands in the air and laughed, and I laughed with him, to the bewilderment of the gathered crowd. "You're quite ridiculous."

"I know," I said with a wink. Oh, how bold he made me!

"Wait right here," he said, and disappeared into the square. His attendants shouted after him but remained in place, perhaps uncertain whether the order had been for them or me.

Moments later, William returned hauling a child's wagon that contained the largest pumpkin I have ever seen in my lifetime. "Will this do?"

He winked back, and it was my turn to gape. For once, I was at a loss for words.

"I'll send someone to retrieve the wagon," he said, tapping its handle. "And I'll tell them to use the front door this time."

But as we had played one for one thus far, I thought to end it on a note in my favour. For though my heart was glad for his company and delighted at his attentions, I held no illusions as to the meaning of this festival.

He should not concern himself with me. That had been made quite clear last night.

I placed the toy bird in my pocket—bent my knees—reached into the cart, and hoisted the pumpkin into my arms. I'd thought only to lift it for show, but once I held it, I was shocked at its comfortable weight and the strength in my limbs.

It seemed I had gained something of use from Celia's tasking after all, however unintentional.

William exclaimed in surprise, and bent to catch its fall from my arms.

But of course, it did not budge.

"If you could be so kind as to place the hatbox atop this pumpkin," I said, feigning a demure composure, "I'll be on my way."

"But you can't possibly—"

"Are you saying I'm weak?"

"I—" He stopped, and his grin returned. "Let's not start that again."

He placed the hatbox gently on the pumpkin, and his eyes twinkled with mirth. "Are you sure you won't stay? Or allow me to help? Now that you're, ah, properly attired? It seems I could use your assistance in some of the festival's feats of strength."

I felt immensely grateful for his tact amid the gathered crowd, though I rolled my eyes for his final comment. "Thank you, but I can't." I bent my knees as I could not curtsy with a pumpkin in my arms. "Another time, perhaps?"

He stared at me, unresponsive, for several moments. I shivered under his gaze.

An attendant cleared his throat and William roused.

"Another time, then," he said, all playfulness gone.

I turned without another thought to begin my journey home.

"Wait," he said, when I'd gone but three paces.

I stopped.

"Will you attend tonight's ball?"

Oh, how I wanted to tell him the truth. To lose all pretense and hear my name from his lips, seeing me, the *true* Ella. But no.

I could not. For the sake of Edward's life, I could not.

And so, with a heaviness in my heart—and in my arms, truth be told—I offered the briefest of smiles and didn't respond.

At the very least, I would not lie.

So I said nothing, and simply went home.

25

The Dressing

I hid the pumpkin in the stables, with plans to bring Edward out to see it as soon as he'd gained enough strength. After delivering the hatbox to Celia, she directed me to help Charlotte immediately. To my good fortune, she didn't remark on the lateness of my return, and I presumed she'd been too occupied by her own doings to notice my absence.

As I laced up Charlotte in her dressing room, I found myself feeling bolder and less cautious than usual.

"How did you enjoy the ball last night? Did you see the Prince?" In truth, I wanted to hear her speak of *me*.

But thinking I hadn't heard the full story of Victoria's collapse, Charlotte sniffed and spun her own tale.

"It was glorious, couldn't you tell? Victoria exhausted herself so completely that she needed a royal escort home. They gave us all one, of course, because Prince William found us both so enchanting he couldn't bear to see us leave in a common carriage. What a pity you weren't able to attend. Though you must admit the punishment fit the crime, *sister.*"

Indeed it did, but not in the manner she thought. "So you danced with him, then?"

"Oh no, not last night. I plan to save my appearance at his side for tonight—let him taste the wine of cheap, desperate women first. Tonight he'll have rich cream, and never look back."

I pulled her strings with a little more force than perhaps necessary. "Then what of Victoria?"

"Strategic," she grunted, "and just what we needed to take his mind off that brainless tart he—"

I pulled again, harder this time. "Sorry, almost there. How handsome you'll look with a waist like this. You were saying?"

"Good. I mean to make him forget she ever existed. I hope she stays abed tonight."

Once more, I couldn't resist. "You mean Victoria? Of course she will, after such ... exhaustion."

"No, you bloody fool. Mother won't let *her* stay home. I mean that foreign princess that the Prince kept mooning over after he—" She stopped and spun to face me. My heart leapt three feet in the air, I swear it. "But why should I tell *you?* It's not as if you'll be there. It's none of your concern."

That, I hadn't decided. "Well, I don't know."

"You have another gown?"

I saw the glint in her eyes and refused to play her game. "Of course not."

"You'll stay and play nursemaid to that snivelling brat, I suppose."

I stiffened. "Edward is unwell, yes."

"Better get used to it. A nursemaid is all you'll be good for, at this rate." She pulled a gold necklace from a trunk on the floor and held it up to her neck.

I gasped. The necklace belonged *to my mother.*

There could be no mistaking. I remembered those delicate gold leaves and filigree as well as the day we'd found it in the shop of Liesl's father, when Father and I had chosen it for Mother as a gift during my thirteenth Advent.

Charlotte looked over her shoulder and cleared her throat, as if I should clasp it around her neck.

"That does *not* belong to you," I said instead.

She narrowed her eyes. "Of course it does. What would a cinder-wench know of it?"

She asked, so I answered. "I know it belonged to my mother. Did you really think I wouldn't notice?"

Charlotte shrugged as if it were the least important thing in the world. "It's not as if she's using it."

Rage bubbled up from deep within my chest. "Take it off."

Charlotte laughed. At me. "You want it back?"

I blinked in surprise. Could she truly have had a change of heart that quickly? "Yes, of course."

She held the necklace away from her body, dangling it above my outstretched palm. Hope rose to quell the rage, and in that one moment, I wondered if we might learn to live in harmony with each other after all.

Until she dropped it to the floor, lifted a shod foot, and stomped on it with all her strength.

The thin gold leaves crunched underfoot. Charlotte's smug grin didn't leave her face as she lifted her boot to reveal my mother's necklace, bent and in pieces, on the dressing room floor.

"There it is, if you want it so badly." She took a wide step to bring us face to face, and I held my breath that I might not spit forth the fires that boiled in my belly. "Only remember, *sister,* that small bones are just as easily broken."

My breath rushed out, unbidden. Unlike her sister, Charlotte had no need of subtleties. She would not hurt Edward. Would she? The coldness with which she'd crushed the necklace suggested she might.

"You'd do well to remember that." Charlotte swept out of the room, leaving me with a broken necklace and a savaged heart. The rage returned, slow at first, but I stoked the flames and let them burn, hot and thick.

And so, I did not care when Celia piled chores on me for the evening's duties. I did not care that Charlotte continued to spare no opportunity to humiliate my family's memory. What I did care about what this: Charlotte's insistence on proffering vague threats to our well-being, and the inexplicable realization that Victoria fully intended to attend tonight's ball. Indeed, she would do so despite what—by all accounts—had appeared to be a near-fatal incident the evening prior.

This, I knew, simply did not make sense. It should not have been possible. She should have been abed for days before rising—weeks, perhaps, though I am not a doctor—let alone before attending a royal ball.

Nothing about what had occurred made sense, but answers alone would not bring protection. For that, I had another plan in mind.

Thus, I waited and waited and waited.

Finally, the time came.

And so I retrieved *The Book of Conjuring* once more.

26

The Second Ball

They left. I did not hesitate.

I set up the parlour as if by rote, though the ease with which I fell into the routine stirred a concern. I buried it.

The spirits did their work, and I would do mine.

I had no doubt of my power, though if anyone had asked, I couldn't have explained why I continued to tempt my eternal fate. I was as though driven by some force—something unseen—to use the ability, now that I had it.

I don't excuse what I did. I only wish to explain why I continued to seek retribution despite my misgivings.

What is more, I longed for something deeper. Harsher. More severe, for a part of me believed that no matter what, I still held control over the spirits and what they did. And that same part of me wanted to see Charlotte suffer.

And so it was with this in mind that I turned further pages in *The Book*, knowing full well what I sought.

"To inflict harm," I read, "make an image of wax on the day

and in the hour of intent, in the name of the one to be harmed. Thus, you should use wax of candles burned at a funeral, and on the likeness, fashion hands in the place of feet, and feet in the place of hands."

And so I did. With candles from my room that I had saved from Mother's funeral, I molded a crude figure of my stepsister. With my fingernail, I inscribed Charlotte's name on the wax doll's forehead, and on its chest and shoulder, carved the book's images of circles, planets, and five-sided stars.

Then I called my spirits. With the bridle still, I had no need of the first spirit. To the second, I had only to repeat my request. And to the third, I gave the wax doll, which he consecrated with spit smeared over the doll's eyes.

"What would you have me do?" Oliroomim spoke with an unsettling eagerness.

From my hair, I drew a pin. With a hollowness in the pit of my belly, I pierced the spine of the doll.

The spirit frowned as if disappointed. "That will not kill her. You must place it through the head and down to the spine, touching the heart. Do it again."

And as much as I knew the evil of my actions, I couldn't go so far as to take a life. I simply wanted to exchange hurt for hurt.

"I don't want her dead. Harmed, yes. But not dead. I won't be responsible for her demise. I'm not a monster."

The spirit giggled. "Afraid of the flames, mistress? They already lap at your heels."

"Enough." I couldn't bear to hear it. "Will you do this?"

He nodded. "As you wish. Is this your only request?"

No—I had need to know one more thing. "Tell me, spirit, did you once live?"

Oliroomim's eager smile wavered, then vanished. "It's too late to save me, mistress. Thinking on it will accomplish nothing."

"So you did live, once." I shuddered to think of it. "How is it you ended up here, called by a few simple words—"

"Simple?" The spirit's childish voice deepened to a roar, his razor sharp teeth descending to flash in the moonlight. I stumbled backward as he lunged for me, jaws snapping, tethered only by the cord of the circle which prevented me from harm. "You play with powers you don't understand, mistress. It is *you* who does not allow my relief. It is *you* who calls the dead forth from their resting place."

His voice lowered to a hiss like a thousand snakes. "It is *you* who keeps *us* shut out of the gates of heaven."

And with that, he vanished.

I fell to my knees and wept.

I met Liesl on the palace steps once again, though she didn't appear as eager to see me as the evening prior—and in truth, I felt a strangeness at seeing her twice in one day, as two different people. Tonight, she wore a gown similar to her first, only in a flattering shade of pea green.

She gasped at the sight of my own, pure silver gown—silk, lace, and crepe—with sparking emerald gemstones adorning the bodice and cascading down the skirt in thin, swirling patterns that created the illusion of climbing vines.

They shimmered with every step I took, and yet I didn't feel quite so uncomfortable as the night before. Though perhaps that may have been due to my attentions being focused elsewhere, particularly on what the evening's events might bring.

Liesl elected to enter the hall with her brother this night, though she wished me luck with a great embrace and a tender kiss on both cheeks. I asked that she be announced before me, so that she might be given the chance to reach the bottom step and complete her entrance before they announced my name.

And then came my turn.

As soon as my false name resounded in the ballroom, the room quieted—and though I tried not to become overwhelmed by it all, the hall appeared even more grand than the previous night. More food, more wine, and to my bewilderment—despite last night's surprise ending—more guests.

I descended. Before I reached the bottom step, he was there. Waiting.

Wearing silver and emerald.

I both cursed and thanked the spirits, for doubtless I would be accused of conspiring for the Prince's favour.

In a way, I suppose I had. But I did not care.

"Lady Aleidis." William's words flew out in a breath, and I shivered at the strangeness of my mother's name on his tongue. For a moment, I thought to reveal myself, but I resisted. In due time, I would.

"Your Highness, a pleasure to see you again." I took his hand as he offered it.

"Would you honor me with another dance?" He drew my hand once again to his lips, and a flurry of delight rose to cover all the evening's other emotions. "Since we were, after all, cut short last night. I suspect you have more to say concerning my public comportment?"

"Why, Prince William, you're far too kind," I said, matching the amusement in his gaze. Mild annoyance at his disarming sense of composure and something else—something deeper and not altogether unpleasant—took hold, and I followed his lead to the dance floor.

As the music rose, I felt comfortable enough to speak without being overheard. "Surely you must have other ladies who want for your time. Why spend another moment with me?"

Puzzlement, mirth, and sadness flitted across his face. "You truly don't know?"

I shook my head. "Unless like draws to like, I don't see why."

He did laugh then, hearty and true. "I might accuse you of having spies in the palace."

"And I might say the same of your folk amidst mine."

"*Touché*, Lady Aleidis, as the French say."

"Please," I said, drawing a deep breath, "just Aleidis is fine."

His grip tightened and my head spun. "Of course. Aleidis."

We continued the dance in silence, until I could bear it no longer. "The woman who became ill last night—is she all right?"

Concern drew his features into a frown. "I believe so, though no one can explain what happened. I have heard of that particular affliction only once before, but … "

My throat tightened and the fear must have shown on my face, for his voice trailed to silence and he reassured me with a smile and gentle touch on the small of my back.

"It's not important. My father knows something of it and its cause, is all. Don't trouble yourself with it."

How could I not? "Your father is a physician, too?"

"No, of course not, he—" William caught himself and started again. "Aleidis, why do you insist on making this so difficult?"

"*This?* You mean conversation?"

He shrugged and grew quiet. "That too."

A less prudent part of me wanted to bait him further. "Have you had opportunity to enjoy the rest of the festivities, Your Highness?"

"I went into town today," he said, without hesitation. "The main square was crowded like you would not believe."

"I might." I glanced around us as a shiver crept up my spine—but this time, it was not for seeing Celia, or Charlotte, or Victoria. "Did you meet anyone interesting? Though I don't suppose you had much time to interact with the common folk, being who you are."

He sighed and dropped my hands, only to grab them again upon realizing that it would be quite irregular to cease dancing in the midst of the song; we would likely be trampled under whirling pairs of feet.

"Why are you doing this? Do you really think I'm such a terrible prince that I have no thoughts or feelings of my own? I'm no pawn, Lady Aleidis, and I'll thank you not to view me as such."

A lump of guilt formed in my throat, and the air grew warm. Why did he make me behave so? "I apologize, Prince William. I'm sure you're a very kind person who looks out for those in need."

"Now you're being patronizing."

"No, I speak honestly!" Several heads turned our way, and I lowered the volume of my speech. "It's only that ... perhaps you'll understand better if I explain."

"Please do." A smile played at the corner of his lips, and I drew confidence in the fact that he still held me close.

"I have a ... friend, at home. This girl is somewhat impulsive, and she cannot check her tongue, no matter how hard she tries. Even in the worst of moments."

"I understand how you might get along." The sparkle in William's eyes returned, brighter than the chandeliers above us. "A *friend*, you say? Do go on."

I did. "She recently, if somewhat unexpectedly, made acquaintance with a young man, whom she initially dismissed in much the same way, ah—"

"As you've dismissed me? I think I understand. Please continue."

My cheeks burned. "If that is the way you choose to interpret our interactions, so be it. But she—my friend—may have developed a certain fondness for this young man, as they have found themselves in similar circumstances on a number of unexpected occasions."

William frowned, and I am certain he suspected the truth of my tale, but I wanted—no, needed—to hear from his lips that which would never be.

It was a futile endeavour of a foolish, heart-stricken, young woman. "And, she suspected he held a fondness too, despite their difference in station."

He chose his words carefully, regarding me with a curiosity that kept my cheeks aflame. "That's a blessing for both parties, isn't it? Few matches are built out of romantic attachment these days, and more out of prudence."

"I haven't finished, Your Highness. Unexpectedly, and without warning, this young man chose to take a wife—at his family's urging, or so my friend understood. And what is worse, he did not choose *her*. In fact, she didn't even come under consideration, and while she thought at first it mattered not at all—that perhaps her hope had risen on false foundations ... "

William tilted my chin upward, so that our gazes locked as firmly as a horse hitched to a wagon. "I am not the sort of man to give a lady false hope, only to crush it underfoot. I swear it."

I shook my head. "But isn't that exactly what you're doing here? Look around, Your Highness. All of these ladies attend a ball at your home, for one reason alone: that they might be chosen to be your wife." With few exceptions—I thought of Liesl, content to see the wonders of the palace and snack on rich pastries. "I simply do my part to guard myself against disappointment and heartbreak."

He grew pensive as the music drifted into softer strains, drawing this particular dance to a close. William escorted me off the dance floor, and I was surprised to notice the pounding of my heart, thudding in my ears like a beaten drum. We stopped only several paces away from a table of giant-like proportions, loaded with sticky sweets and goblets of rich, dark wine.

"I do not intend to lead you on, Lady Aleidis. I can't deny your beauty and the richness of your gown, but please understand—there's something different about you. Something familiar."

I swallowed the cry that ached to burst forth, and allowed him to speak his part.

"I don't know why I feel comfortable telling you these things, but … most of the other women here, they barely speak a word to me and when they do, it's only to raise a compliment about the festival, or to praise the King's social policies. I swear, half of these women have been coached to say things they don't mean, and the other half seem to think that I'm here for a pretty face and a well-formed pair of—"

I cleared my throat, lest he become *too* familiar in public. "Your Highness?"

"Oh." He appeared stricken for a moment. "Oh!"

And as though we sat again in the dim light of the tavern, or in the graveyard against my mother's stone, or in the town square with a pumpkin at my hip, we laughed together. Well and truly, and loud enough to disturb the guests who lingered nearby. I caught several glares from other women I both did and did not recognize, but also furtive smiles from those who, perhaps like Liesl, felt relief at seeing Prince William spend his precious few moments with anyone but themselves.

Perhaps it was a good thing we'd come to such a point, for it meant one of the royal advisors could seek us out in the crowd and draw William away to his other duties for the evening.

"Your Highness," said a broad-shouldered man with the royal

insignia on his coat, "there are a number of visitors here this evening to whom the King would have you introduced."

To me, William rolled his eyes, before turning his attentions to the man who'd approached. "I'll be right with you, Fritz." To me, "You'll manage without me for the rest of the evening, I suppose?"

I could not help but smile. "Indeed, I will."

"You may not be rid of me yet." With a subtle wink, he slipped into the crowd of guests, following his father's advisor.

I played our conversation over in my head to reassure myself that I was not quite so much of a fool as I suspected. That my fondness for William grew unbidden, there was no question, but I also knew it would be all the worse if—when—he chose another. Whatever had led me to tell him such a story of my "friend?"

Despite any affected pretence, I pretended to be someone I was not. Would he feel the same way as I, if I lifted the veil? Above all things, in regard to his attentions, I felt thoroughly and utterly confused.

I may be a young woman in body, but within my heart rests the flighty uncertainty of a little girl. How is it I could be strong in so many things, but one glance—one touch—from a boy could reduce me to scattered fragments?

Lost in my deliberations, I barely noticed Liesl come alongside me with a tiny, glossy pastry between her fingertips—and several chocolates clutched in her other hand. For her sake, I hoped they didn't melt and give her away.

I didn't wish to end the evening on an awkward note with my friend—even if she thought me someone else—so I closed the small gap between us and gently touched her elbow. "Liesl?"

Liesl regarded me with alarm before her eyes softened, and I wondered—who had she seen? "Sorry, for a moment I thought you were ... " She laughed, realizing her parallel error.

"We're even, then." I pointed to a tray of ruby red cherries in honey glaze. "As delicious as I'm sure those are, they look like a dress stain waiting to happen."

"Oh, they are." She spoke with an air of authority, as if the pronouncement came from experience. "But they're just about worth it. Have you tried any of the oranges? I thought I might faint for the wonder of it."

I had tasted oranges before, once. Father had brought one home as a gift from one of his journeys, and refused to disclose to Mother just what price he'd paid for the rare delicacy. I'd never told Liesl, simply because I knew how deeply she'd wanted to try one. And I would not burst her enthusiasm on this day, either.

"It sounds glorious," I said. "I must admit, I hold some envy for your lack of concern."

"Oh, but Aleidis, you have the Prince's attentions. That is something everyone here envies *you* for."

If only she knew. "In a way, yes. But I'm afraid not much will come of it."

"Because of how far you've come? I wouldn't want to live that far from my family, either. I don't care if it's the 'lot of a woman,' I'm not leaving this city if I can help it."

Oh, my dear, dear friend. How I have missed you. I would have loved to spend the remaining hours in my friend's company, but as I reached across the table for a sugared biscuit, movement of a familiar sort moved across the edge of my vision.

Celia. Chatting with one of William's attendants. Lorenz? No, Cromer.

Not again.

Liesl's voice grew distant as I strained to catch the refrain of Celia's melodic speech. Could I interrupt? Save William's attendant from becoming an unwitting pawn in her schemes? But even as I questioned whether such a thing would be possible, she loosed a girlish giggle—something more befitting one of her daughters, I thought—and reached forth to place her hand over his.

Cromer stiffened and I bit my tongue to stop from crying out.

Hesitation begat failure. I could only watch, helplessly, as Celia led this man through the crowd, smug satisfaction clear and bright across her face.

Charlotte and Victoria followed behind.

Victoria, alive and well, her visage appearing as bright and full of life as it had ever been, new hat perched delicately upon her head.

She should not be here.

It did not make sense.

And when the crowd moved to hide their progress from me, I did the only thing I could do. I followed them.

I realize now, poor Liesl must have wondered at my rudeness, for I left her mid-conversation—but what else could I have done?

Seconds felt like hours as I searched the room for their presence, finally spying their target: William. Of course.

If I pushed through the crowd, I would be too late to see or hear their meeting. If I circuited the room along the outskirts, I might make it—so I did the latter, stepping as quickly as my uncomfortable, heeled shoes would allow, all the while praying to reach William before Celia and the herd of bodies under her control.

They returned to my view just as Celia placed Charlotte's arm across Cromer's, as if to have her introduced directly. Victoria followed with a morose expression, appearing less enamored of the situation with each step. And Celia?

She, no doubt considering herself the cleverest of all, circled the place where William stood in deep discussion with men who were easily recognizable as foreign visitors and royal advisors. How curious. Should he not have been dancing with eligible women instead of conducting palace business?

I drew closer, hoping to gain some sense of understanding of Celia's intentions—and understand I did, as she and Charlotte approached from opposite sides. Celia intended to subdue William with the same touch she'd used on Cromer, and Baron von Veltheim before that, and my father before that.

The woman had some sort of magic, that much was clear, and I would learn the truth of it for the sake of my family—but now? What and how did not matter.

It only mattered that she did not succeed.

I pushed through the crowd, excusing myself as best I could. I am sure I stepped on at least several toes.

I watched as she lifted a hand, reached forth toward William's clasped hands at the small of his back—heard Charlotte being introduced as Cromer interrupted the small gathering—

And at that moment, I 'stumbled' on the hem of my dress and pitched forward to plant an elbow in Celia's back. She, too, lost her footing in the assault, and whirled to see from where the attack came … but I had already drawn away, and stood behind another guest.

While this did not foil her grander plans—for William's hands were now occupied with greeting Charlotte—at the very least, I had bought a little more time to consider how I might stop her from using that seductive touch on the man I cared for.

But there was still Charlotte.

The spirits had yet to carry forth my commands, but surely it was only a matter of time. Besides, it was too late to change what I'd set in motion, and so I closed my eyes where I stood, and waited.

I did not have to wait long.

A wail pierced through the gentle melody of violins, soft at first, growing in strength, and rising to a feverish pitch until the rumble of the crowd became overwhelmed by her—yes, Charlotte's wails—and I heard the music no longer. I pushed back through the crowd until I had her within my sight, and oh, what a sight it was.

I couldn't look away. She appeared as an image from an awful dream, one that seems to last for a lifetime and from which you can never wake.

Her mouth gaped like a chasm, eyes grown wide and round and unfocused ... no, they were focused, but on what?

I looked to the crowd and to William, who stood still as marble, composure broken by the second girl to have lost herself in his presence, and most unfortunately for him, not in the way one might hope for a future wife.

The thunder and clank of the palace guards in their heavy garb rose from the far corner of the room, but even then, Charlotte's wail shifted as if playing a measure of music, becoming an unearthly scream that resonated throughout the hall.

She lifted one finger. At William? At the balcony? No, she pointed at the ceiling, but when I looked, I saw nothing. My eyes roamed back downward with the crowd's attentions.

Charlotte lay in a heap upon the floor, but none so calm and still as Victoria had the night before. Where she lay, my stepsister writhed and twisted, clutching hands to her head, eyes opening and closing amid her screams. I made out one small phrase within the noise, and felt a pinch of alarm at the words: "*Save me.*"

I rushed forward, pushing aside those who surged ahead to see clearer the suffering of another. Oh, how I wanted to run once again, but more so—even more so—I felt sorrow for William, who'd had his second ball disturbed by my doings.

Charlotte screamed once more as I fell to my knees aside her thrashing form.

"Char—" I stopped, for I'd nearly given myself away. "Miss? Miss, can you hear me? What is it?"

In an instant, she ceased moving. My heart skipped a beat. But rather than acknowledge my words, she lifted her face to the elegantly high ceiling of the ballroom, and raised one arm with finger cast to follow. I looked up and again saw nothing, but a cold breeze brushed against my cheek, even though I saw no windows or doors open to the night air.

Next to me, in the softest whisper that only she and I might hear, Charlotte spoke one word.

"Demons."

The breeze became a blast of wind, rushing past my ears like waves on water, and Charlotte screamed once more as a rush of air that smelled of rust and the musk of deepest night blasted across her body and into—merciful heaven, *into?*—her throat. A sharp crack resounded from somewhere on her person as her back arched off the floor, higher and higher as though drawn by some otherworldly master of puppets.

But demons? I imagine those who watched believed she'd gone mad, and I admit, at first I doubted whether this could even be my doing at all. I had no dealings with demons. To my knowledge, anyhow. Believe me, if that had been my intention, I would have found another way from the start. The words of Oliroomim, the child-spirit, echoed through my skull ... the flames, already lapping at my heels? No. I wouldn't accept it.

And then William was shouting, looking to his father the King upon the balcony. I only saw him vanish into the crowd, for as the palace guards reached the place where Charlotte and I remained on the floor, she screamed once more, her back bending and twisting and cracking no doubt every rib in the corset of her gown. I hoped that was all that cracked.

Of course, that's a lie. One small part loosed a private smile, to see her broken and crushed as my mother's necklace. To see her in pain by my hand, rather than being at the mercy of her will and her indifference to my life and the life of my brother.

"Mother … " she squeaked.

I regarded Charlotte with curiosity.

"Mother," she said, louder and with an urgency in her voice.

Where *was* Celia? She'd orchestrated the introduction of Charlotte and William, so surely she and Victoria should be gloating somewhere nearby. Where could she have gone that she wouldn't know of this, or—

"Mother, they pull me back!" Her cry sounded of panic and fear and deepest hate. "Don't let them take me, you promised!"

"Who?" I shouted, forgetting myself. "Who is trying to take you, and where? No one has laid a hand on you."

Wild-eyed, she reached forth and grasped my arm, her fingernails driving into my palm with the force of a hammer against an iron spike.

"All the demons of hell, come to drag me back," she wailed between screams, and I leapt to my feet as in an instant her eyes rolled back to reveal blank, white slates. Her lips pulled away from her teeth to loose one final cry, a primal scream that forced me to rip away from her grasp and cover my ears.

She arched like a wild beast, limbs limp and flailing, hair and garments driven by wind that we couldn't see or hear or smell and now could barely feel, but for a coolness and a gentle breeze like a summer's eve.

And with that, she dropped fully upon the floor as a ragdoll tossed away by a child. A prickle along the back of my neck caused breath to catch in my throat. I didn't dare move to look to understand why, and so I pledged to remain by her side until the palace guards came forward to finally take Charlotte from the ballroom. Her face looked pale as death, and I feared the worst.

Had I not *demanded* she live? Had I not forbade the taking of a life?

I looked but did not see her chest rise or fall in those moments before she vanished from view, hauled to her feet and lifted into the arms of two strong men.

And then—only then—did I allow myself to engage the dread that formed the moment the hairs had raised along the back of my neck.

With a deep breath and growing unease, I turned and scanned the crowd around me, which now moved away from the finished spectacle. Seeing nothing, I looked higher.

And there, on the second floor balcony, overlooking the very place where both her daughters had fallen, stood Celia.

27

The Learning

I flew to Edward's room, first.

"How does he fare?" Breathless, I took in the scene: Gretel, hands to my brother's cheeks, and Edward, whose pale face should have been so full of life, joy, and not of the pain that contorted it now.

I stumbled against the door frame, bracing myself with a still-gloved palm. Gretel took me in with wide eyes and no doubt more than enough confusion for the both of us.

"Miss Ellison?" She looked from Edward to me and back again. "No matter, that. I'm of the mind to not want to know. I cleaned the room once again, but I can't—"

I didn't care about the rug, or my dress, or whatever else.

"Can you do anything for him?" The words came out soft and stuttering, nothing like the self who'd left hours before.

Gretel snorted. "Course I can. The doc's been here, the moment that blasted woman and yourself left the house." I started to protest, but she hadn't finished. "I didn't want you t'stick around worrying."

I understood, though still I wished I had stayed behind. But then, how could I protect my family from behind closed doors?

I had a thought to ask Gretel. "Cook, have you noticed anything … strange about Celia?"

She coughed to stifle a laugh. "Where t'begin?"

"No," I said, moving to sit on the bed and stroke my brother's cheek. "Beyond her cruelties and her daughters. Something … more?"

Gretel squinted as though I'd lost a marble in a bowl of cream. "What d'you mean?"

I heaved a sigh and wished for Father's return. "At the ball tonight, Charlotte … well, she had a fit. A horrible, embarrassing fit, right in front of the Prince. Honestly, I thought her full gone, though now I'm not so sure."

Gretel gazed at me with an intensity like as I'd never seen before. "Go on, child."

I tossed a sharp glance, for her tone held none of the questioning or curiosity I'd expected. Instead, she sounded rather … sad.

"Through it all," I said, "I wondered where Celia might have gone, why she hadn't come to see to her daughter. After all, one might expect her to remain diligent after Victoria's episode last night. But when I looked around to find her, Cook, she stood nowhere near her suffering daughter, but rather on the balcony overlooking the crowd. And I cannot believe what my eyes saw, but it was as if, well, as if she didn't care."

Gretel remained silent.

"Her daughter, in the throes of death, and she did nothing."

With a sigh, Cook cupped my chin with warm fingers. "Was the crowd too thick? She couldn't see otherwise?"

"No," I said, urgency welling up from some unknown place. "No, that can't be true. I've never seen someone so—"

A door downstairs slammed with such force that the whole house echoed. Muted voices carried from below, and I realized with horror that I sat on Edward's bed in my spirit-woven garments. For the ball, the spirits had assured my lack of recognition, but at home, I felt certain the illusion would be ended the moment the three laid eyes on me. And as curious as I was regarding Charlotte's well-being, I couldn't risk discovery. Not yet.

"Go, quickly," Gretel said, leaping to shut Edward's door—but leaving it open a crack for my exit. "Before you're found. Go, and I'll stall her call for you."

Grateful, I hurried to the door, only to hear the clack of feet upon stairs. Gretel closed the door and looked around, frantic as I felt inside.

"Under the bed, or in the closet, quickly." She pointed at both in turn, but little good a closet would do me if betrayed by my own nose and a speck of dust.

Delight at the home's cleverness sprung to heart. I raced to Edward's own wardrobe and pressed two fingers underneath. The passage opened, too slowly by far, for when one lives by seconds, even a moment seems like an eternity.

Gretel's worry shifted to a smile, and believe me when I say I'm sure I saw her eyes fill with tears. "Go, Miss Ellison. You have much of your father in you. He'd be proud, I'm sure."

And although I didn't understand what she meant then, I believe I do now.

I think she saw what was coming, perhaps not in the manner of a mage or a mystic, but clearly she had enough knowledge of *The Book* and the house's secrets that she sensed a shifting.

A change in the wind, perhaps.

I raced into the passage, and rather than attempt to climb the attic ladder in my gown, I made haste to the laundry … and that is where I hid the second of my beautiful gowns, where it would rest until becoming a plain white shift once today became yesterday.

I changed back into a plain cotton dress and scrubbed my face with a small bit of lye that sat upon the washtub. With hair suitably mussed, I proceeded to the front hallway. Victoria stood alone at the base of the steps, clutching her gloves and staring into nothing. I fought the temptation to run the other direction, to return to Edward, but her gaze locked on me before I could change my mind.

"Bring me some tea," is all she said, and she stepped into the parlour.

At this hour? I wanted to ask after Charlotte, but—

"Two teas, girl." Celia descended the steps, expression blank and vague. A hollowness opened in my stomach at the sight of her. I nodded and left to do as told, despite the lateness of the evening. At least, that was my intention, but it occurred to me that if Celia and Victoria waited in the parlour for tea, no one was watching over Charlotte—if indeed she had returned home with them.

I slipped back into the laundry, through the passage, and upward to the room that Charlotte now called her own. And, without regard for safety, for discovery, or for what I might be risking in that moment, I pulled the lever and waited for the door to open.

It did.

I remained in the passage, taking deep breaths and praying that Curson's promise to hide the passageways as asked functioned just as well as the actions of the other spirits. With the passageway door wide open, I looked through toward the window, for I could see only a corner of the room from where this passage opened.

Charlotte sat in a velvet chaise by the window, curtains drawn back so that only a hint of moonlight shone on her face. However, with her back to me and seated, I couldn't see if she had indeed been injured by the evening's ordeal.

Temptation grew. I could creep to her door and pretend to knock, or perhaps I could even come back with tea before the others noticed what I was doing or—

I stopped myself with a mild rebuke. What did I hope to gain by coming here? What would I learn? It was Celia whose actions were the strangest of all, though the very simple fact that both Charlotte and Victoria still lived after what happened—it was enough to make me, yes, fearful.

But not as fearful as I should have been.

I pulled back into the passageway, but in my haste and lost in thought, I slammed my elbow against the outer wall. Stinging pain spiked up my forearm and into all five fingers, and the sharpness of my breath did exactly what I had intended to avoid.

Charlotte's gaze snapped to the right.

"Who's there?" she squeaked. "Mother? Is that you?"

I dared not take another breath. Another step.

And just when I thought I could wait no longer, her gaze turned still further. Over her shoulder. Across her back. To the other shoulder. As an owl spins its head to see throughout the night sky, that is how my stepsister Charlotte looked from one side of the room to the next.

Fear and disbelief grasped at my chest.

I couldn't believe my eyes, and yet, how could I not? And worse came still when she stopped, head turned to look backward as a doll in a careless child's hands, for it was then that I saw her eyes. Even in the pale moonlight, there could be no mistaking—no white remained.

Pools of liquid black stared directly at the place I thought to hide, where I stood near-helpless between the walls.

And yet, she did not see me.

"I can hear you," she said, high-pitched squeak lowering. She stood. Turned her body to meet her head. And stepped forward.

"I can smell you." Her voice lowered to a hiss, and I swallowed hard.

This wasn't the Charlotte I knew. The Charlotte I knew should be lying abed, if alive at all, after what I'd seen. But *this* Charlotte? She advanced, step by silent step, toward my hiding place.

"I know you're there."

She drew closer and I couldn't help but slink back, ever so slowly, into the darkness. Perhaps some part of me knew that I had still to close the passageway, once opened. Not that it would be difficult, but I wonder if perhaps the other half of me wanted to know—needed to know—that I was safe within the walls.

That Edward would be safe, should it come to that.

She moved close, and I saw her with clarity. One arm, she held loose by her side, and the way she stood, as if … as if some part of her middle had been pulled apart from the rest, and then put back together in a hurry. Like dishes stacked by an inexperienced scullery boy, piled too high.

The black pools of her eyes were what frightened me the most. Even more than the pointed, sharp teeth that brushed her lips as she spoke. Even more than the bluish tint to her skin, which the night's gleam revealed as so pale that dark veins popped from her neck and hands. Even more than the rasping voice with which she spoke, so different from the mouse-squeak I knew her for.

No, the eyes told me everything, and struck me with a terror beyond all I'd felt so far, for Charlotte's eyes were the same as those of the spirits I had conjured.

And those eyes—those dark hollows—revealed a soul of true and pure evil.

Her arm swung forward, hand reaching, spiked talons where gloved fingers should have been. As she reached for me, I came to my senses and pulled the door back, swinging her heavy wardrobe back into place with every ounce of strength left in my being.

It latched, but I didn't wait to be sure.

I turned, and I fled.

28

The Disappearing

*E*dward, Edward, Edward.

I burst into his room, limbs shaking, breath quick and shallow and dizzying. Charlotte, by truth or by design, was no longer the girl we'd thought her.

Lord Almighty, save our souls.

I paced back and forth in front of my brother's bed. What would we do? What would I do? I could not keep him here, not with that … that …

Charlotte was not human.

Had she ever been?

By God, had we lived in this house with …

No, it could not be. I would have known.

Would I?

Victoria, first. Then Charlotte. Both, by all rights, should be dead upon the ground, their souls headed toward judgment.

And what of Celia's touch?

Sick crawled up the back of my throat at the thought of it all.

It would be all right. We would be all right. Perhaps Gretel and I could escape with Edward, travel … where?

Gently, but in haste, I drew Edward's head into the crook of my arm and sat him up, though still he slept. His blankets, I bundled around his form, and tucked a toy soldier into the front folds for company. He began to fuss and mumble, twisting in the sheets, so I drew him closer, seized by worry. He felt far too light for a boy of his age and size.

"Hush, Edward," I whispered, "you'll be all right soon. We only need to—"

The door flew open with a crash and I leapt to my feet, Edward still wrapped and in my arms.

"Ella." Celia stood in the doorway, arms folded across her bosom. "Did I not ask for tea?"

It was then I realized—Gretel no longer sat in the room. In my panic, I'd forgotten about her.

How had Celia known I would be here?

"I set the water to boil," I said, voice and words coming stronger than I felt. "It'll be ready momentarily."

She came into the room, head shaking. "I'm afraid not, girl. It will be ready now."

And then she stopped at Edward's bedside, reaching toward us, fingers outstretched, and I froze with uncertainty as I recalled Charlotte's reaching hand only moments before.

"The ball," I shouted, "how was it?"

Taken aback, Celia withdrew her hand and gazed at me with something akin to thoughtfulness. "Delightful. There will doubtless be a wedding soon enough."

The audacity of her!

"Oh?" I played the coy, naïve child. "To whom?"

Celia snorted, reminding me evermore of her daughters. "One

of mine, you blundering gnat. We'll be living at the palace within the month."

My stomach sank, though my mind raced to make sense of her words. We? And how could she be so certain?

"That *is* delightful," I murmured, holding Edward tighter and inching toward the still-open passage entrance. What would happen if I stepped through while she stood in the room? Would we vanish like ghosts, or would that very action break the enchantment that held her blind?

"Such a loving sister," Celia cooed. I stopped, feet rooted to the floor. "Where do you plan to take him? Surely it'll be difficult to serve tea while holding him in such a way."

"He's unwell," I said, "and he'll find more comfort near me than in this room alone."

Celia's blank expression twisted into a smile. "I'll stay here with him. Don't you worry."

But there was no power in heaven or on earth that could force me to leave him alone with *her*. And especially not with Charlotte—*that* Charlotte—nearby.

So I thought myself quite clever when I asked, "Will Charlotte not be taking tea with you?"

The smile flickered as a candle flame caught in crosswinds. "No. Not tonight. It's quite late and she has decided to rest for tomorrow's event. We will do the same, momentarily."

A scream tore through the house.

Celia and I exchanged a wordless look, and she knew that I had won this round. With a huff, she withdrew from the room in haste, and I, in my hurry for Edward's safety, closed his door and dragged a chair over to push beneath the handle. I tilted the chair in such a way that it would take some effort to shift the chair and open the door, but in case this failed, I also dragged two wooden toy boxes to the door and stacked them across the entry and under the chair for leverage, surprised at how easily I now moved such large and unwieldy objects.

If anything, perhaps it could buy a moment of time.

With a kiss on Edward's forehead, I left again through the passageway and emerged with caution in the library. Dangerous, perhaps, but where else could I guarantee not to be seen? I crept to the kitchen, where I planned to ready the tea and catch a few words between Celia and Victoria.

Where *had* Gretel gone?

As I prepared the tea, the night began to call to me, and I yawned without ceasing for what felt like hours—though of course it was not, for once the kettle began whistling, my eyes opened enough to pour the water and set all that was needed on the tray.

Only then did I notice that a pot set upon the stove, which I had taken for empty in my tired stupor, held now-boiling water inside. Someone had placed it there before I'd entered the room, but for what? The need to prepare any sort of meal could surely wait the few hours until morning … unless Celia had demanded a dish from Gretel out of her own selfishness.

And because I couldn't see Gretel in the kitchen, and because I have a penchant for caving to the temptations of curiosity at the most inconvenient moments, I chose a wooden ladle and plunged it into the pot.

I stirred, hitting a large item in the murky, boiling water. Boiled roast? At this hour? I couldn't resist and drew up the item, though through the haze of impending sleep, what I saw didn't make sense.

Long, fleshy knobs like fingers. Four, attached to a central root, with—

I dropped the ladle with a crash and fell backward, scream caught in my throat. Bile rose to splash my tongue and I pressed my lips together.

A hand boiled in that pot. A *hand*.

I couldn't hold back any longer, and emptied the contents of my stomach—which mercifully contained very little—onto the kitchen floor.

I recognized that hand. It had touched my cheek earlier that night.

I felt nothing.

Numb and hollow, I knelt in my own sick and watched the rivers of fluids seep into the cracks along the floor. Smelled the stench of my insides.

I hadn't believed them. Not truly, not until this moment.

I hadn't understood the depths to which they would dive. Oh, my head knew. My heart had not.

A moan rose from the deep of my innermost places, but even as I squeezed shut both eyes and clamped down upon my tongue to keep from crying out, buckets of salted water flowed in heavy streams across my face, joining the same that pooled in the cracks beneath the place I knelt.

And then I felt everything all at once, as if the whole of me turned inside out, as if hot brands seared every inch of skin, as if ... as if ...

I had no words. Utter torment diffused through my being, for in this moment I knew that only a monster could do such a thing.

I had three.

Racked with heavy, silent cries, I pitched face-first onto the hard floor. Both fists pounded upon the ground, sending spikes of pain to jar my bones, but what did it matter?

Gretel, dead. But *why?*

And with a horror that grew from a tiny seed of long-held

doubt, I understood.

Miss Mary. Our butler. The scullery boy, barely of age to ride a horse on his own.

All of them, gone.

I blinked until my vision cleared, and saw bright red eddies that slid across my battered fists, but instead of my own blood there was nothing but Gretel—panicked and afraid. Miss Mary, confused and terrified.

Did their blood flow as mine, in their final moments?

Lord Almighty, why?

Might I blame the terrors, instead? Perhaps I was wrong—how I wanted to be wrong—but no, nothing so obscure as terrors had done this.

Celia. Charlotte. Victoria.

These terrors had names that tasted of death.

These three, deliverers of destruction to the undeserving.

Murderers.

Gone now, everyone else, all but Edward and I, alone.

No one would come to save us, for they were all dead.

Every last one.

I rinsed my mouth of its bitter tang and cleaned the mess. Better not to reveal what I knew, little that it was. I picked up the tray of tea and, with shaking hands and a stomach that threatened to empty itself of nothing once more, took careful steps to the parlour.

I stopped outside the entrance, as whispered words wafted through to my listening ears.

"Patience, girl," said Celia, for there could be no mistaking the alluring lull of her voice, harsh and beautiful even at a whisper.

"You're lucky your impatience hasn't cost us more than it might have."

"That's skill, mother, not impatience. And I can't help it. The streets are empty in the night." Victoria sniffed, and I imagined her haughty expression and nose pointed to the sky. "And after what has happened these two nights, fewer still will venture forth. I thought you said this would be naught but a simple snatch of power."

A slap echoed throughout the parlour, sharp enough to ring in my ears where I waited.

"You forget your place, you impudent creature. There have been … certain unforeseen complications. Someone is here, someone who I had believed long gone. An old foe. But the coward will not face me, it seems … so I will draw him out myself."

He? My stomach tightened, and the taste of bitter bile returned.

"Your power—"

"—is certain. As like draws to like, I believe half the task may be done for me." There could be no mistaking the smile that surely showed upon her face, though I didn't understand what she meant by it.

"If you're so powerful, why didn't you stop it—"

Another slap, and I gasped at the snarl that came from within the parlour, like a wild beast unchained. I couldn't help it—my hands shook with a violence that rattled the cups on their trays. I released a breath of fear as the parlour became silent once more.

"Ella?"

I hated that she still called me that.

"Ella, sweet child, is that you?"

No. Not me. If I could have given my soul to vanish in that instant, surely I would have.

The tray rattled again, and so I couldn't hide. I stepped into the parlour with head held high, presuming to exude calm, though certain the entire kingdom could hear the beating of my heart against my chest.

Celia and Victoria were seated at opposite sides of the room. I served both, and Celia thanked me—a strange gesture, I thought.

Victoria, however, looked at me with a wry knowing that halted my breath and nearly caused my hands to falter in presenting her cup. I thought of Charlotte's words: *I can smell you.*

"You have such lovely skin, sister." She took the cup and stared me down.

I couldn't help it. I looked Victoria in the eyes. They were black as pitch and hard as stone. I didn't cry out. I didn't drop the tray, nor did I wish to turn and run as I had mere moments before. No, in that instant the absurdity of every echo of their presence, from the second each woman and girl walked through our front door, fell across my shoulders like a soft blanket. So, I did the one thing Victoria did not expect. I smiled.

Her expression of surety faltered. Then darkened. Then became angry. Perhaps I had overestimated my cleverness and bravery.

I left the room, delivered the empty tray to the kitchen, and fled back to the library—through the passages, and back to Edward's room.

I curled up next to his feverish form, and slept.

29

The Protecting

I awoke several hours later at the sound of pounding on Edward's door.

"Ella? Edward?" Celia banged once more, jostling the handle. She pushed and the door gave an inch before sticking against the braced chair and toy boxes.

I flew from the bed and re-entered the passage, pulling the wardrobe shut behind me. I didn't want her to discover me with Edward for the same reason a cat cleans its paws after a fall—I wanted to appear as though it was not as important to me as in truth, hopefully diverting attention from the very thing that was the most important of all.

I exited the walls through the library, grateful once again that I could traverse the passages alone and in silence, despite all else. I mounted the stairs with speed until I stood directly behind Celia— who continued to call into the room, turning the door handle again and again.

"You called?" I asked, clasping hands across the front of my dress.

Celia whirled around and stared. "Where have you been?"

Perhaps I hadn't thought this one through. "I went to check on the horses," I blurted, "and see to the garden."

Celia's eyebrows lifted as one. "Did you?"

My spirits sank. Had I fallen into a trap? "Yes, of course."

She nodded once and touched a finger to her lips. "And you saw nothing? Noticed nothing?"

And that is why he that utters a lie is a fool. "I'm rather bleary-eyed this morning. I saw little and accomplished even less, thinking to return to the task after breaking my fast."

"Oh no," she said, drawing her fingers together. "That won't be necessary. However, both of your sisters require assistance today."

Not what I'd wanted to hear.

"Charlotte first, please. We'd like to dress early and arrive well before any others. More time with the Prince, you see."

Why tell me this? "I'm sure that will be very beneficial for the impending proposal."

Celia squinted at me. "I do hope you're not mocking me, girl."

I wouldn't. Not now, anyway. "Of course not, but you did mention a wedding—"

"I did." She dropped her arms to her sides and regarded me with an uncomfortable scrutiny. "You're certain you won't attend tonight, Ella?"

Her sudden use of my name last night I had ignored, as my exhaustion had obscured judgment. But now, it sounded foreign and unclean, coming from her lips.

"I'm certain," I replied, pulling back to stand at the top of the steps, away from her reach.

"You'll miss the chance to see this elegant, far-traveled princess everyone has been talking about. Surely my daughters have mentioned her."

I ceased breathing. "Charlotte did mention someone yesterday."

Celia stepped closer. "She has such lovely, sable hair. And pale, gleaming skin. Much like yours, under all that." She waved a finger at my face and dress, and I forced myself to offer a pleasant smile in return.

"How lovely. Where is she from?"

Celia placed a hand on the railing next to mine, and it took every ounce of remaining strength not to pull away. I didn't want to show the growing worm of doubt and suspicion that crawled about in my gut.

Did she know?

"We haven't the faintest," Celia said, waving her other hand in dismissal. "Won't you come? You'll miss the engagement otherwise."

I shook my head and used the final line of defense left, though it drew attention to the very thing I'd been trying to avoid drawing attention to.

"Edward isn't well, and I really must stay to care for him." I took a deep, strong breath before continuing. "I might have asked Cook to care for him tonight, but I'm afraid she may have also succumbed. I haven't seen her this morning."

Celia regarded me with silent scrutiny, and I felt liken to wilt under the probing gaze. Finally, she spoke. "I imagine you haven't. Go tend to one of your sisters. We'll discuss your attendance later."

I coughed in surprise. "But Edward?"

She snorted. "He won't die to be without you for one evening, girl. *Go.*"

And with that, she folded her arms and backed against Edward's door, as if to bar the entry to my own brother.

She hadn't asked about the blocked door, either. Perhaps my efforts had bought some time after all.

Daylight has a peculiar manner of washing away memories and images from the darkness of night, and so it was that I entered Charlotte's room with little trepidation and a bravery that surprised even myself.

I reasoned that, if Charlotte and Victoria had become something else ... something *other* ... had I not dealt with such things already and come away unscathed? Certainly, I thought, a conjuring of spirits under one's control had to be different from those that existed in this present plane of their own accord, but spirits were spirits—if indeed they *were* spirits or spirit-possessed—and thus I didn't approach them with blindness or total lack of expectation.

I could win this fight. For Gretel. For Mary. For Edward.

Still, to bolster my confidence that I might survive the day and see Edward safely away and well again, I pulled a piece of ribbon from one of my few remaining unsoiled garments and threaded the bone key onto it like a string. I placed this around my neck and secured it with knots, hiding the key itself under the collar of my clothing and out of sight. Although without power, as told to me by Curson, the feel of smooth bone against my skin brought forth a flood of memories of Father and his quiet confidence in all things.

If ever I had need of his strength, it was now.

And so, with bone about my neck and calm in my heart, I entered Charlotte's chamber to assist her preparations for the third ball.

I found both Charlotte and Victoria in the same room, laughing together over goblets of deep, red wine. Thick, too, for I watched a droplet slide like fresh custard along the side of the glass.

The scent of roast meat and the tang of metal filled the air, as both plucked morsels of some treat from a tray near the window. Wherever they'd obtained something to eat was beyond me, for without Gretel to assist in kitchen preparations, I would have figured them to starve before venturing into such a place on their own—let alone know how to use anything but a knife.

Thoughts like these made me shudder, for *what* they might be consuming was another thing entirely. My confidence faltered, and I shook it off. I couldn't dwell on what I knew it might be, lest I flee from them both and leave the task incomplete, risking my chances at a private moment later on. There was a quiet safety in denial, however false. I'd tend to the needs of the day and bide my time until the moment the three left for the evening's activities.

And then I would protect my family.

Victoria noticed me first, and beckoned with a bent finger. "Do come in, sister. Would you partake?"

She lifted the tray and extended it toward me. When I didn't respond, she sighed as though exasperated by my presence and set the tray back down. "Very well. Do as you like. I have no need of you."

That hadn't been Celia's instruction. "Your mother intends for me to help you both dress today."

They looked upon me with something akin to disgust.

"You won't touch me," Victoria spat, "you'll try to steal my things again."

"She helped me just fine," said Charlotte, sipping the wine. "You only have to tell her what to do."

"And did you not collapse from your strings being too tight? No, she won't touch mine."

Did Victoria seriously imply that I'd tied Charlotte's corset so tight that *it* had been the cause of her collapse? Or more likely, that had been *Celia's* explanation.

"You fell in front of the Prince, too," Charlotte said, bottom lip protruding. "It's not as if he prefers bleeding orifices to seizures." She slammed her wine glass down on the table, breaking the stem and sending the glass tumbling to the floor. It cracked but didn't shatter, only spilling the contents upon the rug at their feet.

Charlotte giggled at the sight, while Victoria rolled her eyes.

"My exit, at least, looked all the more sympathetic. Yours simply appeared desperate. Mother will choose me, in the end."

Charlotte's bottom lip pouted even further as she folded both arms across her chest, the very picture of a child denied her own way.

"You don't know that," she hissed, slouching back in her seat.

"I do, and you'd do best to stop acting like an imbecile. I'm sure Mother has other plans for you." She took a delicate sip, looked at me, and wiped the corner of her mouth with a bare finger before licking off the contents. "But you may have use of her pet for another day."

"I hate you." Charlotte stood, stomped a foot, and pointed at the door. "Get out, *sister*. I have to dress for *my* prince."

Victoria rose with a sigh, placed the goblet on the table, and levelled her gaze at Charlotte and me in turn. "Have a lovely day, sisters. And if I see either of you near my room today, I won't hesitate to—"

"Just *go*," Charlotte urged.

Victoria left, nose high in the air, and stopped only once in the doorway to address me. "And how is the brat, girl? Long for this world?"

If I could have struck her down in that instant, believe me, I would have. Instead, I offered a polite curtsy and a reply of untruth. "Edward is a strong and hearty boy, dear sister. Most children are. I imagine he'll be up and—"

Victoria waved her hand as she interrupted. "I can't possibly be bothered to care. Good day." She swept out of the doorway, but who remained was sorry comfort indeed.

With a screech, Charlotte grabbed the tray of unrecognizable meats and hurled it at the door. To my amazement, rather than landing in a heap only inches away from her attempted strongman efforts, the tray flew through the air and slammed against the doorframe with a crash. It fell to the floor, making an awful mess to join that already under her feet.

"Well," she said, after the final morsel had fallen. "I don't care what *she* says. I shan't go back. I *will* have the Prince and the life I deserve."

And I had not a clue. "Go back where? To the castle? School?"

She stared at me then, remembering she shared the room with another body. "And why Mother has bothered to keep you around, I haven't the faintest. You're quite hideous."

Color rose to my cheeks, though I bade it not. "Shall I dress you, sister?" I had no need of her insults or conversation today. Not after what I'd seen last night. "The red, today?"

She ignored me and bent to pick the broken goblet off the floor.

"My, my," she murmured, turning it to look upon all sides, "how careless of me." Her gaze slid to meet mine. "It does seem that I am unaware of my own strength, at times. What a pity. A lovely goblet it was, too. Did you not think so?"

I replied that I did. What else could I say?

Her tone shifted again, from mouse-like to a harsher, deeper version of Charlotte. My heart nearly stopped as she stared at me, inching herself closer with each word. "And if I should so happen to learn that someone has breathed a word of my private conversation with my sister to our mother, I will reward that someone with this—"

She took one step closer, palm wrapped around the goblet's bowl.

"—same—"

Another step, and her grip tightened.

"—caress."

The goblet's bowl shattered in her hand, and she dropped the pieces without her gaze ever leaving my own. Several shards of glass stuck deep into her palm, blood oozing through the places where they pierced. Her eyes grew black as night, while a grin swept across her face.

For once, I found my senses and moved to leave with a cry in my throat, but Celia stepped into the room and blocked my retreat.

It would be the one and only time I would ever feel relief at her presence.

"Charlotte."

The white of Charlotte's eyes returned in an instant.

I didn't dream it. I swear this. Truly, it happened.

Charlotte pulled both hands behind her back, as though intending to hide her bloodied hand from her mother. Celia raised one eyebrow, looked from her daughter to me and back again. "Stop being a wastrel and get dressed. We have work to do."

"But—" Charlotte's squeaking whine returned.

"You would have me choose another?" If words were knives, we both would have been slain on the spot. Charlotte remained silent. Celia turned on her heel and left, leaving her daughter shaking with fury. Charlotte ran forward and slammed the door closed, cutting off my plan of escape. I didn't want to be in the room with this angry ... *being*.

Choose another, Celia had said. Another what? Another *whom?*

And besides, how could she? Edward and I were all that remained. And yet, a nagging in my skull whispered other words

I denied hearing for the longest time. Perhaps she meant another *daughter*—another creature, or monster, like them? Were there others we had yet to learn of? Or worse still, were these girls not her daughters at all?

I suspected I was being played for a fool. Whoever the others were, I would doubtless learn soon enough—and if not, I'd still have Charlotte. Ah, the joys I lived for.

"Shall we?" Charlotte growled, yanking a bulky, bead-laden, red velvet monstrosity from her wardrobe.

I saw no other option.

30

The Stand

I could not shake the image of Gretel's hand, boiling on the stove, as I readied Charlotte yet again. I remained silent and carried out her requests, for with every demand came a reminder of *her* hand, pierced and bloodied and as it had appeared, free of pain. She had not hesitated to risk her own injury to prove a point.

Such a thing was not human.

My mouth grew dry as I worked, the scene playing over and over in my head, constricting my breath though I wore no corset.

Might I secret Edward away somehow?

Out of the house, or away from town. Perhaps we could find work on a ship or with traveling merchants. It would only be a matter of time before these three struck again, of this I felt sure. And how long would Celia's patience for me hold?

I needed to get Edward away from her, *now.*

And Father.

Oh, Father. What if he returned to find our absence? What if we left, only to leave him to face the full brunt of Celia's wrath?

Despite Gretel's suggestion that he knew some of the power I had found, I could not leave him to meet her alone.

And what if he lived but remained under her spell, too far gone to remember his own kin? I could not allow that. That is not a life, for a life under duress is no life at all.

Or what if he *never* returned?

What if Celia had already killed him?

Oh, Blessed Lord, save us. I repeated this prayer, over and over, blinking away the tears of memory and swallowing the hot, bitter taste of fear.

For my father's sake, I had to do something. And for Edward's, for after tonight, if Celia had her way, she would no longer have need of us to continue her ruse. With access to the King through the Prince, and thus to the throne, by God …

And … why?

Even as Charlotte admired herself in the mirror, turning this way and that, I no longer saw a young woman with whom I shared my home.

No, I saw Gretel's murderer. *One* of them, a beast capable of carrying out every threat and more.

I glanced to the newly formed scabs on her hand, where the glass had cut and she had bled.

She'd *bled.*

Did that mean that she, too, could be killed?

The thought drew forth a whispered memory—words read from the Scriptures by my mother time and time again. They came to mind so clearly, I swear it was as if she stood there with me, speaking words of comfort: *To everything there is a season, and a time to every purpose under the heaven. A time to be born … and a time to die.*

*Every*thing.

These remembered words and the strength of memory fuelled my resolve. I would not run, not yet. Tonight, I would attend the evening's ball, but this time—*this* time—I wouldn't ask the spirit child to hold back.

My family's protection remained in my hands alone.

But William, he wouldn't see the darkness coming—Celia would have her way in the blink of an eye, and no one else knew of it but me. Treasonous, her plans, but what did that matter? Lives were at stake, and I was the only person who knew.

I drew a shuddering breath as Charlotte pulled on her lace gloves and blew a crude kiss in my direction.

It smelled of putrid flesh.

I would likely die, this night. But if I did? I would do it defending the lives of the ones I loved, and avenging the lives of those I'd lost.

I couldn't simply arrive at the ball and expect events to unfold as before. No, with this greater knowing, I needed to prepare, to be ready for Celia's schemes—and to find a way to protect those who needed protecting at the same time.

But of course, such a thing is easily said—more difficult to carry through.

First, a weapon.

I am well aware of the impropriety of a woman carrying a weapon, but desperation reveals many truths about one's self that often remain unknown save for moments like these. My truth? I did not care one whit for the uselessness known as propriety.

The moment Celia and her daughters left the house, I raced to Father's study. In it, he'd kept swords, daggers, knives. I'd assumed these for decoration, as souvenirs of his travels, but the moment I crossed the threshold to his office, I saw his private place of work in a new light.

His desk still remained in the center of the room, sturdy as a foundation, but the shelves which lined the walls ... to the unaware, the items upon them appeared as a haphazard jumble of trinkets and curios. To my new sight? *Purposeful displacement, to confound one who may suspect ... what?*

No matter. I would think on that later.

For now, two crossed swords—one very large and one very small—were mounted on the wall behind his desk. Perhaps that would do? I raced to them and chose the smaller.

I gasped as the smaller sword's hilt seemed to warm to my touch. I wanted desperately in that moment to take it, hold it, understand its meaning ...

But no, I could not.

Even a smaller sword, the length of my arm from elbow to fingertips, would be quite conspicuous inside a crowded ballroom. As for understanding? Such a thing would have to wait.

I pawed through the assortment of items on his shelves with growing alarm: an obsidian blade with jade-carved handle; a thin, ivory ring, carved in the shape of teeth; a shelf full of texts by Origen of Alexandria, Erasmus of Rotterdam, and several priestly prayer books used for Mass.

Vials of powders and liquids, labeled with whimsical phrases like "unicorn dust" or "fairy tears" appeared far more sinister than they had only weeks before—what did they truly contain?

On a shelf to my left, I found a small, sheathed dagger, and two shelves below that, a strap which—after some manoeuvring—wound around my leg. Cumbersome, but it would do in a pinch. I slipped the sheathed dagger into the strap, where it sat snugly against my skin. I would only have to bend and lift my gown just above the ankle to reach it.

And though I continued my search, looking for anything else that might assist my cause, it was not until I reached the lowest shelf in the room that I found a plain leather satchel in its furthest depths—it could not be seen unless one crouched upon the ground and strained to see into the shadowed ledge.

I opened it, for I am a fount of curiosity.

Inside the satchel? A pile of polished, white bones.

My breath caught and I dug further inside the bag, drawing forth a cord of thin rope, a wound ball of string, a stick of charcoal no wider than my smallest finger, and—if that had not been enough to affirm the meaning behind this discovery—a palm-sized leather pouch that contained nothing other than a handful of powdery, gray ash.

The world grew still and quiet.

These things.

I had suspected, but I had not *known*.

Even Gretel had known something, hinted more than once, and yet …

"Why? Why, why, *why?*" I shouted at nothing, pounding a fist against the floor. My scabbed wounds of the previous night, broken open by my fury, sent sparks of pain shooting through my wrist. "Why, Father? What have you done … ?"

In that moment, I realized two things.

My father had called spirits, as did I.

And Celia thought him returned, somehow—and a threat to her own plans.

Nothing about this made sense, and I could not see when he had done this, or how, or why I should have found the book, or why he had not shared such a thing with Edward or myself.

Had Mother known?

I had little time for answers, sore little, if I wanted to reach the ball in time to do any good. I closed the pouch of ash and returned it to the satchel, along with the rope, string, charcoal, and bone. But as I drew out my hand to pull the drawstring and close the bag, my fingers brushed against an item which crinkled under my thumb.

A slip of paper?

It had been folded over itself many times, creased with age, and the ink smudged in small circles across the sheet as though someone had ... as though someone had read this—written this?— with tears in their eyes.

I read the name at the top and the name at the bottom, and these names caused the world to collapse and bury me beneath it.

My Beloved Josef,

May this letter find you safe and unharmed, and may the Lord have seen fit to grant us one day more. Beyond that, I cannot say.

I remain unwell, my love, and I say this not to put within you a fear or desperation, but to spur on your resolve—our resolve—to the cause of peace, justice, and God's glory. We must use our time remaining wisely, for what little time there is, may we use it to build a future that is safe and whole for our children.

They are so innocent, Josef. They weep at my bedside and I try to be strong, but some days this is beyond my control. On those days, I do not resent my condition, for I know it means you do good works.

Accomplish the task which is set before us, my love. Push back the shadows so that our children may live in the light. Know that I am with you even now, though my body fails me and my spirit often feels weak.

Gretel has been kind enough to compose this from my speech, so any strangeness of form in this message is my own. We are blessed if we find true friends where it is least expected.

Carry out your calling, my love, but do it quickly so that we may have one more day together. One hour, even, would be enough that I might see our Lord with happiness in my heart.

Remember that I have accepted this fate willingly, for the sake of our children, our children's children, and for all creatures who may receive His grace.

The children send their love. Would that I might explain to them the sacrifice we make, but I fear that Ella will not understand. In time, perhaps she will come to know the truth.

For today and these remaining days to come, I choose to believe that all things work together for good to them that love the Lord, to them who are called according to His purpose.

Come quickly, beloved. I am waiting.

Your Devoted Help Mate,

Aleidis

I do not know how long I knelt on the floor in my father's office, reading this letter, tears streaming down my face like a tide.

What did it mean? Why would my mother write such a thing?

Sacrifice and calling were not words I had ever thought to associate with my parents, and to learn that Mother had hidden something from me on purpose …

She must have known. She must have known of Father's *Book* and these tools, and perhaps that is the calling of which she had spoken. More than ever, I ached for Father's return.

Where was he? Were he here, he could help. He could tell me what to do next, and he could—

Movement outside the window, at the edge of my vision, interrupted these thoughts. A flash of alarm shot through my senses—it couldn't be the terrors come calling, for I now felt certain Celia and her brood were somehow responsible for these things … but terrors were not the only dangers to a young woman on a dark night.

Despite better judgment, I stood at the window and squinted into the fading twilight—for it is in the spaces between sunrise and sunset that we see little and find much to fear.

Across the drive, at our gates—someone moved toward the house, a dark, hulking shape obscured by the streaming rays of a disappearing sun, stalking slowly until far enough beyond the light to reveal—

William?

What? My eyes must deceive me, I thought, for he should be nowhere but inside the palace, greeting the guests as they arrive and choosing which among the many women he would take for a wife—not riding atop a horse on my father's land.

But when presented with another curiosity, I do not shy away. I threw open the window latch to push back the shutters and whisper into the descending night air.

"William? Is that you?"

There was silence, except for the chirp of crickets and the brush of a gentle breeze amid the trees.

And then he spoke. "Ella?"

Fewer things made sense with every passing moment, and my head ached to bear the burden. "William, why are you sitting on a horse in my yard?"

He dismounted and his footsteps crunched on dirt and stone, coming closer. And I, beyond rational thought, found myself leaning halfway out the window of my father's study, face-to-face with the kingdom's Crown Prince. He wore a riding coat similar to the one I'd borrowed on our first meeting, and his medallion shone as always, despite the fading light.

"Ella, I could ask you the same thing."

"The same thing? I live here. And I'm not on a horse, nor in the yard."

He laughed gently at that, but I could not share his light spirit.

"I had a meeting outside the palace that ran late," he said, "and my father is greeting everyone in my stead. The meeting was, shall we say, unavoidable."

"And this meeting required your presence in my yard?"

He pursed his lips and looked behind, toward the open gate, before speaking in a voice soft and low. "Why aren't you at the palace? I've looked for you at the balls, but I couldn't find you. The last we met, you had a pumpkin at your hip."

Oh, how my heart ached. "My brother is very ill. He can't be left alone." It was most of the truth, at least.

"I'll send a doctor," he said, as soon as I finished speaking. My composure began to slip, and I fumbled for a reply.

"I have nothing to wear. And no time. And there is no horse here, and the others took the carriage."

"Then come as you are. Please, Ella." His eyes pleaded, the sincerity causing my chest to ache and my limbs to weaken. How could he be so kind? So caring?

And what had I given him in return? Doubt, anger, and accusations. Ah, but that was Aleidis, mostly.

Still, he'd come for me.

I thought I might climb out of the window into his arms just then, wrap my own about his neck and speak the truth—but there were far greater things at stake here, and only I could accomplish the task.

Perhaps this was the sort of sacrifice my mother spoke of.

"I'm so sorry," I whispered, hoping he wouldn't hear the tremor in my voice. "I can't. Would that I could, but I can't … you've been so very gracious, and I … " I stopped my words before I spoke aloud something that could not be repealed.

"Go on." He returned my whisper, and came close enough that no one existed in that moment but the two of us.

But it could not be, and so I shook my head and begged my troublesome heart for release. "I can't. William, please. You have a ball to attend, duties to perform, women to dance with … "

I heard the twinge of bitterness in my words, but he didn't seem to notice.

"I don't want to dance with other women."

How could something so intangible hurt so much? "Surely there's someone? One woman, at least, who has caught your eye?"

William paused and looked away, and I knew then who he thought of. I felt sure of it, but only for a moment. Doubt strikes like a viper at a woman's heel, and I wished to end this now before the wound could fester.

"Go, William. Go to your ball and your women in their fancy dresses, and leave me alone."

"You don't mean that," he said, confusion marring his beautiful face. "Maybe at first, but not anymore. I like you, Ella, and I don't care what anyone says. You're irreverent and honest and clever and you don't care who or what I am. I'll bring you to the ball and dance with you if I have to climb in the window myself and draw you out—"

"Beware of a woman in a mauve dress and foxtail stole. I suspect she has designs for the throne, and her touch is both seductive and cruel." I spit the words forth, for I did not trust myself. I wanted to go with him. Needed to go with him.

But I could not.

"Goodbye, William." All at once, I grabbed the shutters and pulled them shut, threw the latch to lock them in place, and drew the curtains closed.

Then I grabbed my father's satchel and fled from the room, deeper and deeper into the house until I could no longer hear him calling my name outside the window, nor the pounding of his fist against the front door.

I sat, knees to chest in the library passageway, until the pounding faded and I heard his voice no more.

Too much. I bore too much.

I felt I would collapse under the weight of it before night's end—but at least, William's bizarre appearance had bought me some time.

For Celia could not have acted without him there.

With my father's satchel in hand, I began the ritual preparations— this time made easier, faster, with the items from his bag.

How many times had his hand held this rope? Or this bone? These thoughts would only distract from my purpose, so I pushed them aside ... and yet, as I bent to write the names of the spirits, I stopped and thought to look through *The Book of Conjuring* once more.

Just in case.

In case there might be something better. More effective. After all, had my stepsisters not lived? Such things should have brought them so low that they might never rise again. Instead, they lived and thrived, if a monster could be said to *live*.

They had killed, and they had threatened, and I had every

reason to believe they would do so again.

The game had changed.

I found many other spells in the book, conjurings for riches which I did not need, for divinations that I did not want, and for power over life and death that I did not dare read for the fear their first words struck in my heart. But oh, how those shapes, names, and phrases sent tremors down my spine, and built a different kind of longing in my heart. But I would never speak those words, for they called to me as a silver coin to a scavenging crow. They promised a revenge, harsh and severe, and a death beyond the dead.

While I could not speak those words, I would find a way to stop Celia, and as I read, I happened upon a most gratifying recitation that struck me with gladness and delight. Better yet, the book did not specify who among those many spirits might do this for me, and so I acted as before.

I called those known spirits for a third time, Lautrayth, Feremin, and Oliroomim, that they might bring me a horse, a gown woven of illusion to bring me honor, and this time—only this time—that they might carry forth a most particular request.

I knelt in the circle and held the bone aloft, this time the skull of an unfortunate sparrow or robin who'd given its life for Victoria's vanity.

There would be no more sacrifices on their behalf. After today and the night prior, I didn't trust them to allow Edward and I even one more breath in this world, should Celia's plans come to pass.

Tonight, I would alter my course of requests and demand a different arrangement, pushing aside the trepidation that came with those thoughts.

I began as before, with some slight variation to prepare for the enhancement of my requests.

"I conjure you," I said, "those aforesaid spirits, by He who will come to judge the living and the dead, and the whole earth by fire, and by that Day of Judgment and by the sentence upon your head that day, you must be compelled to come here without delay and fulfill my every command."

And they came as before, in black smoke and radiant violet fire, extinguishing all hope and devouring the light of the setting sun, so that the parlour appeared as deep and dark as night.

And as before, I obtained what I required from the first two spirits. A horse, and my illusion. The third, the child, waited with folded arms and blood-red lips.

"Oliroomim, my request." I swallowed, if only to prevent my own bile from spilling forth, for when he smiled, I saw chunks of bleeding flesh still impaled on his tiny, dagger-sharp teeth.

He laughed, licked his lips, and swallowed, eyes glowing with pleasure as a child's when given a new toy. What toy had made *him* smile so, I prayed I would never know.

"Yes, mistress? Back so soon? I suspect there is more to this night than before, if I judge by the words of power that called us forth."

But I had other curiosities to discuss first. "My sisters. I asked they not be fatally harmed, and yet the punishments you sent were enough to lay low any mortal being. Why?"

He averted his eyes and pulled a miniature pocketknife from a pouch in his torn, dirtied pants. Were the spirits not allowed unblemished clothes, even in death?

Edward had a knife just like this. A gift from Father, two Christmases ago. He'd taught both of us to whittle that day, and we carved small trees that still are placed upon the mantle each year in memory of that day. Truly, Edward could barely hold the knife that year—and he could not make it work alone—but I still remember his infant hands curved around the handle, and the excitement in his eyes as Father guided his hand to shape the little wooden tree.

The spirit flicked open his own blade and began to draw the knife tip under each fingernail, as though my presence was but a mere annoyance to him.

"They remain unharmed, do they not?"

"Yes, but that isn't what I asked." That, I *did* want to an answer to, but not yet. "Why send a fatal trial against my wishes?" For if I couldn't control what he might do, how could I be sure that both Edward and William would remain safe as well?

He flicked his gaze to me as though my stupidity begged disbelief. "They *did not* die. Your orders were followed. *Mistress.*" He didn't bother to hide his disdain. "What do you ask this time?"

It still didn't make sense. "But you couldn't have known they wouldn't die. They should be lying abed, taking final breaths at the very least, and yet they left just now for a third night of revelry. *How did you know?*"

He ignored me.

"Tell me."

Still nothing. Petulant child.

"By my command, tell me."

He spat at my feet and lunged forward, teeth bared. I gasped and flinched in return, but held my ground as I dared not break the circle and send him back. Not without what I needed first.

Besides, he couldn't hurt *me.* I hoped.

"You, mistress, are ignorant as a newborn babe. Why is it they cannot die by my hand? Why is it that a fatal affliction serves nothing? You know the truth of it, and yet you refuse to see."

I did refuse. I know it now—I didn't want the truth. Yet it clung to my soul as a leech, despite my yearning to refrain from its acceptance.

"What *are* they?" I whispered.

The spirit's smile returned. "That, mistress, is the right question. What would you have me do?"

I shook my head, impatience returning. "What are they?"

"You already know."

And perhaps I did. Still, I could not accept the thought that my stepsisters were one of *them*. Oliroomim's kin, so to speak. "I need protection, spirit. There is a plan afoot, and I must stop it."

He shrugged, small shoulders lifting and dropping with a sigh. "And?"

I had hoped for his assistance, but for whatever reason, he resented me openly today. Had my questions of the previous meeting remained at the forefront of his mind?

Did spirits *have* a mind of free will to think on such things?

I flipped through *The Book*, turning to the page which presented my new course of action. If someone had asked me even a fortnight prior if I would ever do such a thing, I would have laughed and called them a fool.

Ah, but who is the fool now?

I spoke the words on the page, and any regret I felt at the beginning was replaced by the knowledge that I did this not for myself and not for selfish reasons, but for the safety of others. For those who could not keep safe themselves.

"I, Ellison, supplicate you and beg you, by the hand of the only Son of God, that by my words and will, you will bind the King's son William to me in such a manner that he will revere me above all mortals, never wavering from agreement with me, but always obeying my commands. May he take pains to please me, by our same Lord the Christ who reigns forever and ever. Amen."

Silence enveloped the room, but only for a moment, because once the words ceased their ringing in my ears, another sound replaced them.

Oliroomim *laughed.*

Cruel and too deep for a small child. His lips curled back from his teeth and I shrunk inside the circle. Of all things, I hadn't expected laughter. How could I?

I drew myself up to full height—which I admit, is not much for a woman of my size—and thrust a hand forward to touch, yes, touch the spirit-child Oliroomim.

I closed my fingers around the collar of his worn shirt and willed myself to forget the childlike appearance. To forget how deeply he reminded me of my own brother, for Oliroomim was a spirit first and no longer a child, and therefore subject to *my* commands.

His eyes grew wide and all laughter ceased as I yanked him forward, pulling him closer into the circle.

"No, mistress," he said, voice quivering.

I will not deny that it pleased me. I felt tired of being subject to the spirit's whims.

"Why do you laugh?" I hissed the phrase, my lips inches from his undoubtedly false display of weakness. "Have I not commanded you?"

His head shook. "To conjure love, mistress, is a complicated thing."

I didn't care. "I don't have a choice."

"You play with free will and forces beyond your understanding. Love isn't as simple as many believe."

That was not what I wanted to hear. "Can you do this or not? It need not be permanent, but a life may depend on it."

He took a quaking breath and I hardened my heart at the sight of it. "I will try, but I cannot guarantee what you seek. I may be powerful among spirits, but to conjure love … that is deeper and darker than I."

"I care only for protecting my own. Tonight, someone will seduce the king's son and I'm afraid this means he will come to harm."

"Because you love him?"

My chest grew hot and tight. "Because he doesn't deserve to be forced to love *them* ... "

I realized the idiocy of my own actions once the words left my lips. If Celia would deign to manipulate the Prince's affections with her power, how did what I planned to attempt differ?

Truly, it did not.

I would be no better than she if I carried it forth. Yet, *I* didn't place threats upon the lives of others. If Celia and her daughters left our home for the palace, perhaps then I might believe us safe, but what of William? And after what I had seen and heard last night? I couldn't believe Celia had finished with Edward or me.

We were not safe, nor William. And only I had the power to prevent future affliction.

"Can you do it?" I released the Oliroomim from my grasp. "Will you do it?"

He grimaced like a baited bear. "I can't make him love you, mistress. That sort of deep enchantment is beyond my control. There may, perhaps be another way."

I nodded. "Speak."

"Would you accept an elimination of choice?"

Elimination of choice? Such as the removal of certain personages? "Tell me what you mean, exactly."

His smile returned, reserved and yet with a touch of eagerness unlike before. "I cannot change his will, but I can ensure that you, mistress, are his only choice when the night comes to an end."

Certainly it sounded like what I wanted, but Oliroomim hadn't exactly proven himself trustworthy in all things.

"Might another spirit be able to carry out my wishes?" I thought of Curson and shivered.

The spirit stomped a foot and crossed his arms like a spoiled infant. I hated that I pitied him still.

When he didn't respond, I relented. "Fine. You may carry out this and only this. If only I remain, he must choose me. Whether I accept or decline is my choice alone."

Oliroomim bowed his head. "As you wish. The Prince will consent to marry the last woman standing when the clock strikes midnight and brings forth a new day."

A wave of relief flooded my senses. In only a few hours, William would be safe from Celia's influence, and with it, Edward's and my future secured.

In fact, I felt more trepidation at the thought of marriage than anything else … but if the offer meant protection for my family, so be it.

31

The Third Ball

I arrived as before. Crowds of attendees still swarmed the steps to the palace, as I should have expected, even though I'd been delayed far longer than my arrival on the evenings prior—well after sundown—for tonight's entrance. However, on this third and final evening of celebration, it appeared as though no one in all the kingdom or kingdoms beyond wished to refrain from partaking in a moment of spectacle. Truly, the people would gossip about this night for years to come.

I searched for Liesl upon arrival, scouring the crowds for her youthful features. I thought I saw her once, traversing the steps in a gown of peaches and crème, brother chaperon on her arm. I thought she saw me and I waved in greeting, but she turned away with such speed that it couldn't have been her.

Though of course, it was. I shouldn't have abandoned her last night. I did not blame her resentment, for my unintentional rudeness remained at fault.

Still, I had no shortage of those who sought to assist my ascent, but upon reaching the landing, I felt abandoned as before. Every other woman had a brother or cousin, father or uncle on her arm. I stood alone, despite the extravagance of my gown and the open stares at my person.

They couldn't be faulted. After all, I wore a gown of spun gold, jewelled with rubies and diamonds, paired with slippers of the most delicately gilded glass. Uncomfortable to be certain, but further proof of my delicate and distinguished personhood—under the illusionary effects of spirit-bestowed dignity and honor, that is.

Once announced, I descended the ballroom steps for a third time, admiring the further prodigality of such an event. Gold and purest white stretched across the hall from floor to ceiling, and the dance floor had even been given new tiles of purest white marble and inlaid gold.

The room shone like a vision of heaven, and before I reached the bottom of the steps, there stood William. Of course, he also wore a suit of gold that matched his ever-present medallion, and again I wondered how the spirit always knew. I should thank Feremin, one day. But unlike other nights, William held both hands behind his back and stood as though jolted by some kind of shock.

Fear shot through my belly. Had Celia already acted? Had I come too late?

"Lady Aleidis," William said, bowing stiffly at the waist. "Welcome."

He took my hand—which I offered—and once again raised it to his lips. He did not release me and instead moved closer.

Only then could I see the sweat on his brow. The trembling of his lip, the wild uncertainty in his eyes.

William felt afraid.

For what? My William of the graveyard hadn't been afraid, nor had the William who'd ushered me to safety after witnessing a murder or the William who had slunk around my family's stable and courtyard at strange hours of the day and evening. But this William, he feared something. I ached to ask what, but before I could, he glanced upward and I followed his gaze. The King watched from the balcony above, looking over the crowd with a palace guard on either side.

Curious. Perhaps William's nerves were due to the two incidents of nights past? Still, it was most disconcerting, more so than it may have been otherwise, for tonight I would remain his only choice, though I knew not how.

I nearly cursed aloud. I should have asked *how*.

"Lady Aleidis, I'm very pleased for your return." His greeting sounded as stiff and formal as the starched coats of the palace guard.

"Simply Aleidis, please, if you recall. And I thank you, and likewise." I pulled my hand from his grasp. "I should say, best wishes on the day of your birth. You are one year older, and if the old superstitions are true, one year wiser, though I have yet to see it. How fares the evening?"

He startled a bit at the loss of my hand, but dropped both arms to his sides as if planned. "I … thank you. Your consideration is very kind. Shall we dance?"

I shook my head. "Thank you for your offer, but I'd rather not dance with a gentleman whose attentions are forced beyond his own will."

As much as I longed for his touch and his company, I preferred his safety and my diligence even more. If he was unwilling to dance, I would place my attentions elsewhere. Keeping an eye on Celia, perhaps. Or him, from a distance, to ensure Celia could not make her move before the spirits.

"You … decline?" Sharp breaths from surrounding eavesdroppers woke William as if from a daze.

I nodded. "You don't seem all that excited to dance with me tonight, so I'll spare you the forced invitation and decline. Now you're free to—"

"No," William shook his head, "no, it's not what you think, look, it's just—"

Our eyes locked and my heart leapt despite myself. "Then explain."

The corners of his eyes crinkled and he stared as though I spoke some foreign language.

"You're asking me to explain why you think I don't want to dance with you even though I actually do?"

"Yes." Oh, how the true Ellison struggled to the surface, beyond the spirit-woven façade. I couldn't hold her back. "No one's forcing you to dance with anyone, so if you don't want to, I won't indulge what you believe to be an obligation. Therefore, I officially release you from any obligatory actions toward me."

His mouth opened into a small "o," and I couldn't help but smile.

"No," he said again, "it's not you, and I have to say you're the most forthright girl I've ever—"

"Woman." I glanced pointedly at my dress, among other things.

He cleared his throat. "Uh, yes, woman."

"Do you have other duties to attend to?"

"Yes. No! Wait … " He pressed two fingers to the bridge of his nose and I found the laughter slow in coming. How I loved making him fluster, but tonight of all nights, it annoyed rather than endeared.

"Look," he began, extending a hand, "I do want to dance with you, and I apologize if I seem distant. There's something I have to do tonight that's rather … how shall I put it?"

"Critical to the future of the family's legacy in the kingdom?"

I wanted to take back the words the moment I said them.

He stared openly, then, as my hand slid into his. "Yes, it is. But how did you … ?"

"Rumors." I waved my free hand and forced a girlish giggle, sounding more like a choking cat than a mysterious princess. My stomach hurt. I missed Gretel.

"I see."

He led me onto the dance floor and we stepped lightly to the center, just as in nights past. Perhaps I could survive one dance— just one—fully present with him. One, only one.

Part of me hoped it was possible, that I could enjoy these final moments with William in peace. Another part of me berated my foolishness.

"Have you enjoyed our festival?" William placed light fingers across the small of my back and heat flew to my cheeks.

"More or less." I responded with truth and honesty, but also because I wondered if a less-than-favorable response might pique his nerves even further. "The fainting and bleeding ladies have certainly been a highlight."

He laughed at that. "My apologies again. My understanding is that one poor woman lost her breath and the other ate a bad bit of meat that caused some terrifying hallucinations."

"You don't say?" Now *that* intrigued me, for it placed blame squarely on the palace, freeing Charlotte or Victoria from fault. A scowl formed on my face. Had I sabotaged my own efforts?

"What have I done now?" William sighed as we turned, separated, and drew together in yet another court dance, this one a simple but energetic piece from a northern region.

"Nothing, this time." I offered what I hoped was a reassuring glance.

"You're quite impossible, you know that?"

We continued to dance through the wafting strains of the orchestra, and only when the music had long ended and several newly-bold ladies' chaperons demanded the Prince's attentions did William bid me a good night.

Freed from his arms, I wandered the ballroom, feeling the strangeness of the dagger's leather sheath against my leg. None of the assembled guests seemed daring enough to engage the woman that Prince William had shown attention three nights in a row. But it was for the best, I thought. The fewer I spoke to, the less likely that I should stumble over my tongue and reveal my true self. Thus, I remained an outcast in a sea of admirers.

Does the Queen feel this way often? I should still love to ask her one day.

As I stood beside a pillar, off in a far corner that I might observe the guests without feeling further out of place, I felt rather than saw someone draw close.

"Congratulations," said a familiar voice.

Of course Victoria would find me here. Well, this version of me.

"For what? And good night to you as well." Even jealousy didn't excuse rudeness.

She snorted, an oddly delicate sound that reminded me of her mother. "You appear to have won Prince William's affections over everyone else. Well done."

"Thank you," I said, "but I wouldn't be so certain. There's still time yet."

"Indeed." She moved closer and I tried to step back, though I couldn't—with a wall of people only a few steps behind and a pillar to the other side, she had me closed in. "I *will* give you a tip, however."

She lowered her voice and leaned forward, as though possessing some great secret.

Something about her didn't sound as typical of Victoria. Rather, her voice was more akin to Charlotte's when I had visited her in her room. I moved to look in her eyes and indeed, they had filled to liquid black. I recalled the need to bend and reach my dagger, but the thought had barely occurred before—

"He won't have you if you're dead."

Pain tore through my side. Victoria stood aright, pleasant smile perfectly in place, looking all the more as a beautiful, innocent guest in the palace.

And she walked away, sliding into the crowd.

My vision swam and I felt like a draining pitcher. At the bottom, the pain came in waves, and while I didn't want to look, I did. The world became hazy and tilted as I moved.

I backed against the pillar to keep from falling and looked a second time. Blood stained the right side of my dress, and I pressed both hands there. Red liquid oozed from between my fingers. My head felt heavy and light at the same time, and I began to slide down the pillar as my legs refused to stand upright.

In the distance, someone screamed, and cold hands touched my forehead, my arms, and my side.

I couldn't see anything but red, everywhere, hot red that pulsed me into darkness.

A black maw opened across my vision, deep as the night, calling.

My eyelids fell.

32

The Reckoning

Bright light flashed beyond my eyes.

"Lady Aleidis."

A voice called to me, far away. I ignored it, for it penetrated the warmth and comfort of where I rested.

"Lady Aleidis, can you hear me?"

I wanted to tell them to leave me be. To go away. Couldn't a girl sleep? So, so tired. Only someone of immense cruelty would draw me from this.

"Lady Aleidis? My God, is there anyone who knows who she came with, or where she's staying? Surely we must contact her father—"

Father? No, Father is not here, I thought, *he's long gone. Perhaps I will see him, where I'm going.*

"A chaperon? Brother? Anyone?"

Brother.

My eyes opened in an instant, and I gasped at the pain that returned without warning. And then I remembered Victoria's words, the pain, the dark—

"Aleidis, I'm here."

Prince William crouched by my side, and only then did I notice that I no longer slouched against a pillar in the great ballroom. I'd been laid on a small couch in an alcove, off to the side of the guests and their revelry. A wall of palace guards blocked my view into the hall, and the guests' view of myself.

"What ... " I began, testing my voice.

"Have a care," said William, taking my hand. "You had a bit of a spell."

"No," I shook my head, wincing at the pain. "My ... another woman, she came to speak to me." I sought the place on my side where Victoria had touched and recalled Charlotte's claw-like fingernails of the night prior. Had Victoria *stabbed* me?

I remained a complete stranger to her under my illusion, and she'd stabbed me. Simply because I vied for the Prince's attentions. Regardless of Celia's assurances that she would secure the palace's offer of betrothal. Had *this* been the plan I'd heard her speak of?

I tried to sit, but William rested a hand on my side and prevented me from rising. Warmth spread through the place where the pain should have been, and I gasped at the softness of his touch as—I simply can't explain it any other way—muscle and sinew, the fibers of my flesh, knit together to make me whole once more. I felt it, piece by piece, and a pure sense of bliss enveloped my being as the pain ebbed away. I looked to William to ask what he had done, but he held a distant expression, serene and so peaceful with closed eyes that I could have lay there forever, watching.

He moved his hand away and I do swear that I caught a glimpse of an object in his palm. Gold, round—his medallion? I looked to his neck and noted its absence.

When he finally opened his eyes, before a word left my lips he stood and offered both hands to help me to my feet.

"How do you feel?"

He knew very well how I felt. "What did you do?"

"Are you well enough for a final dance?"

It seemed that tonight had been designated an evening for unanswered questions. "Your Highness, a woman ... she stabbed me in the side. I can't dance with my dress soiled as such."

He scratched his head like a curious ape. "I see nothing."

I looked down and exclaimed in surprise. My dress shone as it did before, pure and whole. No stain, no tears.

William's expression remained clear and innocent. "I'm sorry, Lady Aleidis, but you must be mistaken. You must have hit your head when falling."

"Falling!"

"Perhaps you should rest another few minutes?"

I opened my mouth to demand the truth, rage rising at lies from this unexpected source, but before the first word passed my lips, the sound of lightning cracked throughout the nearby ballroom.

I sprang to my feet as William and the guards surged forward into the open hall. He glanced back at me once, but another crack took his attention away. I'm sure he saw I stood without effort, and I cannot fault him for leaving under the circumstances.

"Stay there," he called over his shoulder.

"Not likely," I replied, though I doubted he heard.

As I followed him into the hall, screams formed in the mouths of guests and released as the candles and lamps in the ballroom extinguished as one. The air grew cold.

I knew this. I'd felt this before, even once already this night. The spirits were coming.

But *why?*

I pushed forward, through fainting ladies and piss-soaked men of lost courage, and followed the upward gazes of those who remained standing. The sight weakened my legs despite my renewed strength, for in the air above us, a gaping hole opened with cracks of lightning and ripples of thunder. Silver-lined edges pulled apart to create a chasm between floor and ceiling, sending swirls of black mist shooting through the darkness into the throngs of people below.

We stood staring, uncomprehending, at the opening form.

And then the words became clear as I recalled what the Oliroomim had said. *The last woman standing.*

God Almighty.'

This was the spirit's doing.

I touched my father's bone key safe around my neck, thinking for some way to stop this before—

I didn't finish my thought, for a monstrous sigh ripped the gaping blackness open even further and a surge of black mist poured through the center—mist that shifted, twisted, and took shape as it dove through the air toward the crowded ballroom.

Despite the lack of illumination, I saw flashes of claws and fangs, leathery wings, and bloodshot eyes. Hideous forms swooped from above toward shrieking, stunned guests, and I did nothing but watch in horror as a host of vaporous spirits swarmed a woman in green silks.

In the next instant, she floated off the ground, screaming for help, and I looked around for a soul who might be tall enough to pull her back to earth.

And then they dropped her.

Without warning and without time to break her fall, her body smashed against the floor with a sickening crack, and I fell to my knees as a redness seeped from behind her head.

My doing.

This was *my* doing ... but how?

The spirits guaranteed my success, but not through death. Never death. Had I not demanded as such?

Another woman collapsed at my side, sobbing, begging the Lord for mercy,

And had I not called on the Lord's name for this? Had I not demanded the service of spirits by his power? Of course I had—and surely the fires of hell awaited me even now, for I could deny it no longer.

I had not conjured simple spirits, nor angels, none of those creatures in the manner one thinks when supplicating the saints or the Holy Mother.

No. By my father's book, I had conjured a horde of demons.

And as if that were not enough? They no longer listened to me. They were not following my commands, of that I felt sure.

Something had gone terribly, terribly wrong.

I ran.

I am not proud, nor regretful. I ran, and I did so as quickly as I could. But I wasn't the only one, for we all swept toward the grand staircase, each of us praying—I am certain—that we not fall, nor be trampled, or worse yet taken by the demons before then.

I had to leave. If I couldn't be found, the spirits—demons—could not complete their work. Or so I hoped. Perhaps they would cease their malevolence with their conjuror absent. It did not make sense, their violence.

How could *I* have done this?

A girl to my left stumbled, but as I reached out to help her stand, a familiar face swooped down from above. *Curson.*

"*Hello, mistress,*" he said, and my limbs both froze and became quivering jelly at the same time.

However, this time, I didn't want his presence and I resented the growing craving. I needed to move, to escape. But oh, this spirit.

"Leave us," I forced in a whisper. "I didn't ask for this."

He reached out and touched the straw-colored hair of the girl who'd stumbled. She sighed, jaw growing slack as her bosom heaved.

"Leave her," I said, and fought to suppress the rising tide of unbidden jealousy and yearning.

"*My regrets, mistress.*" Curson leaned forward and placed a smoky finger on my lips. I shuddered despite myself, my whole body aching to remain, but my inner self screamed that I had to leave *now*.

A drop of salty liquid formed in the corner of my eye as I strained against the hold on my will. And as it slipped from its place, down the side of my nose, trickling toward my mouth, Curson bent to gently—ever so gently—kiss away my tear.

I could stand it no longer. I couldn't afford this delay, and neither could those who sought to escape the mission carried forth by the demon host. As it was, I needed to end it before others suffered at my expense.

With a shout to fuel my strength, I pulled with all my might against his hold on my will. I did not move. A second time, I tried to block out all thoughts of him, holding back the tide of desire as sluice gates upon a river. His neck strained as if pulling against my resistance. I couldn't allow this, not here and not now. This desire was neither pure nor welcome, and the cost too great.

I gathered my will once again, holding firm, thinking only of the pain of those around me, and loosed a second shout— louder this time, and felt the give of unseen chains. Harder then, I strained, and my limbs tore through their bonds. I plunged my hands through his smoky flesh like a knife through butter, and his eyes widened in shock. My anger grew. How *dare* he?

My fingers closed around some solid lump inside his chest, and though I fought a growing tide of revulsion, I pulled back as hard as my new-formed strength would allow, drawing the object out as mist fought against force, slippery and hard and soft and sharp and this moment formless, that moment hard as stone.

I held tight and received my reward, for from Curson's chest came a gooey, blackened mass. It writhed in my hand as small white creatures twisted about, tasting the air.

Curson looked from me to his rotting, maggot-infested heart. Fear reflected in his beautiful eyes, and yet I didn't care.

I felt glad.

I threw the heart to the floor and pressed my heel into it.

"Go back to hell," I whispered.

With a fiendish shriek, Curson's form pulled backward through the air, into the darkness above us, and through the gaping hole in our indoor sky.

And in that instant, three more demons were also sucked through, and I clutched at the key around my neck. I had not done *that*.

A flash of light in the ballroom revealed William, his father, and two other men—Peter, and perhaps Lorenz—standing with hands raised on the marble floor. The two held staffs, the King a sceptre, and William, his medallion. For an instant, I wondered if *they* had wrested control of my spell, but no ... for as I watched, a second flash of light burst forth from the King's sceptre and William's medallion, together, sending a swooping demon spinning backward—back, back, back, and up, until the gaping darkness above reclaimed its own.

William. He had worn that medallion *every time* we'd met.

He had "saved" me from the town terrors, and been there when they'd struck. Knew its patterns, behavior. That night, he'd known it had killed and would not strike again. Certainly, it was no coincidence we'd met so many times after I'd found *The Book*.

He had spoken of the King, of being beholden to a family legacy, even during the festival.

But what did it mean?

Too much, too many questions. My head throbbed with the ache of frenzied dismay, and it would not be abated until I had answers and so, unthinking, I took a step toward them—

And lost my footing on the steps, falling into the arms of a stranger who assumed I also fled the room. I shouted for release, but over the growing din of screams and cries from both people and demons, no one could hear a word—and if they did, they didn't care. The crowd dragged me up the rest of the steps, and in the moment before the onslaught of bodies pushed me out the grand doors, I saw it. Saw *them*.

On the balcony—just as she'd been the night prior, watching her daughter thrash about on the ballroom floor—stood Celia. But this time, flanked by a daughter on each side.

Celia's arms stretched forth toward the writhing black mass on the ceiling, and her mouth moved in a silent chant I could not hear. At her sides, Charlotte and Victoria. Eyes closed, mouths open with expressions of rapturous delight upon their faces.

They remained undisturbed by the spirits … no, far from it.

Lord Almighty.

Celia controlled my spirits.

Somehow, she had taken my command and twisted it, perverted it, and as she spoke, I saw her daughters point and laugh at the fleeing crowd as though directing the demons' attacks like a game at a carnival.

And as another set of stranger's arms wrapped around my middle and dragged me across the entrance plaza, toward the second staircase that led down to my waiting spirit horse, I did not resist.

The scene played over and over. William, the King, royal advisors and attendants, fighting the demon horde ... and Celia, with her daughters, controlling them.

The demons *I had called.* Who were supposed to be under my control, carrying out *my* demands.

I would not ride my spirit horse tonight.

I wanted nothing more to do with spirits.

From afar, I spotted Liesl in the crowd, limping, with bloodied cheeks. Her poor brother cradled his hand, and when I stopped to call her name—which reveals more about my own imprudence than all else—someone in the surging crowd slammed into my back and threw me forward, sending me tumbling down the steps. I drew in my arms and rolled, step after step, unknowingly kicked and stepped on by others as they too tried to escape.

I didn't blame them. In fact, I didn't hurry to stand. I deserved it.

I had done this and I needed the pain ... for what had I now but Edward and some small semblance of freedom? Surely someone would soon discover what I had set in motion. Perhaps William, and the King, already knew. Perhaps that is why he'd pretended at being my friend ... and alluded to more.

Oh, Lord.

I could do no more. I had to flee the kingdom.

And while I welcomed death as punishment for my actions, I couldn't allow Edward to suffer for it too.

We would leave tonight.

33

The Cost

Home.

As always, to Edward's room.

I flung open the door, calling his name, fumbling with my dirtied, golden skirts, desperate to tear them off and make our way free of—

I froze in the doorway. Edward was motionless.

Breath held, I crept to his bedside, praying he had only fallen into a deep sleep, but the fear ... believe me when I say I have never felt so afraid.

Even at his side, I saw that he didn't move. His small chest didn't rise or fall, and so in disbelief I lay my head upon his chest to listen.

I did weep then, for his heart still beat, and yet ... and yet he barely breathed at all. His skin, cold as a storm in the dead of winter. His fingers, stiff and blue. But he *lived.*

I couldn't stem the flow of tears, for now I saw the way things were. Our lives ended here. I couldn't move Edward in this state, nor did I have the strength left to do so even if I had wanted to. More so, I doubted very much that *The Book of Conjuring* contained any remedy for illness. Cursing and making others ill, certainly, but healing fell beyond the book's ability and mine.

I knew this. I had already searched the book in vain.

"Edward?" I whispered and gently shook his arm. "Edward, wake up. Please. You have to wake up."

But he did not.

How long I sat at his side, listening for the rise and fall of his breath, I cannot say. But I admit, I wept until I was certain the wells were dry, and then I wept still more. How fair was a God who'd allowed such an innocent to suffer? Who'd brought such calamity on my family? Surely, we didn't deserve this. If anyone should be punished, it should be me alone.

Edward, only a child, to be taken in his earliest years—did purity of the soul count for nothing? Did all my cries for mercy go unheeded?

I had seen this all before. It was only a matter of time before Edward left me, too. Everyone else had.

Perhaps he would see Mother, where he went. Perhaps he would be happier there, in her arms. Or perhaps she could petition the Almighty on behalf of her son.

A thought struck me—surely being in the presence of God would allow her this one request, if the saints didn't already kiss her feet and seek her comfort. I had to speak to her one final time and beg that she do this one thing for me, since no one else listened.

And she *would* speak to me. I had seen her face, when last I'd visited her stone ... had I not? It could not have been a dream. I *had not* imagined it. I had to believe it. I had to try.

Though I felt loath to leave my brother for even the blink of an eye, I saw no other way. I tore off my skirts and stuffed them once again in Edward's closet, kissed his too-cold cheeks, and left through the passages—ensuring his doorway remained blocked and closed to Celia, should she or the others return—and plunged into the crisp night air.

I only hoped that I returned to collect Edward long before their arrival home, if indeed they bothered to come back at all.

Once more in my undergarments, I tore through the town, caring not for decorum and no longer in fear of assault by terrors. It was even easier to ignore the stares of the few who undoubtedly peered from behind closed curtains, perhaps wondering at the influx of citizens returning from the palace at utmost speed, with wild fright in their eyes.

Past the Church of the Holy Paraclete and its spires I ran, through the gate—closed, but unlocked—and into the field of stones. I left the gate open and stomped through the field, welcoming the stabs of thorns as devil's weed pierced my toes, digging into soft flesh.

"Mother." I stopped in front of her stone and raised my face heavenward. "Mother!"

Silence.

I waited, breathing in hazel and lavender. Believing she would appear. I *would* see her again. Why had I not thought to call on her so many months before?

I called again.

And waited.

And called once more.

With no reply, I leaned against the stone, sliding my back across its weathered surface.

I couldn't leave until I had received some kind of sign, some assurance that Edward would live. For if he did not? Neither would I.

I called and waited and called again, praying and begging and bargaining with every possible thing. My life for his. My soul for his. All earthly things, if only Mother would speak to me but once.

My lids grew heavy as the night wore on, and my heart began

to fray with the loss of hope. Surely, Celia and her daughters had returned to the house by now. Found Edward. Relieved him from his earthly body.

Doubtless my time, too, was nearly through.

I felt sure of it.

And just when I had given up all faith—when I knew, beyond all doubt, that my mother couldn't hear me and I had only imagined her presence those times before—the world shifted.

The cool damp of the night air changed. A warmth spread through my fingertips as the earth around me began to glow with a white, radiant light that I had seen once before this evening. The scent of hazelnut and lavender grew thick and strong until the air became like a thick fog that overwhelmed the senses.

I scrambled from the place where I sat and stood before the stone, watching. Waiting. I reached to the bone key for reassurance and comfort, and shock ripped through my belly as I touched an empty space. The key was gone, the ribbon no longer fastened about my neck.

I dropped to my knees and searched the ground where I'd sat, where I'd walked, the place by the gate—

"Ella."

A gentle hand reached toward my cheek, robed in a white glow that radiated peace. Calm. Trust.

And hope.

I rocked back onto my heels and stared at the vision before me. "Mother?"

She looked as beautiful as I remembered, and even more so. Flowing chestnut hair and skin as smooth and pale as cream, and the whole of her enveloped in a light that proved her glory.

Her hand moved away from my face and I cried out at the pain of loss.

She smiled and clasped both palms together, eyes sad and yet ... not. I couldn't place it, but it seemed as if she felt ... content. But that couldn't be true, for how could she *ever* be content without *us*?

"Mother, is that really you?"

She nodded, and her expression turned grave. "Ella, you must listen."

"No, please," I cried, "I have an urgent request. Edward is deathly ill."

"I know," she sighed, and my heart cracked. "That's why I'm here."

"Then you know I need your help. *We* need it."

"On the contrary. You must help yourself."

I heard the words, but they didn't make sense. Could she not hear my urgency? My desperation? "Mother, Edward is dying. I believe he has the same illness that claimed you, and with Father gone, I don't know what to do."

My voice cracked and shook, and I yearned to run into her arms and remain unto eternity. But she hadn't opened them, and I feared to test her patience. I had miracle enough that she stood before me.

She bowed her head for a moment before lifting her eyes to mine. "I know, Ella. I know. But there is something you must understand first. I cannot help you. Not even if I wanted to, and my words will have no sway."

The crack in my heart split in two and I sank into the earth, down and down, at the sound of her words.

"Ask Father," I pleaded, "if he's there with you. He'll understand."

"He's not here."

"Mother, please." Why did she deny me? Why refuse one request? This couldn't be my mother, no, my mother was gentle and loving and strong—

"Ella, *you* are the only one who can save him."

And now she mocked me. "He's going to die, Mother. At any moment. He may be gone now, for all I am aware."

"He lives, dear heart. I would know otherwise. He lives."

I swallowed hard, wincing at the ache of a dry throat. "Please, I beg you. Ask on Edward's behalf, beseech the throne of heaven to save him. Just this once."

Mother's eyes filled with tears, and yet they didn't fall. I wondered if, in truth, there would be no more crying in heaven. I wondered if I might ever see the radiance of her spirit from the other side, and if we would weep without our tears falling at the waste of life in this moment.

"Ella, I can't, and I didn't come to break you to pieces. I came to warn you, dear child, and though I may pay dearly for it, I cannot watch—"

"Pay?" I sat further upright. "What do you mean, pay? There can be no price worth your soul, Mother." And it came to me, then. "Your sacrifice. I found a letter, sent from you to Father during your illness ... it spoke of sacrifice. What did it mean?"

She shook her head, and in her eyes I saw the many things she could not tell me. Still, in death, protecting her children. Perhaps she spoke truth to me after all.

"I had hoped it would not come to this, daughter. I had hoped you might escape your father's calling."

Ah, yes. This, I understood, and my anger began to rise from deep within. "Gretel knew, and she paid for it with her life. Miss Mary, too, and the others. If only you had told me yourself, given me this one means of protection, I might have saved them before—"

"There is a reason we did not tell you, Ella. You must believe me. You must understand the meaning of this sacrifice."

"I cannot understand if I am not told."

None of this made sense. I felt as though I'd been stuck in a horrible nightmare since the moment of her passing, and thus I told her so. Still, she smiled her sad smile and spoke.

"That book is more powerful than you realize. *You* are more powerful than you realize, daughter."

I had no doubts about the book. But myself? That power had not shown itself to be as beneficial as I had hoped upon first discovery. It had been twisted, taken away from me this night without my knowing until it had been too late.

"For every action, there is a consequence. Do you understand this?"

"Yes," I said, for I did. "When one throws a stone in a still pond, the waters move outward from where it strikes. When one is cut, he will bleed. These are consequences."

She nodded in affirmation. "Yes. Your father taught you well."

"You helped," I reminded her.

"I did. But no matter. Just as a stone strikes the water and creates ripples, so does speaking the words of the book—and calling for assistance from the world of the dead—cause ripples in the world of the living. Herein is the moment of sacrifice."

Oh, no. These were things I didn't want to hear. These were not wonderful things to remind me of my mother's love, or even words that might affirm I had done the right thing by coming here. I thought I could bear no more, but truly, I knew little of myself then as compared to now.

"Mother, I can't. Please, no more."

"You, Ella, must listen."

I squeezed my eyes shut as if this would make her words disappear, but couldn't keep them closed. Not while she stood in front of me as light and spirit.

"The consequence for conjuring forth spirits of the dead is far greater than you ever imagined. I know this. Your father knew this.

And now, you must know before it's too late to save him. It is imperative that you be given the choice."

Now she spoke nonsense. "Father knew what? Save who? Is Father in danger?"

My mother, in all her awe-inspiring glory, regarded me with a deluge of pity. "Necromancy—for that is what it is—draws on the life of the living, dearest daughter."

I could not breathe.

"For every conjuring of the dead to life, someone living must give up a portion of *their* life in return."

No. I wouldn't hear it. I refused. I covered my ears with my hands, but still I heard myself ask, "*Whose* life?"

"Oh, child." She slipped down to rest on her knees, and I worried that her purity might be marred by the dirt-packed ground. But she cared nothing for it, and held my gaze so firm I couldn't break away. "The price, dearest Ella—the consequence, the sacrifice—is the life of the one most loved."

"No."

"Yes, my love. That is the cost. And that is why it is both dangerous and powerful, for the most loved by the one who calls on these darkest powers must pay that terrible price."

An alarming, sickening, unbelievable truth crept into the base of my skull. It sneaked and crawled as I held my blessed, celestial mother's gaze and recalled once again, with utter revulsion, that I had seen Edward's illness before.

"Mother?" My voice trembled and shook.

"Yes, Ella. But I knew the cost, and so did your father."

"No." A tremor ran through my body, head to toe. "The letter ... but I would never hurt Edward, and Father would never—"

"Listen to me." Her voice became stern and terrible. "A great evil was loosed in this world, and no one but your father could stop it. We knew the cost and I paid it willingly on his behalf."

I rose and backed away from her form, swaying with unsteady gait as she confirmed the words of her letter, and of Gretel's hints toward understanding, made far clearer now. But it couldn't be true. "I don't believe that. *Nothing* is worth that. Father wouldn't ... and *I* wouldn't ... "

She stood and reached to grab my shoulders, but the instant we touched, my skin burned like fire and she cried out in pain. I pushed forward to help, but she backed away, clutching her hands to her chest.

I stepped back and she dropped her arms, revealing black scabs that formed over raw, luminescent flesh in the very places she'd touched my skin.

She *couldn't* touch me. That purity couldn't be a part of me. She stood cleansed, whole, and I, already damned, for I had called forth hosts of demons and paid a wretched price.

"Nothing is worth this," I whispered, as the weight of my actions fell heavy on my shoulders. "What have I done?"

Mother's form shook as she covered her face with both hands. When she pulled them away, I saw nothing but strength. Forgiveness. Understanding.

And perhaps worst of all, for it terrified me even more: affirmation.

"You, too, are fighting a great evil. But I promise you, your father never intended for you to be a part of this."

Then he should not have left me alone with that woman. "He left. He left us, alone, with *her* and her spawn. Why not take us with him?"

"To protect you, daughter. So that you might be safe."

Anger rose once again as her words drew an ugly portrait of yet another unbidden truth. "We weren't, though. And he didn't protect us at all, nor you if all is as you say. He failed. You gave your life and he failed. You died for *nothing!*"

"No, Ella, listen." Her voice grew stern and her words, fervent. "Your father loves you, but now you must be strong for him. And for Edward. Evil still crawls through your world on fleshly limbs, and your father's fight isn't over."

"Nor mine, it seems." I thought I began to understand. "But if I act, Edward will die. Unlike you, he hasn't had a choice. How is that fair? I can't, Mother, for his death will be on my hands and I *cannot* lose him."

"I'm so sorry, child." She drew up to full height, the blaze of her being setting the field of stones aglow with white light. "Beyond this, I can't help you. My time is done. I came but to warn you and let you know, one last time—"

She couldn't leave now, not yet. Not before I had answers, for what could I do that might not jeopardize Edward's very life? "You can't go, I need you still. Mother, tell me what to do! I have nothing, no one here to speak for me, and I'm afraid."

"—I love you."

And despite my pleas, my screams, my grasping at air, and all cries and supplication to the saints and angels, she vanished. One moment she stood before me, the next, gone. The ache of loneliness returned, and I remained unmoving as the clarity of her memory faded with each passing moment.

I no longer knew how to save my family, for what could I do that would not cause further harm?

She had left me with one terrible, agonizing truth.

I, for all I thought I did to protect him, had been killing my brother instead.

34

The Announcement

I must have fallen asleep after that, for I woke in the early morning hours with a crick in my neck and scratched elbows from lying against the stone in place of a bed.

Memories of the night before returned in a flood, and though I had wept all my tears for Edward, for Father, for Mother, and for myself, it didn't stop the fresh rivers that fell as I pushed from the stone to stand upright. I would do no good sitting here while my brother still suffered. I would return to him and carry forth my plan—to leave and never return. I would find a way.

I couldn't fight this evil, even if I wanted to, for to do so meant that Edward would die. My brother's life for the sake of the world? I was not yet ready to make that sacrifice.

Not *yet*.

I was not as strong as Father.

I walked home with speed and determination, though not before stopping to call at the doctor's house. I woke his door maid, for she answered with sleep in her eyes and surprise on her face, though my questionable garb may have contributed to the latter.

"Tell the good Sir Doctor that Ellison and Edward require his presence immediately, please."

The door maid blinked and wiped sleep from her eyes. "The hour, miss—"

"Matters not one whit. Go and tell the doctor, and I assure you, he will be grateful for the disturbance. Tell him that Edward requires immediate care, and that I have requested a transfer from our home to a more suitable location as quickly as possible."

"I'll retrieve him momentarily," the maid said, yawning.

But I couldn't wait around for him. "Tell him I had pressing matters to attend to, but that I will assure his arrival isn't interrupted." I would do so even if it meant fighting Celia with physical force. Not that I had another option. "He should come to the house the instant he rises. Do you understand? He cannot wait."

I felt certain he would arrive in due time.

I would have the doctor move Edward from the room while I gathered what we needed, and perhaps with his help, we could make our escape in safety. Far, far away from our own terrors, keys of bone, and memories of the breaking of our family.

But as I raced down the path to our home and slipped into Edward's room from the passageway entrance, I stopped short and nearly perished from shock.

The door to Edward's room stood ajar, and Celia rested at the edge of his bed, cradling my brother in her arms as though she'd birthed him from her own flesh.

He looked paler still than when I'd left him, though perhaps that was my own dread projected upon his limp form in her arms. As I moved forward, seized by a mad boldness, she looked me firm in the eyes and grinned a wicked grin of ivory teeth and wine-dark lips.

"A most unfortunate situation," she said, drawing a slender finger down the side of my sleeping brother's face. "It appears that you continue to disobey my orders and left the house at night. What depravity have you indulged in this time? You missed quite the excitement at the palace."

When I didn't respond, she took up one of Edward's hands and drew it to her lips. "Poor child."

"Put him down," I said, hoping she did not hear the tremor in my voice or see the shaking of my limbs. "He's unwell and needs rest. It isn't wise to move him about in this state."

"Oh, I'm sure it isn't." And to my complete bewilderment, she did just what I asked. She placed him back on the bed and covered him with his blanket, folding it back just so. "Now tell me, girl—where is your father?"

I coughed in disbelief. "My father? You think *I* know where my father is?"

She looked from Edward to me and toward the passage entrance.

Could she see it?

"I have reason to believe he is nearby."

Lord Almighty, did she *know?*

"It is imperative that you tell me the instant you hear from him, do you understand?"

I nodded, if only because she rose from the bed and it appeared as though she would leave the room if I simply agreed to her demands.

But my tongue doesn't always do as my mind tells it. "What if I refuse?"

In the beat of a bird's wings, she opened Edward's window and looked out. "It's quite the fall for a young child at this height. It would be most unfortunate if he were to trip while wandering about."

I didn't doubt she would do it. Indeed, that she had not already snuffed out his life was surprise enough. But no—she needed us to catch Father in her trap. I swallowed all pride and objection and relented for the sake of my brother. "I'll tell you. I promise. But he isn't here. Why would you think such a thing?"

She gazed at me as though my head had been filled with air. "Certain … events have led me to believe … " She blinked and tutted like a school matron. "It's not your concern, girl, only that you *will* tell me if you receive any knowledge of his presence or whereabouts. I miss my husband."

I'm sure she missed having a witless peon even more. But I agreed and she smiled the satisfied smile of a cat with a mouse between its claws. I loosed the breath I held as she moved to leave the room—but in that final instant, she turned and regarded me with a wryness that churned my stomach.

"Ah, one more thing. If you finish your tasks today, I may allow you to return to your room."

My room? Whatever did she mean? I'm certain the confusion showed on my face, for she sighed and continued.

"My daughter is getting married, you stupid twit. Do you recall nothing?"

"Married!" I blurted without thinking.

She scowled, the expression marring her exquisite composure. "To Prince William. This evening, in the palace chapel."

"So soon." My mind raced to make sense of it. Victoria? Marrying William after all?

But how?

"It's natural that such an important union be confirmed as quickly as possible. Charlotte and I are having our dresses made today in town, so we won't be needing your assistance."

My chest grew tight and Celia's words faded in my ears, replaced by Oliroomim's childlike voice: *The Prince will consent to marry the last woman standing when the clock strikes midnight and brings forth a new day.*

I'd fled the ball thinking to remove myself and thereby cancel the spell, despite what I had seen, despite what I knew. Once put into motion, it could not be revoked. I had tried to find a loophole, and I'd failed.

I should have realized. Since Charlotte and Victoria were some kind of unearthly creature themselves, of course the demons could not hurt them. For all I knew, my stepsisters shared in their likeness.

And so by my actions, Victoria had remained for William's affections, and undoubtedly Celia had used her influence and powers of persuasion on the King's son.

On the one I loved.

My heart seized at the thought. I did love him, after all.

He couldn't marry Victoria, not today, not ever. Let him choose another woman, let him choose a princess from the most foreign land, but not *her*. Not my stepsister.

"Bid her my congratulations," I offered, for I could think of no other words to say. "And many happy returns on the day."

And with that, Celia swept from the room, leaving me with a broken heart, a life nearly gone, and but one choice to make … how would I stop the wedding without use of *The Book*?

I took the passages down to my father's study, trying to recall if I had seen something—anything—on his shelves that might offer a hint of protection, or perhaps a force of destruction that wouldn't harm any but the one intended. Or, if need be, the intended and myself.

However, when I entered the study, I took no more than

three steps before being stopped by the disastrous sight before me. No longer was the room the pristine, orderly sanctum my father had treasured. No, someone had seen to that, and left no corner undefiled by their touch.

Books and papers lay strewn about the room, collected in haphazard piles as though the one who'd taken them from their places had searched through each and every page before tossing them aside in a furious rage.

And not only were his precious books forever destroyed, but all his trinkets and treasures from his many travels, far and wide … smashed upon the ground, thrown across the room, or simply dumped from their resting places onto the floor. Whoever had done this must have been looking for something, and I began to suspect I knew both who and what. And with Father's implements in my possession, I had beaten her to it.

Celia wanted to know if Father had contacted me. She needed us. She knew something of Father's work, that much was clear—work that I now realize fell easily under the guise of a merchant's dealings and travels—and she likely believed *he* had called the spirits.

She thought he had returned and fallen out from under her spell.

I smiled, despite the direness of all that had befallen us, for in that instant I thought of a plan. A poor, untested, and dangerous plan to be sure, but a plan nonetheless and one which relied on my task-birthed strength. With a plan came hope.

Leaving the disaster, I retrieved the dagger I'd found in the study and strapped it to the inside of my wrist. Then I dressed in a pale, rose-colored gown—*my* dress, from *my* wardrobe—and took a cloth sack from the kitchen. In the sack, I placed three things: *The Book of Conjuring*, my father's leather satchel, and my bundle of the

Prince's belongings, both coat and ring.

Then, with much quiet and care that I might not disturb Celia's own preparations for the wedding, I crept to the stable and saddled a horse. I would *not* ride a spirit horse today, not when our own were available and while Edward's life lay forfeit. I also cannot deny that I hoped a lack of a second horse might cause some delay in Celia's leaving, for our carriage required two to easily pull its weight.

I rode to the palace, perhaps unthinking in exactly what I intended, but I couldn't sit by and sweep ash from the hearth while William fell under the same spell as that which trapped my father. To that end, I would sweep ash no more after this day—not for Celia, and not for myself.

In a way, I felt grateful for the loss of the bone key. No risk for temptation, and no longer had I to worry about demons and spirits and my own eternal soul. I resolved, from this day forward, to win the battle through my own strength.

So I rode and rode, and in a grove of trees before reaching the palace, I hid my horse and my bundle. On foot, I did exactly what William had instructed me to do—I followed the path around the stables until I came to a large oak door, the service entrance to the kitchens.

Guards stood on either side of the door, which must be a sorry post for a palace guard. What would one have to do to be relegated to such a dull position? Yet, seeing them there bolstered my resolve. If a king would see to the safety of those who worked in even the humblest places, how could I allow his son to come to harm when I might have the strength to prevent it?

"I've come for a service post," I told the guards, who stared straight ahead as though I didn't exist. "I've heard there's need."

They said nothing, but one knocked on the door with such force I feared it might fall off its hinges. Moments later, the door opened to reveal a kindly-looking woman with apple cheeks and crinkles around her eyes.

"Eh?" She peered at the guards, and then noticed me. "Who are you?"

I curtsied for the sake of respect, and wondered for a moment if I should have worn my tattered shift after all. The rose-colored dress would stain easily, and I would have no opportunity to change my clothes.

"I'm here about a service post," I repeated, "as I heard a rumor the kitchens have need."

Without another word, she waved me inside, pointed at a nearby stool, and thrust a paring knife and a potato in my hands. "Go on then," she said, and wandered away.

Bewildered, I peeled the potato. What else could I do? At least it afforded me the opportunity to survey the room, where at least twenty other women both old and young worked on one task or another. The kitchen wasn't as large as I'd expected, but there appeared to be no wanting for space regardless.

Still, the ladies stayed a distance away from me, taking long routes around rather than walk across my aisle. I wish I could have reassured them somehow, but I imagine they saw me as an intruder, come to take their wages when I could already afford a dress lovelier than their finest piece. I don't know that for a fact, of course, and from William's comment to me I am certain the palace workers are paid well for their positions, but I looked suitably ridiculous seated among the vegetables and I didn't blame them for their whispers and stares.

After some time, a girl of about twelve made her way across the room toward me, onions piled high in her arms. "Fancy dress you got there."

She dropped the onions on the counter next to me, and pulled a long knife from her soiled apron. Her limbs were thick and her face full, and her cadence reminded me of Gretel.

Oh, Gretel. Would that I could have saved you from such a monstrous fate.

"Yes," I said to the girl, feeling perhaps a bit too light-hearted for the occasion. "I stole it back from someone who'd stolen it from me."

The girl snorted. "What, you a thief?"

"Not exactly. It's more like the one who took it from me was the thief, and I simply returned it to its rightful owner."

The girl nodded as though she understood completely. "An' so when I take this potato home in my pocket t'feed me sisters, it ain't stealin' either 'cause them royals already stole me money in taxes!"

Although I doubted very much a young girl like her had yet paid a cent of tax, several women nearby erupted in laughter, and with it the mood lightened. Finally, I felt I could ask what I'd come here to learn.

"Is it true, then, that the Prince is to be married this evening?"

I held my breath.

The woman who had allowed me into the kitchen and given me the paring knife slapped my shoulder. "If he weren't, you'd still be outside the door. We have need of many hands today to prepare for the wedding feast, and the more help the better, no questions asked. I'll pay you a fair wage for the day, don't you worry."

I hadn't considered wages, but at least it would give me a paltry sum to present to the doctor as a lean against his care for Edward. "They certainly didn't give you much time to prepare."

"No, but it ain't just the wedding that's bringing a hurry." She scooped up a handful of flour and tossed it into a wooden bowl. "I heard there's more to it."

"I told ya that," said the younger girl. "They be settin' a trap to stop them terrors for good."

My focus snapped away from the potato. "What? Stop the terrors? How?"

The girl threw an onion peel in my direction, though it floated rather than flew through the air and landed only a step from where she'd tossed it. "They find some kinda demon-bringin' stone after everybody ran away. They gonna catch him tonight."

My heart beat faster in my chest. "Catch who? What kind of stone?"

Rolling her eyes at me, the girl learned from her mistake and tossed a whole slice of onion that landed on the hem of my dress.

"Watch yourself, we need all we have," someone scolded.

"Aww, shove it!" said the girl. "Why you so curious? Fancy ladies ain't supposed to care about them things. It's that one who caused the terrors they're gonna catch."

"But who?"

She shrugged. "I ain't seen him. But they're sure convinced he'll be at the wedding, after what happened last night."

I leaned forward too far on my stool, and it wobbled. "How do you know this? Who told you?"

She snorted again and tapped the side of her dirt-encrusted forehead. "People talk around me. Don't think I'm not listening."

I laughed at that, for recently I had come to know what it meant to be taken for weak and slow.

"An' what's more," she added, "the messenger boy, he likes me, so I give him tarts for kisses."

My employer sighed and tossed a grimy cheese cloth at the girl. "Ain't that the truth."

"I ain't finished, y'old hag."

The two smiled at each other, and the tenderness which they shared brought back to mind the vision of my mother. My throat closed and I swallowed hard, bidding the memory to leave me be.

I couldn't be distracted in this moment, for a suspicion nagged at my thoughts. What else could they have found but the lost bone key? Of course, it could do no more good than to open *The Book*, but they didn't know that.

And I no longer needed it, so it meant time wasted to think on it further. I had other, more pressing matters to ponder.

"Please, go ahead," I told the girl.

"I said, the messenger boy, he said he delivered a message t'day, straight from the border—"

"The border! That's a long way off," I mumbled, for I was more distracted by the thought of how I might slip into the chapel unnoticed … and how I might end this day's kitchen tasks without a gown so stained I'd be thrown out in an instant.

"—saw the man they suspected fer them terrors all along," she said as I glanced up, slipping out of thought.

My little paring knife froze against the potato's skin. "Excuse me, what do you mean? Did you say something about a *man?*"

"Yep." She grinned like a mouse with a piece of cheese. "They say he be headin' back to town, and they gonna trap him good at the wedding."

The knife and potato fell from my hands.

I knew who that man was, and I didn't doubt it for an instant. If they had found the bone key and suspected someone, who else could it be? Who else might return from far off and be suspected, if not someone under suspicion already? Someone who, perhaps, might have had to leave town to protect his family.

The man who returned, who they plotted to trap, was my father.

35

The Wedding

I finished out my tasks in the kitchen, for the work came easily to me now and I had offered my services for the day. It would have been an injustice to leave them shorthanded after their generosity in allowing me there. Truly, I admired those women who worked their fingers to the bone and would never see the inside of a fancy ballroom or receive an invitation to a royal wedding—but who still seemed content and proud of their hard work, all the same.

Of course, I didn't have an invitation to a royal wedding either, and so while in the kitchens I had bided my time in hoping for some revelation of how I might enter the palace chapel without being turned away or worse, arrested.

What I needed was the bold Aleidis of the nights prior. Surely *she* wouldn't be denied entrance, but that would require use of *The Book*, which I could not use without the key. Nor would I, even if I had it.

But neither lack of invitation nor unkempt appearance would keep me from entering the chapel to stop the wedding, not while so many lives rested in the balance. I had no doubt that the palace's instructions were to strike down Father on sight, and who could blame them? They believed him responsible for not only disrupting last night's festival celebrations, but for the terrors rumoured across the kingdom. How they could believe him responsible when he rode from afar to return to the kingdom this day was beyond my ken, but I doubted those in the palace knew much of the workings of spirits and conjuring. For all they knew, a conjuror could call up evil from across the seas. I couldn't fault them for this, for even I had little understanding the truth of what I did until confirmed by the words of a letter and the assurances of a ghost.

So if my suspicions proved correct, I decided, I would give myself in his place. I deserved the consequence. I couldn't go unpunished for what I'd done.

The kitchen staff, full of curiosity and gossip, believed me a lovesick girl who wished to simply sneak into the chapel and gaze adoringly upon the Prince and his blushing bride … though I doubted Victoria had ever blushed in her life.

Before I left, they helped to wash beneath my fingernails, pinch my cheeks, and clean the spots of grime from the simple but elegant gown I wore. I didn't look perfect, but it would have to do.

As the sun slipped from its path across the sky and sank toward its resting place, I left the kitchens with kisses and embraces and a promise to return—though I suspect they appreciated an extra set of hands, more than anything—and made my way across the palace grounds.

No one stopped me, for I walked as my father had taught a lady of the noble class to walk: head high, shoulders set, and striding with purpose. First, I made my way back to the horse and retrieved William's coat and ring. The ring I placed safely in my bosom—where it would be most secure—and the coat, I folded and held in my arms.

The palace chapel sat across the grounds from the kitchens, adjacent to the main building where I had ascended the steps for three nights prior. It rivalled the size of the Church of the Holy Paraclete, and I had often wondered whether the King's donation to that other spired church sprung from a guilt that he might have caused God to choose only one place to inhabit on the Holy days. But then, I knew very little about theology or things of that sort, aside from the rather common tendency for kings to spend taxes where spending was perhaps undue.

This palace chapel, to compare, had only one spire, though it reached taller and higher to heaven than I think necessary. Truly, I can't say why they call it a chapel at all, but who am I to question the King and his wishes? The windows and doors and ornate decorations were all gilded, and in every window, a glass-pieced image of this saint or that.

As for the outer walls of the chapel, they appeared nothing short of magnificent from near or afar. The whole of the building stood as purest white, like clouds in a clear, blue sky. The steps, inexplicably marble. I noted that once again, there were no rails to hold to for steadiness, though these steps were fewer and more easily traversed than those that had led to the palace balls.

Guest upon guest arrived at the chapel, and though I wondered if it might fill to the brim before the bride took her first step across the threshold, the greater marvel remained in the sheer number of men and women who braved another royal event.

Regardless of whether they attended out of curiosity, perceived obligation, or need, their fine attire—only mildly less elaborate than what most guests had worn to the balls—could not disguise the strained smiles and consternation on many faces.

At the sight, doubt did its best to worm its way into my skull, demanding that I turn from my folly, that I give up, that my plan was no plan at all and that I could not carry it through.

Doubt made an excellent point. But what other choice did I have? I silenced these doubts and steeled my resolve, for I had to believe that by now, the doctor had arrived, taken Edward to safety, and cared for him.

I touched the empty place around my neck and looked back toward where book and horse stayed hidden. I made another check of the ring's safety and held William's coat tighter in my arms. I had but one chance to gain entrance, and I could make no mistakes. With steady breaths, I drew myself up and strode with purpose toward the chapel's wide, gilded doors.

Within seconds, I regretted the attempt, for my plan was as flimsy as it was impetuous. Still, I couldn't turn back, for the guards at the door had undoubtedly seen me and would wonder at the sight of a girl turning and fleeing across the palace grounds.

No, I had to press on, and so I walked up the steps without so much as a sidelong glance from the guards. The moment my foot hit the threshold, a blue-coated gentleman with a funny low-crowned, tricorn hat appeared as if from nowhere. I felt mild disappointment that he wasn't the same man who'd come to our—*my*—home with the festival announcement, but perhaps that was for the best. Undoubtedly he would have recognized me.

He cleared his throat. "Miss? Do you have your invitation?"

I very much doubted that formal, written invitations had been presented to anyone on such short notice.

"Oh, I'm not a guest," I said, rolling my eyes skyward in hopes to encourage his thinking that, of course, I belonged there. "I'm returning His Highness's traveling coat." I held the bundle aloft, that he might check the crest. "I was informed that His Highness might appreciate his favourite coat to wear after the formal ceremonies. For comfort's sake, before the feast, you understand."

He didn't. "Who told you to bring it here? Why isn't a page presenting it? Or bringing it in with the other—"

"I'm to put it in his dressing room, sir, before His Highness arrives at the chapel. Simply to ensure it's there if he needs it."

The gentleman shook his head. "No, no, no. That's not right. I can't let you in this way, there are guests here and they can't see you. Come away from the door. Better yet, I'll take it."

He lunged for the coat, but I had the advantage of remaining calm, while the poor man had clearly been flustered by such a sudden and unexpected event.

"And leave your post? I very much doubt *that's* a wise idea."

"You can't go in."

"Then I'll be sure to tell His Highness's page exactly who it is that denied the King's son a bit of comfort on this, a most tiring and stressful day—"

"All right!" The man threw his hands in the air, looked over his shoulder, and pointed to the side of the chapel. "Go around to the back and find the far door. Knock three times and tell them what you told me. His Highness and His Majesty are due to arrive at any moment, so you'll need to hurry."

"Thank you, kind sir." I curtsied and sped to the rear entrance, for I couldn't allow the King or William to see me yet. Should William recognize me as Ella before Victoria made her appearance, my efforts might be foiled. The entire task would have been made much easier, I thought, if I had use of Curson to hide myself and my doings. But of course I couldn't call him. I had no knowledge of what my actions the previous night had done to his spirit form in this world … and yet the thought and memory of his presence made the very tips of my fingers tingle and my stomach—

"Mistress … "

I could have sworn the earth shook. That voice, like the voice on the night I'd opened *The Book of Conjuring* for the very first time.

I couldn't have heard it, but oh, my body thought otherwise.

"Command me, mistress … "

"No!" I shouted despite myself and spun around, heart pounding, only to find a wisp of black smoke that dispersed on the evening's breeze.

I had dreamed it. Imagined the voice and the feeling, for there was no way that could be possible. No book, no key. Call one forth by will?

That should not be possible.

But if the spirits should be bound to me, somehow … oh, how my soul ached at the thought, for even an instant of death touching life could mean Edward's last breath.

Do not think about spirits.

I knocked on the door, though I must say, it is a rather difficult thing *not* to think about something once you know that you are not supposed to, under any circumstances, think about it.

The doorman who answered allowed me inside the chapel without delay, as I suspect he worried that the royal family might arrive at any moment and find tasks left undone. I slipped inside and made haste toward the room identified as William's, though upon arrival, I checked to ensure no one watched and instead continued along the hall toward the sanctuary.

The sanctuary was filled with guests buzzing with quiet fervor amongst themselves concerning this thing or that. Like bees to honey are the privileged to the affairs of the rich and powerful—regardless, it seems, of the possible threat to one's person. Do they perhaps hope that some measure of that power will be given unto themselves? I wouldn't have wished to be one of them, even if I were not standing in the shadows with a dagger up my sleeve. My preference swung to a book, a warm fire, a chair, and a friend to share them with.

Despite their presence in a holy place, even the gilded crosses, pews, draperies, and altar were not enough to reveal an out-of-place young woman with a bundle in her arms. I slunk among the crowd, invisible to distracted guests who bickered over seating arrangements and Lord knows what else. As each person finally settled into place, I slipped into the final pew at the edge of the row, nearest a corner shadowed by the balcony above.

Here I waited, biding my time until the bride and groom's arrival.

Soon enough, the whole of the assembly rose to its feet with gasps and murmurs and reverent groans.

The King, the Queen, and their son walked the aisle of the chapel. I strained to catch a glimpse of William's face, but too many bodies stood firmly in my way. They reached the front of the sanctuary and took their places, with the King's chosen priest standing in center to conduct the wedding mass.

And as William turned to face the crowd, garbed in white and gold with a purple robe of the kingly line, I saw it. I had expected to see it, and yet, I felt the surprise of truth all the same. Yes, I loved him, in the way a woman begins to love a man—slowly, hesitantly, and piece by piece. And he? Despite his own will, he believed he loved another.

We remained standing though my legs grew weak, for *she* had arrived.

The bride. My stepsister.

She entered escorted by Celia, who stared with eyes forward, focused on the men who stood at the sacred altar. Her arm, she kept rigid and stiff, with Victoria's hand touching only her forearm with a gloved hand.

Victoria's gown, however, stole the attentions of everyone in the room. Ivory and blue with pearl accent, layers upon layers of the most luxurious material, reaching to the floor and split down the center to reveal a rich, deep blue velvet brocade underneath. Her bosom spilled forth from the top of the corseted bodice, and doubtless every lady with a man on her arm gave a swift elbow to the middle if she saw his attention stray. I noticed at least several gentlemen clutching their sides as the bride passed.

I could never have imagined such an elaborate gown for someone whose betrothal had occurred only the night before, and I suspected Celia had planned this for some time without sharing the knowledge. I would wager my left arm that the dress had been complete for days now, if not longer.

While not typical of brides I have seen, Victoria had also chosen to wear a veil—a filmy, flimsy garment that might as well have been sliced from one of Celia's curtains. I wondered why she'd chosen it, but I also wondered whether perhaps her lapses in self-control as of late had caused some aspect of her true self to remain visible beyond whatever illusion she wore each day.

Perhaps the veil was for *us*.

And although the attentions of those in the chapel remained riveted on the bride and her attending parent, I didn't take my eyes off the doorway.

I waited for Father, wishing and desperate to see him alive and well, but praying that he might stay away for only a time longer, that I might take our family's fall and leave himself and Edward free and safe and well.

But he did not walk through the door, and the attending priest began the mass the moment Victoria took her place.

The priest greeted the assembly and we responded, and our voices rose as one to sing Gloria to the Almighty. I noticed that Celia did not sing. Nor Victoria, beneath the veil.

When we finished, the priest bade us bow our heads and kneel in prayer before—

"No," said Celia.

No? My gaze flew to the altar, where Celia stood with hand upon the priest's neck. I wish I could say I looked at the scene in disbelief, but I did not. Her actions were far from surprising, despite the fact that she had interrupted her own daughter's wedding.

"No," she repeated, her voice echoing throughout the room, rising above the growing murmur. "There will be no mass today. No catering to the Divine. You think He cares for us? Think again. The vows, priest."

I looked to the King, whose features I expected to contort with rage at the audacity of this woman, but he too appeared pacified as Celia—without reservation—crossed the stage and thrust out her hand to place her fingers across the clasped hands of His Majesty.

"The vows." She looked to the priest, and although the guards bent to strike her down, the King raised his right arm to cease their advance.

"The vows," he repeated in a voice so barren, so devoid of life, that I knew with certainty he, too, had fallen to her touch.

No longer was only William's future at stake, but something else became abundantly certain: Celia, in devising this marriage, had greater plans. Plans which involved subduing the King to her will.

My time had come.

I slipped from the pew into shadow and crept toward the center aisle. With guards looking outward for intruders—and, I assumed, my father—and guests looking forward at the caricature of a ceremony at front, none looked to the center aisle. No one noticed a girl in a rose-colored dress who stalked toward the Prince and his bride.

Those who did see me, once I passed, did nothing. They gasped and stared but they didn't move. Would no one think to act? Would none dare interfere? Perhaps they feared causing a disruption worse than that already under way. Or to bring attention to themselves, especially after the events of nights prior. No matter, it made my task easier.

Yes, I was afraid—I planned to interrupt one of the most sacred rites of the church and one involving royalty, no less—but with my soul already damned, what else did I have to fear but the loss of my own life? So long as the ones I loved remained safe, I could forfeit all else.

One more step forward, I told myself. This one for Miss Mary. The next, for the butler and stable boy. Our house staff. The next for Gretel, and the next for Liesl and her brother, who I hoped were still strong and whole.

And then I found myself drawn alongside Charlotte, who quaked in her seat. A curious thing, for although I could so clearly recall her unearthly appearance two nights ago, this time, she appeared all the more like a jealous sister.

Jealous enough, I wondered, to help me?

"Charlotte," I whispered. "Don't turn. Stay where you are."

Of course she glanced back. With a sigh, I returned her stare.

"Why are you here? How did you get in?" She glared with a deep ferocity.

"I'm here to stop the wedding." I offered a pleasant smile in return. "Would you like to help?"

Without another word, she stood, causing murmurs and ripples among those seated. "It should be me up there."

"Of course," I agreed, trying to keep my voice low and hoping she would follow suit. Would she truly assist so readily? We were not friends. Her trust should not come so easily.

"Mother promised." She glanced over her shoulder at Victoria, and back to me. "She promised *me* first, not that sorry excuse."

I realized my mistake.

Charlotte wouldn't help *me*.

She simply needed an excuse to help *herself*.

I moved to lay a hand on her arm, to discourage what would surely turn my plan on its head, but she spun around faster than I could anticipate. Her eyes had become black, empty pools. Her fingernails, growing, lengthening, sharpening. Her mouth, full of teeth like knives, gaping—

And she shoved me backward that I might release her arm.

"I won't go back," she hissed from behind a mouthful of daggers. "He's mine. She promis*ssssed*."

Then, with shocking speed, she ran—ran!—down the aisle, toward Victoria, toward William, and I knew beyond all doubt that if she couldn't have him, no one would.

I didn't think. I merely acted. Who can blame me?

For as I leapt to my feet and cried out for her to stop, I pulled the blade from my sleeve and hurled it with all my strength— strength which I'd gained from cleaning the stables, the chamber pots, sweeping the hearth—toward my stepsisters.

I no longer cared which one it struck, only that it might stop one or both of them from hurting anyone else.

In that instant, several things happened at once.

As she reached the altar, Charlotte leapt from the ground and released an otherworldly shriek that pierced my ears, her arms outstretched toward her sister. As she came into Victoria's view, my veil-covered sister screeched in return and, in the space of half a breath, both stepsisters exploded into mist and reformed, but no longer as the girls I knew.

Screams rose from the crowd as two black, sinuous creatures, taller than two horses stacked high—with talons longer than an eagle's span and leathery wings protruding from torn flesh on their backs—appeared where my sisters had stood. They beat their wings and flew toward each other, even as my dagger continued its path through the air toward their now-changed forms.

The chapel erupted into madness.

I screamed William's name as I watched these things unfold and when I saw, with growing horror, that he remained under Celia's spell and could not act, I screamed louder and with every ounce of force in my body, and could not help but think of the horde of demons that had descended upon the ballroom the night before.

And then from all sides of my outstretched hand, from which the dagger flew, came the shrieks of a horde of tortured souls pulled forth from their resting places to do my will.

The ground shook and I dug my heels into the floor, even as from the air above us came the crash of a thousand panes of glass shattering at once. I watched in dismay and terror as a crack appeared in the floor of the chapel, pulling my gaze away from my sisters.

It grew and grew and grew, opening wider than the aisle, becoming a great, gaping maw that stretched down into the earth.

And as my sisters collided, the sound of screaming filled the air as hundreds—no, thousands, or tens of thousands—of demons surged forth from the pit and filled the chapel with their deafening cries.

A great heat rose from below and the ground shook once more. I stumbled and fell forward, a wail on my lips, seeing my own death in the fires of the Abyss. Yet as I closed my eyes to the world, my feet landed on solid ground. I opened them to the realization that I stood whole on the other side of the pit.

Oliroomim, the spirit child, stood before me, sadness in his eyes—a true sadness, of the kind I had never seen. "You called, mistress."

I didn't understand. How could it be possible?

"No," I said, "I didn't. I don't have *The Book*. I didn't draw a circle, or speak your name aloud—"

He glowered at me, and I shuddered at the sight of it. "You no longer need it, mistress. No one does, in the end. Behold your power."

And I did.

Guests streamed out of the chapel, scrambling, trampling, weeping, and clinging to each other in escape.

Charlotte and Victoria—or whatever they were—ripped and tore at each other's throats, my dagger's path long forgotten. The scent of rotted flesh and dung filled the air as legions of the dead dove and struck and ripped chunks of blackened tissue from my sisters' bodies.

William, and the King, had not moved.

In the midst of it all stood Celia.

Staring.

At me.

Her face contorted with rage as our gazes met for the first time.

"You," she said, voice rising to a shriek. "You!"

I held my ground and didn't move. She stepped closer.

"It's *you?*" Disbelief clouded her exquisite features. "*You* have done this?"

I admit, I felt a surge of power. Of satisfaction and yes, of pleasure.

"Indeed," I said, folding both arms across my chest.

With a primal scream, Celia lunged at her daughters, pulled them from one another by brute force, and hurled them toward me. "*There* is your undoing, my daughters," she yelled above the din. "Kill her and you'll both escape the pit. There is reward enough for the both of you!"

They landed on the ground, mere steps away from me in the aisle. I felt their hot breath as they moved before me and the scorch of the fiery pit behind.

I'd been trapped.

Oliroomim stood beside me still.

"What do I do?" I asked.

Calm as a summer's day, he replied, "Simply command."

"But I cannot." *Edward.* "My brother. He may die. He may be dead already."

The spirit shrugged as if he had no care in this. And how could he? The dead do not care for the living. "Your choice, mistress. Your brother's life for the lives of many. These ones will not go easily, now that they've tasted this world again."

I swallowed hard, the heat of flames burning my ankles, the stink of my sisters' breath choking mine. "Why can't I command *them?*"

Oliroomim sighed, exasperated by my ignorance. "They're not yours to command, mistress. They're *hers.*"

He pointed to Celia, whose breathing had turned labored where she stood. But I couldn't focus on her, no—I had to face my sisters first.

"Kill her, you cowards," she screamed. "*She* stands in your way."

"Pretty prince*ssss*," hissed Charlotte, using the title Victoria gave me on the day of the first ball. "Look how she shivers*sss.*"

"Delicious," purred Victoria. A thick glob of slime trailed from her open jaw as she slunk toward me. "But so thin and bony … not like the little waif, so plump and juicy … "

I shuddered at the thought, and although the unbidden demons swooped around us and plummeted at my stepsisters, it did not slow their advance. "You won't have him."

"Tender," Victoria continued, "supple. And so easily broken."

"Together, sister?" Charlotte nudged Victoria with her great, scabbed head. "This one first?"

"Together, indeed."

And as one, my sisters lunged toward me, claws outstretched, jaws reaching toward my neck to surely rend me in two.

They might take my life today, but I wouldn't go without a fight. They could tear my body limb from limb, but *they could not have Edward.*

Their massive forms descended toward me and with a final cry, I thrust my hands forward and thought of Edward, my father, my mother, of William, of everyone I had ever loved and lost, of all those who had perished for no reason beyond the selfishness of these creatures before me.

I thought of meeting William in the graveyard. I thought of holding Edward in my arms as we read his favourite stories. I thought of Father, our jests, our days of happiness before Mother's death, and the strength we found in each other after. And I thought of Gretel, who did not judge but whose only fault had been to help me before herself.

I thought of all these things, of Curson and Lautrayth, Feremin and Oliroomim, of the dead spirits conjured forth, of their loss and how I had forced them to rise from their graves of peace or tortures in hell, and I thought of myself who would join them this day and be called forth by the next and the next and the next ones to find that cursed, God-forsaken book.

I thought of freedom for the kingdom and how desperately I wanted my family to *live.*

I thought of my stepsisters and how they had threatened to take every measure of that away from me.

I took what I knew to be my last breath, and with every ounce of strength which I had gained through servitude to their own whims, plunged both hands deep into my stepsisters' chests, even as their jaws closed around my aching body, and even as the legions of hell descended upon them by my command.

I found that place deep within, and took hold of their unbeating hearts.

And I pulled.

Blood—black and thick, red and hot, sticky and smelling of sweetness and death—oozed down my arms and poured forth from the gaping holes in their chests as I drew out their festering, maggoty hearts.

And I squeezed.

The hearts burst in my hands, sending sprays of white maggots over my dress and shoes and arms as globs of red and black blood burst from my palms, baptizing my cheeks with slate and scarlet.

Closing around my neck and limbs, their jaws grew slack.

Somewhere distant, a woman roared in fury, and somewhere close, a young man shouted as he awoke from a deep, waking sleep.

And that, my dear Father, is when *you* walked in.

36

The Return

My father, William, and the King stare awestruck as I finish my tale. I see the disgust in the King's eyes, but worse, in William's. I am an abomination to their kind, of this I am certain. What they are, I don't know, but it does not matter.

They are safe, and we are whole.

But as my father runs forward to embrace his daughter whose arms and hands and self drip with blood both seen and unseen, I remember.

"Where's Celia?"

She is nowhere. Her body is not among the wreckage of my sisters, nor is she held at bay by my army—the legions who remain swirling above us, held back by my will alone. They fill the chapel sanctuary, and I feel their pain as keenly as if it were my own.

They should not be in such a sacred place. I shouldn't have called them here.

"She's gone," says Father, weariness in his voice—though I can see that his eyes are clear and whole, unaffected. "I never believed it would come to this. I left, that she might—"

"Terrorize the kingdom?" William rouses from where he stands, and comes forward. "It was her, wasn't it? And … those?" He points to the coagulating forms of my stepsisters. They were not sucked back into the Abyss as Curson, and I wonder if they paid a dear price for their human forms.

"They took Gretel," is the first thing I think to say to Father, "and the others. After you left."

I can barely believe he stands before me. There are so many things he needs to know. So many things I want to say, or scream, or accuse, but more than that, I want to throw my arms around him and hear that everything is going to be all right now. Because he is *here* and he is *alive*.

Father sinks to his knees, rivers of salt on his cheeks to match the eddies of crimson on mine. His forehead touches the ground and he raises one hand—his right hand—toward my knee.

It is an ancient gesture, one of supplication—a cry for mercy, forgiveness, and protection.

I cannot bear it. "No, Father, you must stand. I've been strong for you long enough. It's your turn now."

But he is still on the other side of the chasm, and his body shakes, lithe form racked with a guilt I understand all too well. "Forgive me, daughter."

But I cannot, for there is nothing to forgive. He is not a man who should beg on his knees, not to me, not to anyone. "Rise, Father, before I send these legions to lift you up."

And he raises his head to see that I am not angry and that I smile, even though the ache of all that has passed is too much to bear. Would that I were the one on my knees, for I am unsure how much longer I'll have the strength to stand.

And as I reach to take my father's hand across the gap and bid him rise, a shout from behind causes me to spin about.

The King is rushing toward us, bladed sceptre raised, with a battle cry so glorious that I am tempted to welcome the knife and end it all in this moment.

But William shouts, "No, Father!", and raises his right arm, palm open and in it some object I can't see. The momentum of the sceptre collides with William's open palm, and the sanctuary erupts with a bright, hot light.

My demons scream and writhe and whirl with pain beyond anything I have ever felt before, as though every limb is being torn away by wild horses, and I am blind to the world for an eternity until—

The light is gone, the pain is gone, and so are my demons.

The Abyss has closed, and the forms of my stepsisters, vanished.

William stands facing the King. He has defied his Father, somehow—*my* William, who once told me that he feared an act of defiance would shake the fate of the kingdom.

"They've done nothing wrong," he says, holding his palm aloft. Between his fingers, a glint of gold. Did he hold his medallion?

"They've conjured evil spirits, son. Everything we stand against, everything we have a duty to banish from this world, *they* brought forth upon us." His eyes are wild and frantic, but I see that they are also full of goodness and light. Just like his son.

"No," William says, "I know her. She attended the balls, Father, she is a good person. I'm sure this has all been a mistake, she wouldn't—"

What is he saying? I am not Lady Aleidis, I am only—

But I look down at my dress, splattered with gore and entrails, and I see.

My demons have made me glorious, one last time. I am the radiant princess who calls forth the dead.

I am Ellison, girl of ash and cinder and spirits. *Necromancer.*

"It's no mistake," I say.

William turns, though he keeps the King in his sight. "That other woman, it must be her doing."

"She's evil, certainly," I say with a sigh, for every moment I waste in convincing William and the King that they should not kill my father and me on the spot is another moment Celia remains free—and Edward's fate uncertain. "And I am sure that it was she and her spawn who roamed the kingdom as terrors. But all I have done, I have done for my family alone."

I hesitate in the whole truth, but what have I to lose? "And for you."

"Me?" His confusion is immediate, and I wonder if I should have waited.

"Yes, you."

He shakes his head and lowers his hand. "I don't understand. How could you call anything forth? And why for me? We didn't part on the most amicable terms."

"But I know more of your heart than you think."

He gapes like a fish, and I long to engage him with teases and hints and guesses, but there will be time for that later. Now, there is more at stake than a young woman's whims.

Wordless, I draw forth William's ring from inside my dress and hold it in my palm that he might understand.

His eyes grow wide as he takes in the ring, my face, my gown, and my father still quivering at my feet.

"You ... you're ... Ella? Ella!"

I wait for him to see, and he does. The realization drains his face of color as he struggles with the duality of the women he thought he knew.

He shakes his head. "But I thought—"

"That I was something other? I may be a noble merchant's daughter, but I am neither servant nor princess."

He steps forward, brows knit. "I don't understand. If you're Lady Aleidis, then she isn't … but you are … " He pauses, frustration mounting. "Why not just come as *yourself*? I wanted *you* to be there. I looked for you. Asked you to come."

"Yes, but *I* wondered why a prince who so obviously didn't want to take a wife became so interested in one particular girl."

With a laugh and a shake of his head, William plucks the ring from my hand. I am in awe of his bright spirit even in the darkest of moments. "You knew, the whole time. From that first meeting."

"I did." I shrug. "Your coat fell under my stepsisters—over there, see it? I think it may have need of a wash."

He slides the ring on his finger and looks at me—truly looks at me—and sees me as the girl who sat in the graveyard in the early morning hours, alone in her nightdress. Not as some foreign beauty or an illusion of who or what I am.

We are the only ones in the room as he reaches out to touch my cheek.

"My father the King, he meant to trap the conjurer of terrors at the festival. It was my test to seek out the one doing evil, under guise of finding a wife. The fate of the kingdom rested on *that*, not on removing myself from bachelorhood."

"That's a terrible plan," I say.

He laughs again, a true laugh, despite all things. "It is, isn't it? We thought with everyone in one place, the demon caller might—"

"Call down more terrors?" I roll my eyes heavenward, relieved to see a clear and ornately painted ceiling instead of a rolling mass of hellbound creatures swarming the air above. I am reminded of the night of the final ball, and how I had done just what they'd feared. "In that, at least, you were correct."

He looks back at his father the King, whose gaze has softened upon his son. I look back at mine, who is rising to his feet with a determination that warms my soul and heightens hope.

"We are ... protectors, my family." William pulls his medallion chain back over his head. "My heritage, my task, is to defend the kingdom from evil. We bring light where there is only dark, and are sworn to serve the Almighty in the destruction of evil."

I nod. "And your medallion?"

"Saint Michael."

Chief Prince of heaven? Of course. I should have guessed.

"What of your father's sceptre?"

"We all have our own strengths. The King's sceptre serves to channel heaven's favor."

I begin to understand what he's trying to explain. So many things become clear now—why he roamed the streets at night, how he knew of the terrors, and his appearances in our yard. He sought to find and destroy a necromancer—and he'd suspected my father.

"Then by all rights, you should strike me down where I stand."

"Yes," he says, slowly. "I should."

He looks to the empty floor, to the ceiling, and to the place where the pit had opened and spit up heat and flame and spirits.

"But you don't seem evil. You're not what I imagined a necromancer would look like." He points to the place where Victoria and Charlotte had lain, now only a smear of rot and blood. And his coat. "That sort of thing ... that was more like it."

"I think," I say, "that it is not so simple as our elders would have us believe."

"I think," he says, holding his hand out for mine, "that you are rather perceptive. And also correct."

I eye his hand with an intentional scepticism. "What will your bride think?"

He kicks at his coat, and a remnant pocket of maggots sprays across his boot and the floor. Sick laughter at the senselessness of it all bubbles up from some place deep inside my chest.

"I imagine she won't say much." He also begins to laugh, but stops as our eyes meet. "What is it?"

How do I explain? How can I begin to tell him? "It's sad," I try, "No one deserves death, not really."

"No," says another.

We both start in surprise, for the King has moved toward us, his bladed sceptre sheathed. "They were never alive, miss. At least, not as you knew them."

"Lady Aleidis," William corrects his father.

"Ellison," my father corrects William.

"Ella," I say. "And I think they all were, once." I look to the ceiling once more, remembering. "They all were."

The chapel descends into silence but for the soft whistle of the evening breeze outside. I plead silently to the Almighty for a sign, something that might tell me if Edward is safe or if he still lives. I cannot feel guilty for what has happened here—I didn't call the spirits, not on purpose, but still they came.

How is that fair?

Ah, but life is not about what is or isn't fair.

"She's still out there," I whisper, breaking the silence. "It's not over yet."

William looks to his father the King, who bows his head and touches a finger to his forehead in a sign of deference to his son. My breath catches and William nods in acknowledgment. This is William's task now, and I am relieved.

"Maybe she died with her daughters?" William rubs the medallion between his fingers. "Or maybe her powers diminished?"

A roll of thunder, far beyond the chapel, interrupts our thoughts.

Something within me is sure that it isn't actually thunder.

"No," I say, "she lives. We only have to find her and act."

But how? I do not know. I have spent all my efforts on vengeance against my stepsisters and never once thought to bully the source.

My heart seizes in an instant and I'm gripped by a terror beyond all terrors I have ever or will ever face.

"Edward," I breathe, "if she finds Edward ... "

My father places a hand upon my shoulder.

"I'll find him," he says, a sadness in his voice that tells me he, too, is uncertain of what will come. "You help the King and the Prince root her out. I dare not risk falling under her spell once more."

"How *did* you?" I say, spitting the words. "Shouldn't you have known?"

His shoulders slump with a weariness that makes my heart ache. "I did know, my daughter, I did. That is why I married her, at first, that I might keep her close until I could find a way to defeat her. But when I learned the kingdom's paladins—" and here, he looks to the King, "—searched for the source of the terrors and suspected me, I couldn't risk imprisonment or death before I had found a way to defeat her for good."

"You'd seen her before? And yet she didn't recognize you?" The pieces do not fit, and yet my thoughts return to the letter, the task therein, and the sacrifice. Were these one and the same?

Father tugs on his sleeves and taps his forehead. "I have tricks of my own, daughter. Evil takes many forms and has a short memory."

"But Mother?" I can't help but ask.

He nods. "It was her idea, Ellison. She helped me obtain *The Book of Conjuring* from the Royal Archives some time ago. *She* helped hide the path back to me, and *she* fought the good fight by my side, with her strength."

I don't like what I'm hearing. It cannot be true, but it *is*. I know it is. I read the letter—I spoke to the source. "But you lost. Mother died for nothing, and Celia still lives, and Edward—"

He shakes his head and opens his palms toward me. "Not for nothing, daughter. None who give their lives against evil, despite the outcome, do so for nothing. We have each faced it in our own way, and we each pay the cost. Some more than others." He looks to William and the King. "Some are required to make greater sacrifices so that others don't have to."

William's face becomes a mask of confusion, and I am relieved, because I too don't understand *why*. "Then why use this dark magic to fight her? Why not call on the royal family, or even a priest?"

My father sighs deeply, and my stomach roils with anticipation. I ache to know the answer, and yet, I am afraid what his answer might mean.

Afraid of what I will have to do.

"To fight a creature of such darkness," he says, fingers pressed to the bridge of his nose, "one must be close enough to darkness themselves. Only darkness can open the Abyss and return something that evil back into the fires of hell."

He looks at William and the King once again. "Can either of you open the Gates of Hell in the Almighty's name?"

"No," says the King. "Nor would I want to. Purity cannot abide the darkness."

I know this in truth, for I saw it when my mother touched me.

There is silence in the chapel as we all contemplate this meaning.

"And so the darkness must return it to darkness," I murmur.

"Yes," says my father. "We become the damned in His name, that the earth might live in peace." He looks at me with a great, consuming sadness. "And that we might, one day, beg His forgiveness."

I understand now.

It is time for me to kill the beast.

37

The Church

We leave the chapel together, though my father, the King, and William head to the royal stables to find horses for the journey ahead. I walk to the grove where my horse, the book, and my father's satchel are hidden, and we meet again at the gates of the palace grounds.

I learn that William, with great effort, has sent the King away to tend to the needs of those injured in the chapel—to heal any wounds, and to calm the fears of the people. And for the same purpose, because he can be of no use in the battle ahead, I urge William away as well.

"You've no need to remain," I insist. "And you may get hurt."

"You're one to talk," he replies with a frown. "You haven't a clue how to defeat her."

"She's only one woman," I say with confidence. "And no longer has the luxury of demanding that others do her bidding. Right, Father?"

My father is silent for a moment as we move down the road and away from the palace gates.

"She's far beyond that," he finally says, "and the greatest danger is in underestimating what she is capable of. She can take many forms, so be on your guard. Your stepsisters were but another attempt at power in this world, and now that *that* has failed? I imagine she is none too pleased."

We ride down the road, far from the palace grounds toward town, and I know we are all thinking the same thing—where has she gone? I dare not consider that she may have fled, not this time. It must end *today.*

It seems best to think as she might—if she quests for power, how might she gain it? What might she do to ease the threat on her plans?

The weight of the day falls heavy like the burden of Atlas, and a second roll of thunder—closer, this time—gives me pause. The road we're on will bring us to the Church of the Holy Paraclete, and despite the task ahead, I am seized by a sudden urge. I draw alongside Father with my request.

"Might we take a moment?" I ask, though the words sound strange in my ears. It has been a long time since I've asked permission of anything. "I wish to visit Mother once more. Will you come with me?"

Father gazes ahead and I hold my breath. "Yes, this is a good idea. I'd like to see her stone one final time, too." He pulls his horse away from mine, but his words give me pause.

"Final time?" I urge my horse to keep pace with his. "This won't be your final time. You can defeat Celia. You can send her back, and it will all be over. Tell me you can."

He regards me with an even greater sorrow. "I cannot. I no longer know how, for I ceased the use of my powers the day your mother died. My daughter, I kept the evil close to me that I might find some other way to defeat it, but I left before ... " His voice trails with unspoken truth.

"Before you could find someone else to draw from," I snap.

"But you forget, *I* cannot defeat her, either. Edward may already be dead, Father, and if he isn't, for all I know he'll expire the moment I so much as draw a circle in the earth before us."

My anger heats and rises like a kettle set to boil. We're riding toward a foolhardy purpose. Who are we to think we might save this world, this kingdom, from evil? Who are we to take the lives of those we love? Who are we to have to sacrifice for the good of others?

Thunder rolls a third time. It is closer, and I wonder aloud.

"Father, if I were an ancient evil who had just seen my plans of power destroyed at the hands of someone I assumed to be under my control, what would I do?"

"Run," Father offers. "Or hide until I found new minions. Or devise another way to take power."

But it does not sound right. "She has always been sure of herself, since the very moment she crossed our threshold. I don't believe she'll run."

I consider Celia's actions: when I became a nuisance, she pushed me from her way. She'd piled heavy tasks on my head, setting me to do this or that, removing personal possessions and stealing away freedom, until finally resorting to threats on Edward's life.

"Revenge," William says. "In her place, I'd seek revenge."

My father and I speak the same word. "Edward."

But I am looking at him, and he is staring down the road. I follow his gaze, which rests on the very place we travel toward.

"I don't think we'll have to look very far," he says.

With another roll of thunder, closer than ever, the spires of the Church of the Holy Paraclete topple to the ground as the roof pushes upward like a rising loaf of bread and splits in two. Tiles, bricks, and stones drop from their heights, and standing in the center of the wreckage, rising above the church's outer walls, is a beast unlike any creature I have ever beheld.

With a shout, we spur the horses onward, unthinking in our actions, plunging toward a foe we cannot defeat. But I go and I *will not stop*, for as we reach the edge of the church grounds, I see that the beast has destroyed the stones of the field.

They are all turned to dust. The hazel tree stands no more, and the air stinks of crushed lavender, too strong and too pungent to bring calm.

I cry out to Father, but he pays me no mind, for he stares at the beast as we draw close.

It is so much taller than the church's insides that I can barely see its face in the gleam of night. What I *can* see drives a thorn of fear into my heart.

The beast's skin is onyx, scaled and shining, with spikes the size of trees along its spine. Its six limbs are crowned with talons that open and close over the church's brick walls, tearing off chunks and hurling them toward the ground.

As we move closer, I see that the shining of its scales isn't shine at all, but thousands of eyes—one, two, sometimes three on each scale, looking, staring, searching. The skull of the beast is worse still, for it is misshapen and repulsive enough to send bile splashing against the back of my throat. Row upon row of teeth fill its mouth, and mandibles like the jaw of a beetle snap open and shut, tasting the air. A mound of raw flesh where its nose should be drips a yellow liquid that oozes down its face and into its mouth, pouring across its belly and dripping onto the floor of the church where it turns to steam with a hiss.

But the eyes on its face ... I know those eyes, for I gazed into them and saw nothing, many days before.

The beast before us is, beyond all doubt, my stepmother Celia.

And hanging limp in one of her many limbs, clutched so tightly I fear he may be crushed at any moment, is my brother Edward.

38

The Breaking

I am lost. Utterly and completely lost.

I scream at the beast and spur my horse forward, ignoring the shouts of the men behind me. I have no care for myself or this world, for all I can see is my brother in the arms of that beast— that *thing*, who has done nothing but try to claim him since the moment she crossed our threshold.

But I also hold a spark of hope, for why would the beast pay mind to a dead child?

She cannot have her revenge on me if he has already died. No, I would wager my last breath that she would prefer to see me suffer before she claims him.

I am sure of it. I will risk my life, and his life, on this.

I tumble off the horse, clutching *The Book*, as a claw the size of three carriages descends from above. Talons sink into my horse like a knife into butter, impaling the poor creature as it wails once before leaving this life. I am glad it didn't suffer long.

Celia flings it from her hand, across the fields, where it lands with a thud beyond my sight.

My father calls behind me, but I am not listening. I scream at Celia, demanding she release my heart, my brother, the thing I hold most dear in all the world, for Father is returned and we can finally be whole again.

But she, a beast in all forms, only laughs, spewing phlegm and sickness across the crushed stones of the church.

"Give him back to me," I command, for I don't know what else to do. My throat is dry and hoarse, but I will not be silenced. "You have no right to him."

Her voice is deep and grating and scratches across my ears. "He is nothing to me, pathetic creature. But if I am to remain in this world, it becomes clear that *you* cannot."

"I can no longer harm you," I admit, though I know to do so is folly. "I have done enough. Leave us alone, and I will leave you."

It is a promise I should not make, but what choice do I have? If I act, Edward will die. If I don't act, others may die.

I *cannot* make this choice.

Celia roars and the earth shakes, sending me to my knees. Hot tears rise and spill down my cheeks and I grind my teeth as I watch her lift my brother to her festering mouth and place putrid lips upon his face.

I retch, dry heaves that bring up nothing but air and acid. That is not love. She does not know what love is, no matter how she may pretend.

"Stop … " I try to shout, but my legs have grown weak and I can no longer stand.

She will not bargain or compromise.

She will only take power, and when she receives it, she'll seek more.

Deep within, I know she will do so forever and ever, until all those who can love see their loved ones ripped away and devoured by this abomination born of hatred and greed.

I am the only one who can stop it, and now is the only time.

I must love Edward enough to let him go.

I pray that when he sees Mother and she tells him of his sacrifice, that he understands.

With a shaking breath, I lift my head to the sky, and I think of my legions of darkness. I hear the rush of wings. With one finger, I trace a circle in the dirt around me, close my eyes, and press *The Book of Conjuring* to my chest. I do not need the bone key today, for there is a place inside me that knows the words I have to speak. Words I read in the book and swore I would never repeat.

It is time.

"I, Ellison, exorcize you, Celia, by—"

Arms beneath mine lift me to my feet. My eyes fly open and there is William, and my father, standing in my circle and I am terrified, for William surely cannot be here.

"No," I say, panicked, "you can't be a part of this."

"Do you love me?" William asks.

I shake my head. "Why would you ask that? Why now?" Every moment I'm not on my knees in this circle prolongs Edward's suffering.

If I don't act now, I doubt I will ever find the strength again.

William takes my shoulders and shakes me. "Do you love me? Tell me, Ella, do you love me?"

Not now. I cannot. This is neither the time nor the place, and I tell him so.

"Answer," he yells, and I stumble. Of course he catches me with his strong arms that will *always* catch me, forever and ever, if only I answer him.

And I realize this one final truth: I am not alone anymore.

I think of Mother, and her sacrifice for Father. For the world. And I think I know why William demands an answer.

"Yes," I say, for I do.

With haste, but so gently and tenderly that it brings tears back to my eyes, he places a kiss on my parched, bloodied lips.

"Then take my life instead," he says, and grasps my hand.

I shake my head. "I can't. I don't know how."

He smiles and I melt into the earth. So short, our time together, and yet, I would not trade it for a moment with anyone else.

Celia roars above us, and I falter. I am tired, so very tired.

"You don't need to know how," he says, and squeezes my fingers. "I have power too, remember? Think of me, Ella, and we'll save him. Together."

I relent. It is the only way.

And so, with William at one side, and my father's quiet strength on the other, I lift my voice and our arms to the sky.

"I, Ellison, exorcize you, Celia, by the Father, the Son, and the Holy Spirit, the Holiest Trinity, and by He who created heaven and earth—"

Beside me, William stiffens and his grip falters. I hold tighter and will my legions to strike against her.

"—and by all things both visible and invisible, by His power of death and resurrection, that by all these things you are bound to my power—"

And though the demons rip and tear, they cannot hold her attention forever. She notices us, then, and screams with a primal rage that shakes the earth beneath our feet. We are strong. We remain in the circle, for we cannot step aside. She must feel the first tendrils of binding, she *must*.

"—that you submit to me, for I command that you be restrained from this day forward, now and forevermore, under the earth in the fires of hell—"

The shaking grows and grows until we are forced to our knees, and as before, a crack appears along the earth's surface. It opens, splitting with a groan, bringing hot winds and sending streaks of jagged light across the sky.

In her rage, Celia hurls one of the church's stone walls toward us. I see it fly through the air as I speak, and in silence, I beg forgiveness for my failure.

"Don't stop," shouts Father, though I can barely hear him above the din, "the circle will protect us so long as we remain inside!"

The hurled stones whip over our heads and spin away, landing beyond sight. I continue.

"—never again to rise and destroy, forever damned by the power which the Christ destroyed all Hell and by Him who cast you from heaven—"

William looses a cry that rips my heart into a million pieces, for I know it, I can feel it this time—I draw his life and strength not to fuel the dead to life, but to return the dead unto death.

I will lose him, of this I am sure … but in so doing, I will gain everything, for my family will be safe, and that is all that matters.

That is all that has ever mattered.

"—and may all these things be done in His name, forever and ever. *Amen.*"

And just as the earth shakes one final time, the crack spreads to open beneath the church, wider and wider still, and the horde of demons at my command strikes at what my stepmother has become, surrounding and pushing and tearing, forcing her backward, backward, backward, until she stumbles toward the edge. She tilts and sways and I scream for Edward, for as she plunges into the pit with a final roar, in her grasp is the tiny form of my brother who is now falling, falling, falling into the depths of the Abyss and toward an eternity of damnation—

And then the ground closes, seams moving together with

rumbles and scrapes like my passageway doors, and a hole in the sky tears open to pull my legions back inside, leaving blue skies and sucking the darkness from every corner …

And then it's over.

And I am on the ground, and my father is holding me, and I no longer feel William's hand in my own but I am too afraid to look for fear that I have just lost everything—*everything*—and I do not know whether I have made the right choice.

My father holds my face in his hands and tells me he is proud. He buries my cheek in his shoulder and wipes away the tears and holds me as the pain and sorrow of so many days falls down like fresh snow—for although this is over, the memory and aching will not melt so easily.

I do not know how long we sit there. I do know the night turns to day, and still the sun grows tired and falls from the sky as the stars take their turn to light the way once more, and I know the air grows cold, and I know the morning dew smells fresh and sweet and I yearn to quench the dryness in my throat.

And so I sit up, rub my eyes with stiff fingers, and look to the sun's warmth.

And there, amid the sun's rays, is my brother.

39

The True Ending

The spirit child Oliroomim descends from a seam in the sky, a seam which remains despite the ending of all.

But we have not broken the circle, and so it is there still.

In his arms, he holds my brother, and I catch my breath at the strangeness of this spirit carrying the form of Edward who is as small as he.

"Thank you," I say, "for everything."

He lays Edward on the sun-warmed ground, and while my brother barely breathes, I think he lives. I am overwhelmed with joy and a shout rises from within, bubbling forth to culminate in laughter—but I hold back, for I cannot know for sure until I hold him for myself.

"As you wish, mistress," he says, and leaves, sealing the seam in the sky in his retreat. Would that I could spare him, somehow, but to grant heaven to a hell-bound spirit is far beyond even my power. I will not call him again. I pray that will be enough to allow his rest.

I run out of the circle, ignoring every pain that stabs through me, to draw Edward into my arms.

He is alive.

He is alive.

A stirring from behind causes my breath to seize in fright, but when I look it is only William—William!—pale but otherwise well, sitting amid the dirt.

In one hand, he holds his medallion.

"I told you I'd be all right," he says, and I am so angry I want to scream at him, I am so filled with blissful wonder I want to throw my arms around him, but I do neither because Father is here too and we are *all* whole.

We are together.

We are a family again, and will be forever and ever.

And I smile at William and he smiles back, and I know so much more than one simple story can ever tell.

I know that we will, all of us, live happily ever after.

THE END

Cinderella, Necromancer: Historical Notes

When I set out to write *Cinderella, Necromancer*, I had two goals in mind: Stay as true to the original German and French fairy-tales as possible (within the context of the story, of course), and to frame the magic of the story within a relevant, historical context.

"But Faith," you're saying, "necromancy isn't real!"

Ah, but that's where things get really interesting ... so let's start there.

It begins with Richard Kieckhefer, a professor of religion and history at Northwestern University, specializing in late medieval religious culture. He wrote two books that were highly influential on the magic that Ellison performs: *Magic in the Middle Ages* (Cambridge University Press, 2000), and *Forbidden Rites: A Necromancer's Manual of the Fifteenth Century* (The Pennsylvania State University Press, 2012).

Nearly all the spells Ellison performs, and all of the spirits or demons she conjures, are inspired by real, ancient necromancy spells found in the grimoire discussed in *Forbidden Rites*—everything from the circles she forms on the ground, writing the spirits' names between the lines, and facing a certain direction when performing her conjurings. And while the original title of the grimoire remains uncertain (*Forbidden Rites* simply calls it the Munich Handbook of

Necromancy: Clm 849), it contains a smaller text within it called *The Book of Consecrations*. And the whole thing? Written in Latin and German.

Inside the grimoire is a faded stamp that reads *Bibliotheca Regia Monacensis* ("Royal Library of Munich"), which made me wonder, what would a handbook of necromancy be doing in a royal library? Necromancy was a forbidden practice during the 15th century and the centuries that followed, and most of these books were burned by the church upon discovery. Writers of medieval necromancy handbooks were usually clerics—priests or other minor church figures—and late medieval necromancy was more or less a product of a "clerical underworld."

Because of this, the spells and conjuring instructions in necromancy handbooks were written in Latin (assuming the necromancer's familiarity with the Vulgate Bible) and reflect bits of Catholic liturgy, Christian prayers and snippets of scripture. What I found even more fascinating is that these conjurers truly believed that if they were humble enough, God would provide "divine aid" and give them power over the demons they called!

Of course, demons tend to be hard to control—which is why we see in the grimoire the conjurer continually entreating the spirits to appear in a non-threatening, calm form. I made sure Ellison's spirits acted and required the same. The grimoire also mentions that while necromancers need to repeat each ritual exactly, even if they're performing the same spell over and over, they may eventually be able to convince the demons to appear on command—just as Ellison does, despite her surprise at being able to do so.

Now, while it's thought that the earliest versions of the Cinderella story originated in classical antiquity, I tried to pay most tribute to the German version, the Brothers Grimm's *Aschenputtel*, with a few nods to Charles Perrault's *Cinderella*. In the Grimm tale, there is no fairy godmother, and instead Cinderella receives help from a magical bird who calls to her from a hazel tree beside her mother's grave. From Perrault, we learn that Cinderella's mother was "the best creature in the world"—talk about having a lot to live up to! And while only one sister is ever given a name—Charlotte, found in the French version—there are many other little details from both versions that I hid within the story.

You can find these originals online from any number of great websites. I recommend *Sur La Lune Fairy Tales* (www. surlalunefairytales.com).

ACKNOWLEDGEMENTS

I love reading acknowledgements pages. I don't know why, maybe it's the thrill of scanning the pages for names I recognize, maybe it's the affirmation of the truth that there are many, many people whose effort and inspiration goes into taking a story from idea to finished book. I know I always get a little excited when I see an author thanking another author whose work I love—it's this feeling of "Oh, wow! This awesome person knows that awesome person! It's awesomeness multiplied!!!" Also, it's just plain cool to see that people whose work you enjoy are friends with each other.

So, if you're reading this and feeling the same way, you're not alone. I'm right there with you!

And now, on with the show. If I forget someone, I'm sorry in advance. Next time we hang out, I'll buy you a cookie! For reals.

First, thank you to my tireless agent, Bill Contardi, whose professionalism knows no bounds. To Georgia McBride, for taking a chance on my strange, dark story, and to the entire team at Month9Books who had a hand in bringing my book to life. I know that each of your contributions was essential and I couldn't have done this without your hard work and dedication to the process.

Also to E.K. Johnston, for the writing sessions all those years ago, even though I think we did more yapping about books and episodes of Stargate SG-1 than actual writing. It's also because of her that I wrote this book, though she doesn't know that yet. Surprise! And to Emily Zeran, for always believing in me and providing encouragement at just the right times. And to the rest of the G.O.D.S., for meet-ups and marathon TV/movie watching when I needed it the most.

Thanks to Brian Henry, during whose workshop I read the first few chapters of this story out loud. The moment I stopped reading and looked around the room was the moment this strange idea became a real thing. Thanks to Chandra Rooney, whose pep talk made me believe again when I'd lost faith.

Thanks to Richard Kieckhefer for his in-depth research and works on the late Middle Ages which shaped many of the ideas found within this book. Thanks to Charles Perrault, the Brothers Grimm, and Disney for keeping the story of Cinderella alive in the contemporary collective consciousness!

Thanks to the Wrimosaurs for being a constant source of encouragement and inspiration. Thanks to Holly Lisle, whose writing workshops & courses helped shape me on my journey.

Thanks to the 2017 Debuts and the Class of 2K17 Books crew for their constant support. 2017ers, we made it!!!

Thanks to my parents, who never told me I couldn't, and to my siblings, who always told me I could. To my husband, who never stops saying I can. And to God, because without Him, I wouldn't even be.

F. M. BOUGHAN

F. M. Boughan is a bibliophile, a writer, and an unabashed parrot enthusiast. She can often be found writing in local coffee shops, namely because it's hard to concentrate with a cat lying on the keyboard and a small, colorful parrot screaming into her ear. Her work is somewhat dark, somewhat violent, somewhat hopeful, and always contains a hint of magic.

OTHER MONTH9BOOKS TITLES YOU MIGHT LIKE

PRAEFATIO
MAD MAGIC
SACRIFICE
THE REQUIEM RED

Find more books like this at http://www.Month9Books.com

Connect with Month9Books online:
Facebook: www.Facebook.com/Month9Books
Twitter: https://twitter.com/Month9Books
YouTube: www.youtube.com/user/Month9Books
Tumblr: http://month9books.tumblr.com/
Instagram: https://instagram.com/month9books

BOOK 1 IN THE PRAEFATIO SERIES

PRAEFATIO

A NOVEL

"This is teen fantasy at its most entertaining,
most heartbreaking, most compelling. Highly recommended." –Jonathan Maberry,
New York Times bestselling author of ROT & RUIN and FIRE & ASH

GEORGIA McBRIDE

SACRIFICE

"Serpentine's world oozes with lush details and rich lore, and the characters crackle with life. This is one story that you'll want to lose yourself in."
— **Marie Lu, author of PRODIGY**

"A brilliant second act."
— *Kirkus Reviews,*
STARRED REVIEW

CINDY PON

BRYNN CHAPMAN

'Exquisitely written! This book will remain forever in my heart!'
- *New York Times* Bestselling Author Darynda Jones

THE
REQUIEM RED